LADY OF CHARADE

THE UNCONVENTIONAL LADIES
BOOK FOUR

ELLIE ST. CLAIR

CONTENTS

Facebook: Ellie St. Clair

Cover by AJF Designs

Do you love historical romance? Receive access to a free ebook, as well as exclusive content such as giveaways, contests, freebies and advance notice of pre-orders through my mailing list!

Sign up here!

The Unconventional Ladies
Lady of Mystery
Lady of Fortune
Lady of Providence
Lady of Charade

The Unconventional Ladies Box Set

For a full list of all of Ellie's books, please see
www.elliestclair.com/books.

PROLOGUE

NEAR BALTIMORE, 1812

Sarah picked up her musket, hoisting it over her shoulder as she closed the door behind her and walked outside, inhaling deeply as the sounds of forest life filled her ears.

She smiled to herself as she began down the path toward the gathering of houses. She greeted the people she met within the small village as she continued on through it, her boots crunching over the leaves at her feet as she re-entered solitude — from the human variety of living creatures. The forests around her were full of animals of every type. The birds sang to her as she continued along, the rustle of trees around her telling her that there were squirrels or rabbits or something of the like following along beside her. She felt no fear, however — only appreciation for the company. She carried the musket as a precaution, if ever a bear, wolf, or human decided to attack, but she had rarely had to use it, and hoped to not require it anytime soon.

Sarah was well aware that she could have waited for a neighbor to accompany her for her weekly visit into the town, but today she had felt the need for a walk alone. Her mother, gone two years now, would have chastised her, but it was on days like today that Sarah felt her presence remaining with her the most.

She stopped suddenly, seeing long green stems with white fluffy flowers — black cohosh — emerging from the greenery just off the path, and she clipped a bit of it before placing it into her bag. One never knew when it might be required, for she had found it quite effective in treating a variety of women's ailments.

An hour later she emerged from the brush into the cleared land, where the slowly growing town awaited her. Sarah's mother had taken her east to the city enough times for Sarah to know that this town was still rather primitive despite the influx of new residents, but she enjoyed being away from the busyness of Baltimore or another such settlement. She appreciated knowing the names of all who lived near her and of being close to nature, which called to her. She could hardly imagine living in a place surrounded by tall stone buildings and strangers rushing by her, deep within their busy lives.

"Hello, George," she said as she entered the general store, which also doubled as the post office.

"Miss Jones!" he said, his lips beneath his great beard and mustache turning up into a smile. "I was wondering when you might come in. Here for supplies, are you?"

"I am," she said as she began to quickly peruse the shelves for her regular purchases, before more slowly searching the shop for a few additional items.

"Let me guess," George said, leaning over the counter on his thick arms. "You are looking for food stores for not only yourself but also for others in that little village of yours."

"Mabel just had her babe, and Landon has no wish to leave her at the moment," she said with a smile as she thought of the young married couple. "They do not need much, just a few things to get by."

"You're quite a woman, Miss Jones," George said, eyeing her. "My Lois and I worry about you, out there all alone."

"I'm not alone," she said, raising her eyes to his. "There are people settled all around me. I only need to shout and my protectors will come running."

"That may very well be," he agreed, "But are you not lonely?"

"I am far from lonely, George," she said with a smile. "In fact, there always seems to be someone at my door seeking my company."

"Company or treatment," he amended, and she nodded.

"True. But I am happy to help."

Sarah had learned from her mother, Mary, how to use the land to tend to the ailments of others. Her mother had learned from her own mother in England, where she was considered something of a witch. Here in America, Mary had added to her wisdom with knowledge assumed from both villagers and an Accohannock woman, who was married to a white man and had seen in her a shared spirit.

"Well, one of these days, I hope you accept a man who comes calling upon you," George continued, not moved from his mission. Sarah inwardly sighed. He meant well, but she did wish that for just one week she could come to see him without having to discuss the fact that she remained alone, unmarried. It was not as though she had not had any propositions — oh, no, there were plenty of them. But each man seemed to come from a place of wanting a woman to take care of him, rather than being interested in her, Sarah Jones.

"I appreciate your concern, George, truly I do, but I promise you that I am perfectly fine. If the right man comes along, well then, I would not turn him away. But I have yet to find him, and so I will remain alone with my potions and my nearby friends."

"Very well," he said, throwing his hands in the air as if he simply had to accept defeat. "Oh, before I forget — I have a letter for you."

"A letter?"

"Aye. Seems to be all the way from England."

"England?" Sarah raised her eyebrows. She had no ties to anyone in England, as far as she was aware. "You are jesting."

"I am not," he said, holding the envelope out to her. It was slightly torn in one corner, looking as though it truly had traveled all the way from her mother's country.

The moment she had the letter in her hands, every instinct within her was telling her to rip it open to determine just what the contents held, but she decided to wait until she was within the confines of her own home, where she could read and react accordingly. Sarah could tell George was nearly as curious as she was herself, but she simply thanked him, paid for her items, and slung her bag over her shoulder as she left the store, greeting others she knew before she made the return trip home.

She was halfway there when she could no longer resist the suspense. She could practically feel the letter calling out to her, begging to be read. Sarah walked over to a fallen log, and took a seat upon it as she rifled through her bag before finding what she was looking for. She pulled out the envelope, ripping the seal at the back, opening it to find a light scrawl atop a piece of flimsy paper. Crisp bills fluttered out with it, as well as a ticket.

Sarah,

You do not know me. I wonder at how you are — have you made a life for yourself there in America? I can hardly think of living in such a place, but then, your mother was always something of a wild one. She could not be contained, certainly not by her father, nor by any other man.

I have heard of her passing, and for that, I am sorry. I can imagine what you must be feeling. Now that this has occurred, I have found myself wrestling with the thought of whether or not to share the following information with you.

I finally decided, however, that I would want to know, and so I will tell you.

Your father remains in England. He is certainly alive and well, and I am sure he would want to know his daughter. I urge you to return, to make his acquaintance. He is a powerful lord, one who could provide you with a fortune, I am sure.

I have included for you enough funds to help you find your way to New York City, as well as a ticket aboard the Hercules. *I booked it long in advance as I am unsure how long this letter will take to reach you. You have until June 1st to find your way on board.*

Good luck, Sarah. I hope you will consider my words.

Yours truly,

A friend.

Sarah allowed the letter to float to the floor of the forest at her feet. Her father? She couldn't deny that she had wondered about him from time to time. Her mother had always been enough, but in the same breath, she longed to know about the man who had sired her. Her mother had always refused to speak of him, though whenever Sarah mentioned his name, a sad, faraway look came into her eyes.

Sarah lifted her hand in front of her, staring at the ring fitted around her thumb. She had found it after her mother's passing, had known that it must have belonged to her father. It was a man's ring, heavy and gold, an intricate symbol inlaid into its black surface. It had fit perfectly on her thumb, and she became inclined to wear it, despite the fact that it was impractical for her way of life. Yet, somehow, it had never fallen off. She had known it was silly, for the ring should mean nothing to her. However, she had felt a strange tie to it, and to a past that she had never known but could now be there, waiting for her to learn it.

Her thoughts in turmoil, confusion and a strange yearning to know more swirling within her, Sarah carefully tucked the letter back into her bag. June 20th. The date was but a month away now. If she was going to follow the instructions of the letter and find herself on that ship, she would have to make arrangements quickly, for it would take nearly a week to travel to the port in New York City. Her heart began to beat wildly. Could she really do it? Leave all of this behind — her friends, the people who were near to family?

And yet... there was some truth to George's words. She was close to many here, true, but she was the only single woman in sight. Did the people truly appreciate her for who she was — Sarah Jones — or did they simply want her for her healing powers and what she could offer them? She had no idea, but she wouldn't like to leave her villagers without anyone to tend to their ailments. Abigail, the daughter of one of the original families, had been following her for a time now, but she was young, and not nearly experienced enough in the ways of healing. The town was nearby, however, and there was a healer there. Perhaps she could be enough.

"We'll be fine here," Abigail assured her, the girl's eyes bright and innocent when Sarah tentatively raised the idea of leaving the next week. She had been unable to think of anything else but the letter and the ticket since she had first received it. This morning they were foraging for supplies not far from the village and it seemed like the ideal time to raise her concerns.

"Of course you will be," Sarah said, not wanting Abigail to see her hesitation. "I just wish... that I had taught you more."

"You've taught me plenty. And not only that, but there are

others nearby I can turn to for help, if needed," Abigail said before laying her hand on Sarah's arm and proving herself wise beyond her years. "And Sarah, if you do not go, will you not spend the rest of your life wondering about who your father is?"

Abigail's words resonated. For Sarah had no desire to continue to question half of who she was, from where she had come, and whether her father had ever or could ever care anything for her.

"We don't have much time," Sarah said slowly, turning to look at Abigail now, and the girl blinked her eyes a few times, clearing tears, but nodded with a smile. "I won't be able to share all with you, but over the next few days, we have to cover as much as we can."

And so they did. Sarah spent the next week full of nervous anticipation, continually questioning herself as to whether or not she was doing the right thing. This was the only home she had ever known, and how in the world would she go about finding a man she knew nothing about? She had to put her trust in this mysterious letter writer, and hope that when she arrived in England more information would be provided to her.

When she wasn't working with Abigail, she was speaking to all of the villagers who had spent part of their lives in England, attempting to learn all she could about her mother's country.

She didn't feel nearly as prepared as she would have liked, but soon, with nearly all of her few belongings tied in a satchel at her shoulder and the money clasped in her palm, she began the arduous trip to Baltimore. There, she could take a small ship to New York to meet with the ship on which this mysterious messenger had purchased her a ticket, for Sarah had not enough to purchase another passage from Baltimore. She supposed the ticket had been specifically purchased so she couldn't spend the money on anything else, and if she wanted to accept it, she had limited options.

As she finally stood on the deck of the *Hercules* following a quick but wearying journey, looking back at the land that had become her home, Sarah wondered whether she would ever see it again.

CHAPTER 1

LONDON, 1815

*L*ord David Redmond parried the blow from his opponent, quickly flipping his sword up and about until the man was disarmed and defenseless in front of him. He grinned in victory as he heard a slow clap from behind him.

"Well done, Monsieur," said the Frenchman, who had been David's fencing instructor over the past two years. "Once again, you have proven yourself as one of the best."

"Of course," David said, proud of himself. He only wished his father could see him here, where he wouldn't be able to help but find some sort of admiration for his second son. "All because of you, Monsieur Perrault."

"You are far too kind," the small man said, as David bent to pick up the fallen sword and pass it to Berkley, who stood with his hands on his hips, out of breath as he shook his head at his friend.

"One of these days, Redmond," he said, shaking a finger at him. "One of these days."

"A day I eagerly await," David said with a grin, though he vowed the day would never come as he removed his fencing helmet.

"Every time I come a little closer," Berkley protested.

"I would hardly agree."

"Perhaps we should ask Monsieur Perrault."

"No need. Evidence speaks for itself," David countered, and Berkley laughed at that, shrugging to show that on this, perhaps, he conceded.

He and Berkley continued to banter back and forth as they removed their fencing gear. David was well aware that the company he kept was somewhat above his station, as the second son of an earl. A duke and a marquess were lofty companions, but they seemed to enjoy his company, though he often wondered if they were simply living somewhat vicariously through him, both of them now married, though happily at that.

"Where are you off to now, Redmond?" Berkley asked as they walked out into the London sunshine. The weather was slowly drifting into spring. Before long, his family's country homes would be opened, though David was unsure when or for how long he would visit. He found a sense of peace in the country, though in the same breath, if his family was present, they would likely spend the majority of their visit discussing his lack of intentions to marry and their intentions that he do so.

"A return home for dinner, then I suppose I will find myself an engagement of some sort or another this evening."

Berkley eyed him. "And what type would that be?"

"I haven't yet decided," David said with a wink at him. "One of my favorite widows has been rather lonely lately, so perhaps I'll take her up on her offer for a nightcap after a game or two of faro at one of the clubs."

Berkley shook his head, though he seemed amused.

"I'm not sure how you do it," he said, and David shrugged.

"It's fairly simple — you just enjoy yourself."

"Do you never get tired of chasing after these women?"

"It doesn't take much, and they are chasing after me in equal measure."

"I used to think along some of the same lines as you," Berkley said. "But there is something to be said about coming home to the same woman each night — a woman who knows you, and not just the superficial. Who can tell if you need time to yourself, who knows how to comfort you, how to discuss certain aspects of your life."

David shook his head. "I'm glad you have found what you are looking for, Berkley, but that life doesn't suit me. I'm perfectly happy living as I am, and I don't need a woman involved to make things more difficult."

"Suit yourself," Berkley said, spreading his hands wide. "In my opinion, having multiple women would be much worse."

"It's just a matter of keeping them all separate," he explained, as they walked into White's for an afternoon drink before they would go their own ways. Within, they found the Duke of Clarence awaiting them, and as they took chairs near him at the table, Berkley continued the conversation, which David felt was hardly fair, for clearly the two other men would take the same side, the Duke newly married himself.

"What do you say, Clarence," Berkley said, "We are currently in a debate as to what is more difficult to manage — one woman or multiple."

The Duke's eyes sparkled somewhat at the question.

"Had you asked me a year ago, I likely would have agreed

11

with Redmond here, as I believe I can ascertain which of you is taking which side of this argument. However… keeping one woman happy, gentlemen, is far more rewarding than what multiple women could ever provide. Especially if that woman satisfies you more than you could ever imagine."

"You've both gone soft on me," David said despondently as they were served their drinks. "I hardly think that I shall ever feel that way. Though if I do, I know who to turn to for advice."

His two friends just laughed at him. Sometimes David wondered why they preferred his own company to that of his brother, who was far more straight-laced and responsible. He quickly shrugged aside the thought, however, not seeing the importance of it, as he began looking forward to this evening's festivities.

SARAH LET herself into her rooms on the first floor of the tall building. The door, though recessed down a back alley, was accessible to the street, which was both fortunate and not. It made it easy for anyone to find her if she was needed, but at the same time, it put her at additional risk. Not that she wasn't prepared to defend herself, she thought with a smile, as she patted the dependable dagger in the piece of fabric tied around her ankle, before ensuring that her shotgun was in its resting place in the corner of the room, her handgun where she had it hidden next to her bed.

Cheapside was not as dangerous as many neighborhoods, but despite its close proximity to some of London's better-renowned areas, there were certainly risks involved, particularly as a woman living alone on a back street. However, risks abounded no matter where the location for any young woman living alone, did they not?

Upon arriving in London three years ago, she had little knowledge of the city nor its neighborhoods. She had been advised to find a boardinghouse for young women, and in fact had stayed in one for a time. But after two weeks, she had found the rules and boundaries to be suffocating, and had sought other lodgings where she would have the freedom to do as she pleased.

Sarah had thought her stay would be temporary. She had assumed she would find her father fairly quickly, and would know within a month or two whether or not there was any reason to remain in London. But nearly three years later, she was still here — though for how much longer, she wasn't sure.

Without removing any of her clothing, she walked down the small corridor and tossed her bag on the hard wooden floor before throwing herself on the lumpy mattress that passed for a bed. She would have far preferred the furs she had slept upon in America, but then, this was what she could afford, and she should be grateful that she had somewhere to sleep.

Her eyes nearly closed the moment she lay her head back, but she jumped up to attention when she heard a knock at the door. Hurrying over, she opened it but a crack, shocked when she saw who stood on the other side. Her secret, apparently, was no longer that.

"What are you doing here?" she asked, as she opened the door wide to reveal three ladies standing there staring at her.

Soon upon her arrival three years ago, Sarah had the fortune to meet Lady Phoebe at one of the dances Lady Alexander had escorted her to. Soon she had been introduced to two of her friends, Lady Elizabeth and Lady Julia, and despite the fact that she had never quite felt herself worthy to call these women friends, she had bonded with them in a way she had never thought possible. In fact, if it

13

hadn't been for the three of them, Sarah didn't think she would still be here in England. Despite their closeness, however, Sarah hadn't quite shared everything with them.

Elizabeth, Phoebe, and Julia walked the few feet until they stood in the center of her makeshift parlor room and bedroom, looking around them in shock. Sarah nearly laughed at how out of place the three ladies looked in all their finery in the middle of this run-down room. She had done the best she could to provide color to the dingy interior with a few blankets, but there was not much to it — two mismatched chairs stood around the grate, her bed was pushed against the wall, and a wooden screen separated the two.

"Is this where you live?" Phoebe asked, turning her direct gaze on Sarah, who shrugged. "It is — for the moment."

"How could you not tell us, after all this time?" Elizabeth demanded. "We had always assumed you lived with Lady Alexander!"

"I know," Sarah said with a sigh, sitting down upon the bed herself, as she bid the rest of them to take a seat next to her in a ratty chair across the room. "I allowed you to think it."

"But why here? Why don't you live with her? And why didn't you tell us? You could have stayed with one of us!" Julia said, and Sarah leaned back against the wall.

"It's a long story," she said. "But first, how did you find me here?"

"When you didn't attend Lady Nuffield's party this evening, Phoebe and I were worried,"

Elizabeth explained. "We asked Lady Alexander if you had taken ill, and she wasn't entirely sure. As Julia and Eddie were in London, we asked her to accompany us to come to visit you to assure all was well. Lady Alexander's butler was most confused when we asked for you at her home. It was her maid who followed us out and told us where we could find you. We didn't entirely believe her, but decided to follow her anyway."

"I'm sorry to have worried you," Sarah said. "One of my neighbors' boys took ill. I believe it was some bad meat, but we got it out right quickly enough and I think he should be fine. I couldn't leave them and it happened so quickly, I didn't have time to get word to Lady Alexander that I wouldn't be attending tonight."

She looked down at herself in chagrin. She hadn't changed from her evening wear when she had been summoned, and now her beautiful pink gown would have to be laundered or the nobility would smell her coming from far away.

Her friends nodded. They knew of her work as a medicine woman or healer — whatever one chose to call what she did — but they weren't aware of the entirety of it, that she used her skills to survive, although more often than not many of those who asked for her help could hardly afford to pay anything. She typically gratefully accepted whatever they had to offer, be it a loaf of bread or a bag of potatoes.

"You know that I left America to find my father," she said, attempting to determine the best way to complete the story, and they nodded. "Only I didn't come here with the intention of meeting Lady Alexander. It was once I was upon the ship to London that I met her. She was frightfully seasick, and I helped as best I could to ease her stomach pains. In return, she was kind to me, and we became friends. Near the end of the journey, she asked what I was doing in London. I provided a small portion of the story, and when no one met me in London as I assumed would happen, she offered to act as my chaperone. As the widow of a viscount, she has access to social events for which I could never dream of an invitation. I must admit, it has been immensely helpful in order to meet a wide variety of nobles who may be around the age of my father, to try to determine whether any of them resemble me or if they might have any connection to my mother. Not that my strategy is working overly well."

"But why didn't Lady Alexander offer for you to live with her?" Julia asked, and Sarah shrugged.

"She never mentioned it, and her help is incredibly generous as it is. Most people are under the assumption that I am an American relative of hers, and I have found that I do not have to lie about it much — most just accept the fact. Lady Alexander made the offer with the caveat that I ask for no money or further attachment to her, which is perfectly fine with me, for I have no wish for it. I believe she is a bit lonely but had no desire to disrupt her current lifestyle. It works for both of us. She wouldn't want all manner of people at her doorstep in search of a healer."

"That's how you are supporting yourself here," Elizabeth said, more in statement than question, and Sarah nodded.

"I am. Though I would do it anyway, for it seems I cannot help myself when it comes to attempting to heal what causes others pain."

"Well," Elizabeth said matter-of-factly. "I do wish you had told us sooner. Please tell me you have not been living here ever since you came from America."

"I have," Sarah said with a nod. "Nearly three years now, if you can believe it. Though… I have been thinking that it is time I give up on this quest and return home."

"Three years!" gasped Julia as Elizabeth shook her head in disbelief.

"Sarah, you cannot leave us!"

"I cannot believe you have kept this from us," Elizabeth said, as Phoebe sat in the corner watching them, patting her stomach, which had rounded once more with their second child.

"I am sorry to have deceived you," Sarah said, "That was certainly not my intention. It just seemed... easier, and I didn't want you to worry."

"I suppose I can somewhat understand that, though I feel a fool," said Elizabeth. "But now that we know, you can come and stay with me. Gabriel is eager to help you find your father, though we have not much to go on. He has made inquiries, and thus far, there are no connections to a woman and child who left for America — though I'm sure there are more than a few who had some liaisons to which they would certainly not want to admit."

Elizabeth strode over to the wardrobe, opening it to reveal Sarah's dresses, the only items in the room upon which she had spent any money. She had used the additional funds the letter-writer had provided her, though each season she stayed was beginning to stretch what she could afford.

"Do you have a bag into which we can pack everything?" Elizabeth asked, taking charge as she usually did.

"Thank you for your generously kind offer, Elizabeth, but I am not leaving."

Elizabeth swirled around, looking at her incredulously. "Whyever not?"

"I'm comfortable here, and more than anything, those who need me know where to find me. They could never track me down if I were to move, particularly to one of the greatest manors in all of London."

"You do not need to worry about providing for yourself," Elizabeth affirmed. "We will support you in whatever you need, will we not Phoebe?"

Phoebe nodded, though she looked somewhat hesitant.

"Of course we would, Sarah, you know that. However... this has to be what you want," she said softly, and Sarah smiled at her.

"I appreciate that — I appreciate what all of you would

like to do for me, I do," she said. "I know if I ever need somewhere else to stay, I can turn to any of you. But for now, I will remain where I am, content in what I am able to do. And at the moment, as much as I would love you all to stay, I very much need to sleep."

"Of course," Phoebe said, rising from the bed and walking to the door, the other two following her, Elizabeth quite reluctantly as she spun around, continuing to look at Sarah's accommodations. "We shall see you tomorrow."

After they left, Sarah locked the door tightly behind them and fell back on the bed, into a long, dream-filled sleep.

CHAPTER 2

*A*nother evening, another party. David walked around the edges of the room, keeping an eye out for which beautifully coiffed heads he must avoid and which ones were most likely to welcome him. He attended most of these events because his family expected it of him, for the truth was that he far preferred venues where he didn't have to put on airs or maintain any particular facade.

He was so busy looking about him that he almost walked into a marble bust that protruded from a niche in one of the side walls. As he sidestepped it, his foot nearly got caught in the large draperies that hung to the floor over the French windows, and he realized that he had never been much of a wallflower, so to speak. For he had no idea how to navigate the edges of a fine room such as this. The room was large and meant to impose, a fantastic, multi-layered chandelier descending from the clouds painted upon the ceiling. Great mirrors bordered the room to provide an even more expansive look, while gold-framed paintings surrounded the room above blue-and-yellow silk sofas.

The first strains of music began, and David saw Lady

Lochlin coming his way. She was a beautiful woman, sultry and skilled, but she was also becoming a might too attached for his liking, despite his repeated attempts to dissuade her. That was one thing he was always sure of — he never made promises, especially those he had no intention of keeping.

He looked around wildly for an escape and saw the back of a woman he recognized — one who was always up for a spot of fun and was as averse to a permanent attachment to him as he was to her.

"Sophia," he murmured in her ear as he stepped up behind her and surreptitiously ran a hand down the bare skin of her arm showing between her cap sleeve and her glove. "Lovely seeing you here tonight, luv. Fancy a dance?"

Sophia whirled around so fast, she nearly knocked him over. David took a hurried step backward as he realized that Sophia... was definitely *not* Sophia.

The woman, pretty in an innocent, soft way — certainly not his type — narrowed her eyes at him, studying him from head to toe in a way that made him feel quite vulnerable and exposed.

"I believe you have me confused with another, my lord," she said, and he was stunned by the words coming from her mouth, though it was not so much *what* she said, but how she spoke. Her voice was almost... tender in a way, soft and lilting. Her words came out flatter than most, a strange accent that was near to his own way of speaking yet different enough that he could certainly recognize it.

"Ah, yes," he said, his face warming when he thought of the way he had approached her, for she clearly understood the nature of his relationship with this Sophia. "Forgive me, my lady."

"Not, my lady," she said. "Simply Miss Jones."

"Miss Jones!" recognition dawned at her name. "You are a friend of Lady Berkley and the Duchess of Clarence."

"That I am," she nodded, then added, "Lord Brentford."

"Ah, so you are aware of my identity," he acknowledged, rocking back and forth on his heels, unsure of whether this was in his favor or not. "I am simply Mr. Redmond, however, and always will be, being my father's younger son."

"Of course," she said, seeming only slightly embarrassed by her mistake, which was a strange one for a woman of a noble family. "And I am — aware of you, that is," she nodded, and he wondered if that was laughter he read in her eyes. "You have quite the reputation, sir."

So her familiarity with him would not work in his favor then. Ah well. He prepared himself to depart.

"However, I would be happy to dance with you if you wish, my— Mr. Redmond."

"The pleasure is all mine," he said, his manners and charm quickly covering his surprise at her ready agreement, despite the fact his original proposition had been to another woman. Most women would have told him to be gone out of sight, but it seemed this Miss Jones was the forgiving type.

He held his arm out to her, and she took it gracefully as they joined the other dancers who were preparing for the cotillion. They clasped hands, and David was shocked by the jolt that shot through his body at the contact with her, despite the gloves they were both wearing. Her fingers seemed to fit so perfectly in his. David frowned at the thought racing through his mind. Of all the experiences he had with so many women, he was focusing on the feeling of her hands? Ridiculous.

"Is everything all right?" she asked, her pert little freckled nose crunching in concern, and a rush of need to appease her ran through him.

"Of course," he said. "It is simply... the steps of this dance. I was concentrating."

Which was a lie — he had learned this dance as a child

and could likely do it in his sleep. But it was the first thought that had entered his mind.

"I understand," she said with a knowing smile as she leaned into him. "I have trouble with this one myself."

As the music began, he could see that while he had fibbed, she was certainly telling the truth. Her lips moved as she began to count the steps, her head tilting down to gaze at her feet once the couples on the floor began to move in earnest. It was endearing, and so unlike the perfectly practiced steps of most women of his acquaintance.

They didn't speak much — he had no wish to disrupt her timing — but instead, whenever they neared one another during the dance, he studied her.

She was of average height, which put her about a foot below him. He could tell that if he reached out a hand to brush it over her hair, it would be soft, wispy almost, the light brown color reminding him of cinnamon.

Her dress was of a pink so pale it was nearly white. While he couldn't say he was up-to-date on all women's fashion — not like his friend, the Duke of Clarence — her clothing looked slightly out of date, as though perhaps it was from the previous season. Still, the embroidered rosebuds along the bodice and the hem were as fitting on her as anything he could have imagined.

When the dance finally came to a close, her cheeks were flushed, and when he looked at her, all he could think was that if ever he had pictured what an angel might look like, she was standing here in front of him now.

He bowed slightly toward her.

"Miss Jones," he said, "I thank you for the dance."

"Thank you, Mr. Redmond," she responded. "You have been most kind."

"Were you expecting otherwise?" he asked, and she

laughed slightly, a breathy, airy laugh that caused a tingle of pleasure to run through him. He wanted to hear more of it.

"I wasn't sure what to expect, if I were to be honest with you."

"Understandable," he acknowledged, wishing for once that his reputation was not what it was. Perhaps he must make an effort to be more discreet in the future.

He held out an arm to her.

"I will return you to your companion."

"Thank you, Mr. Redmond."

"I hope to see you again very soon," he said once they reached the side of the dance floor and they neared the stately looking woman, who he seemed to recall was a relative of hers. He surprised himself with the realization that he completely meant his words — he was already attempting to determine how to arrange another experience with her.

"And I you, Mr. Redmond."

No sooner had David turned away from the lovely Miss Jones when he felt a tap on the shoulder, and he cringed as he turned around, wondering who it might be.

"David!"

Thankfully, it was his brother, and David responded to his greeting with a wide, genuine grin. He loved his brother, truly he did — it was the comparisons their parents continually made between the pair of them that always drew his ire.

"Franklin," he greeted him, holding out a hand and they clasped arms. "It is wonderful to see you, though I am even happier that you are accompanied by the much more beautiful Andrea."

His sister-in-law blushed prettily, but David knew she enjoyed the compliments — most women did.

"How are you keeping?" Franklin asked, and David smiled.

"As well as ever. And you?"

"Very well indeed. In fact," he leaned into David conspiratorially, "We must tell you of something. Our family will be growing very soon."

If they weren't in a room full of people, David would have crushed his brother in an embrace, so happy he was to hear the news. While their marriage had been arranged by their parents, David knew that Franklin and his wife had truly come to love one another, and he was pleased to hear of their blessing.

Although… he couldn't deny that such news caused a strange stirring within him, a longing. But surely not for children. He knew he would like to have them someday, but that day would be quite far away.

Now his parents approached and David sighed inwardly. He loved them, but he knew what was to come.

"Ah, my family, all together!" his mother exclaimed as she leaned in and kissed him on the cheek. "You look well, David." She lowered her voice. "Has Franklin told you his news?"

"He has, Mother," David said with a nod. "I am so pleased for the two of them, truly I am."

She clasped her hands at her breast. "There is no greater blessing in life than children, as I well know from the two of you."

"And time for an heir, I must say," David's father added, to which David nearly rolled his eyes. Truly, did his father have to ruin every moment with a discussion of what they each must do come the future?

"Now, listen, son," he said, his attention upon David now as he clasped one of his large, meaty hands on his shoulder. "We must have a discussion soon, the two of us. It is time we truly considered what the next few years will hold for you. I know you've had your fun, but that must surely be coming to an end."

David groaned inwardly.

"I believe this moment is about Franklin and Andrea, Father, not about my own prospects."

"Family is family, David. We are all one and the same. Come for dinner soon?"

David nodded mutely. He would, though he did not look forward to the coming discussion.

After waving a footman over to collect drinks for them, Lord Brentford held his glass up. "A toast. To the next generation of Brentford children."

David held up his drink and toasted with them, in celebration of his brother, but with a great deal of perplexing anxiety over his own role in all of this.

CHAPTER 3

"Sarah Jones, was that David Redmond you were dancing with just now?"

Sarah smiled in greeting as Elizabeth approached, nodding at her words.

"It was," she said. Sarah had, in fact, been shocked by Mr. Redmond. She had heard of his reputation, of course, had known that he was a man who enjoyed a rather wide variety of women, as had been apparent by his approach toward her. It seemed she must resemble a… friend of his. The thought had her stomach roiling with a strange sense of jealousy, which was ridiculous — she hardly knew the man. They had danced once together, and a cotillion at that, a set during which they had barely spoken.

While she could tell he hadn't exactly been seeking her out for the dance, she was rather unknown here and didn't receive much opportunity to take to the dance floor. She had studied the steps of the cotillion for some time, and appreciated the chance to put her newly acquired skills into practice.

What had surprised her the most was just how much she had enjoyed her time with him. Perhaps it was the charming smile he continually wore or the way his green eyes crinkled in the corners when he looked at her. He was a man who seemed to know how to enjoy life, that was for certain.

She kept reminding herself of who he was, what she knew of him — and she had a feeling Elizabeth had approached to tell her the exact same thing.

"He is… charming," Sarah continued cautiously, and Elizabeth nodded.

"That, he certainly is," said Elizabeth, taking a sip of the drink in her hand, and Sarah wondered if she was indulging in the brandy she secretly enjoyed. Sarah herself preferred lemonade or something of the sort, for she had seen far too often how the effects of alcohol could addle the brain.

"You will be careful, will you not?" Elizabeth continued. "While he is certainly an entertaining man to converse with or to dance with… he is not the sort of man to whom one should form any attachment. He has no inclination to wed, nor commit himself to any one woman."

"Of course," Sarah said, waving a hand in the air. "It was but a dance. I have recently learned the cotillion, you see, and when the opportunity presented itself, I decided to put my new steps to the test."

Elizabeth nodded, though Sarah could see the concern remaining in her eyes. For some reason, Sarah had declined to mention the fact that Mr. Redmond had initially mistaken her for someone else — someone with whom he seemed far more intimately familiar.

"Of which you did an admirable job," Elizabeth praised her, and Sarah smiled, though she shrugged.

"You are being kind," she said, "At the very least, I know I did not make a mess of it, which counts for something, I suppose."

"You danced admirably," Phoebe said from behind her, joining the conversation. "Of course, when one is accompanied by a man so experienced as David Redmond, it is helpful."

She laughed, and Sarah had no response for she had no idea, in truth, of how a man's experience might affect her own on the dance floor or... as relations of another sort entered her mind, she blushed in spite of herself — where in the world had that thought come from? It must simply be all this talk of Mr. Redmond and his reputation.

"He is a verifiable rake, but a charming one at that," Phoebe said with a smile of affection, showing her opinion of the man, who had long been a friend of her husband's. "Regardless, Sarah, I know you are an intelligent enough woman to be aware to keep from allowing him to charm you."

"Elizabeth has already lectured me regarding Mr. Redmond," Sarah said, surprised at the slight bit of annoyance that filled her at the continued warnings. Did they really believe her to be so naive? So she was a bit attracted to the man. What woman wouldn't be, with his slightly-too-long sandy hair that curled at the ends, his vivid green eyes, and dimples that stretched within his cheeks every time he smiled, which seemed to be rather often? It didn't mean she was going to profess her love to him or plan to marry him one day.

"Besides who he may be, I have other concerns at the moment," she said. "I have been here in England nearly three years now, and I feel as though I am no closer in my quest than I was when I first arrived. Why would I be summoned here by some mysterious letter writer, only for such a person to never contact me upon my arrival? I have attempted to find relatives, but the surname of "Jones," if that even was my mother's true name, is quite common, and anyone I have found does not seem to be any relation. Of course, my father's name remains a mystery, for I was never told anything about him, besides how my mother saw him and what they felt for one another. Every gentleman who appears near his assumed age that even somewhat resembles me seems to have already been married at the time I would have been born."

Phoebe and Elizabeth looked at one another for a moment, causing Sarah to feel like an innocent child.

"I know," she said, holding her palms up to them. "I am well aware that men have affairs outside of their marriage beds. But when my mother spoke of him, she did so with love in her voice. She only left because the man's father threatened to cut off his inheritance should he continue his association with her, and she had no wish to put a rift between him and his family."

Both of her friends still seemed unconvinced, but they hadn't been present when Sarah's mother had told them of her past relationship. Sarah was more sure than anything that her mother had not been a secondary thought to her father, but rather his love.

"I simply do not know what to do next," she said morosely. "What if he is dead? How would I ever know? I am beginning to think it is time I return to America."

"Oh, please do not say such a thing," said Elizabeth. "Whether or not you find your father, is this not home for you now?"

"I must say that I have never had friends such as you at home, but London is... well, it is not where my heart belongs, which is somewhere I can feel the sun on my face, hear the wind through the tree leaves, forage in the woods for supplies, or capture clean drops of water if it might be time for rain. Here, within all of the buildings and crowds, I so often feel... suffocated."

Sarah shocked herself at the agitation that arose within

her when she spoke the words aloud, and Phoebe placed a gentle hand on her arm.

"Perhaps we simply need to find you a gentleman with a lovely country home," she said with a smile, to which Sarah laughed.

"Perhaps," she said, though in her heart she doubted such a man truly existed — for she would have found him by now, would she not have? A man who would own a country home would never be interested in the illegitimate daughter of a nobleman and a healer, and Sarah didn't have it within her to lie about her true origins.

As her gaze flitted around the room at the men filling it, most dressed far more extravagantly than she ever would, far too pleased with themselves and their own deportment, her eyes landed on David Redmond. He now had a woman on his arm, her hair black as night and intricately styled atop a beautiful silk dress of the latest fashion. As he leaned in toward her with a smile, she laughed at something he said, throwing her head back as her hand hooked around his in a possessive gesture.

Seeing him with her only affirmed the words Elizabeth and Phoebe had shared with her. Sarah was aware that she could be far too gullible and naive, and this only proved what she needed to remember — to stay away from men like David Redmond and re-focus on what she came here to do, which was find her father.

And then, she could return home.

* * *

One week later

. . .

DAVID WAS surprised when he heard a knock at the door as he prepared to leave for the evening, with the help of his one servant, who was both valet and butler. Hampton had been with their family for years, and when David took rooms of his own, his father had suggested the man accompany him. David often wondered whether his father used him as a spy of sorts to determine David's current actions, but he didn't overly care. His father already disapproved — what did it matter that he had more in which to be disappointed?

Although David did have to be careful, for it was, of course, his father who had arranged for him to lodge at his Albany chambers within St. James. David couldn't ask for a better location, for he could easily walk to White's and various establishments along Piccadilly and St. James Street — though some of the seedier establishments he frequented at times required a carriage ride out of the area.

Hampton returned to his bedchamber within moments with the news that the Duke of Clarence had arrived. David nodded before continuing out to his sitting room, fastening the buttons of his shirt himself as he did so, greeting his friend wearing only his linen shirt and breeches.

Clarence, of course, was immaculately dressed in evening wear, though David wondered if he had done so simply for this visit. He wouldn't put it past the man.

"Clarence," he greeted him, signaling to Hampton to bring both of them a brandy. "How do you fare this evening?"

"Quite well, Redmond, and thank you for the drink. I must say, you are always well stocked."

"It's required, in order to keep friends like you content," David said with a laugh. "What brings you here this evening?"

"I do not mean to keep you," Clarence said, and then sighed in a manner that was not at ducal. "I am actually here at the bidding of my wife."

"Your wife?" David was wary now as he took a seat across from the Duke in one of the birch wood chairs, which his mother had selected for him for their molded seat rails and out-swept front legs. "If I were a betting man — which, I most assuredly am — I would hazard a guess that this has to do with the lovely Miss Sarah Jones."

Clarence laughed.

"You know of my wife's nature of protectiveness, then?"

"I am aware that following my dance — one innocent cotillion, mind you — with the woman, she was instantly surrounded by her frequent companions, both of whom sent warning glances my way."

"Elizabeth worries for Sarah," Clarence said, one hand splayed wide in front of him. "That is all."

"She seems rather intriguing," David said, not wanting to admit how much she had entered his thoughts following their one dance together. She had not seemed at all like any of the other women within the room, and, in fact, none others had overly interested him after he had danced with her. "She certainly does not seem to be from around here."

"I do not believe she is," Clarence confirmed, and David found his interest piqued. "Her mother relocated shortly before her birth. It seems she returned here with a relative, Lady Alexander, as she is looking to find more of her family."

"Interesting," David murmured, suddenly far more intrigued than he had any right to be. "Who is her family?"

"That, she is still attempting to determine. It seems her parents were estranged."

"Yet she remains part of the world of the nobility."

"By virtue of Lady Alexander, it seems," Clarence acknowledged.

"I am surprised that you are not more involved with the woman's situation, Clarence," David said. "This seems to be one that you would be attempting to control."

"You sound like my wife. Elizabeth tells me that while I am welcome to help Miss Jones in her search for family, what she does not require at the moment is a husband and that I am to keep myself out of any situation involving her and a potential match." Clarence then chuckled. "With the exception of warning you off, it seems."

"Very well," David said, "Consider me warned."

"My task is complete," Clarence said with a smile. "Now, where are you off to tonight?"

"The Red Lion," David said with a grin, knowing Clarence's thoughts on the club — he disdained it, feeling its patrons were far too unruly. "I've had my fill of society functions for a time. They can be rather ghastly, night after night. Tonight, I'm after some fun."

Clarence lifted his drink. "Well, my best to you, Redmond. One other thing before I take my leave."

"Yes?"

"I have heard some... rumblings, I suppose you could say, regarding a certain Lady Houghton."

"Ah... yes?" David swallowed. She had been a mistake, that one. He attempted to stay away from married women, but he was well aware of just how awful her husband was to her, and she had come to him for comfort a couple of months back. He had been slightly in his cups that night and had provided her what she sought, though he sorely regretted it the next morning and had been worried there may be repercussions. He had hoped she kept the specifics of their relations to herself but...

"Houghton seems to have an inkling of what occurred between the two of you. He is a powerful man, Redmond, and not a particularly forgiving one. Be sure to watch your back. I'll watch it for you as I can, but perhaps keep in your right mind when you're within one of your establishments."

"Consider me warned, Clarence — doubly," David said,

beginning to feel like a naughty child who required chastising. "I'll keep an eye out, as well as be sure to not enter too far into my cups — that's a promise."

"Very good. Well, I am off to Elizabeth's parents for dinner. For which, I am glad for the liquid fortitude."

David laughed.

"Good evening, Clarence."

"And to you, Redmond."

CHAPTER 4

*S*arah sat up with a start, every sense on the alert.

She gasped when she heard a loud banging on her door — it must have been what had initially awakened her. She had no idea what time it was, but from the pitch-black darkness she could see through the thin slice of the window in her room, she knew that it must still be the middle of the night. She rose, lifting her wrapper from the nearby chair and tightening it around herself as she padded over to the door in bare feet.

She hesitated when she reached the door, one hand on the handle, the other on the knob above it, ready to unlock it — but should she? She hurried back across the room, picked up her revolver, and returned to the door. Sarah had no wish to turn away anyone who may be in need, but then, she had enough experience to know to be careful.

Sarah undid the lock and opened the door a crack, lifting her revolver as she looked out, seeing no one within her line of sight. What was going on? She was about to close the door when she heard a groan from somewhere nearby, and she looked down to find that the voice belonged to a body piled at her feet.

She looked one way and the other to determine who might have abandoned this person on her doorstep, but whoever it was had departed too fast, especially with the delay in finding her weapon.

Well, it wasn't the first time she had an unconscious body to deal with, though Sarah was a little worried about what might happen once — if — the body woke up, for he seemed the size of a man from what she could tell, though his head was turned over, away from her.

Sarah knelt and gently rolled the man over to his side as carefully as she could, for she was concerned about what type of head injury he might have. Had she not heard him groan, she would have worried whether or not he was even alive, so limp he was. The dim light outside her rooms made it too difficult to determine who he was nor what might have happened to him, so she hurried back inside, where she lit a lantern and brought it out with her.

She held it up to the mysterious man now, worried that she would be too late to treat whatever it was that ailed him. The moment she lifted the light and it glowed off his face, she gasped aloud in surprise, momentarily pulling back.

For the man lying across the doorstep of her lodging was none other than Mr. David Redmond, second son of the Earl of Brentford.

Sarah hastily set the lantern back down in the room before returning to him. Head injury or not, she certainly couldn't treat him outside, for not only would she not have anything she needed, but she feared passersby may see the elegant clothes he wore — in addition to her current state of undress — and attempt to take advantage of the situation. She half-lifted, half-dragged him into the room, grunting as

36

she did so. He was rather lean, but he was still a tall man and far bigger than she was.

Once he was inside, she shut the door, locking it behind the two of them, and then in her usual practiced manner sprang into action before giving herself too much time to consider the situation — that would come later, once her initial diagnosis and treatment were complete.

Sarah wouldn't be able to lift him onto the bed, but she did have a thin mattress for just this purpose, and she dragged him down the corridor, into her bedroom and upon it before lighting her second lantern, setting up the two on either side of Mr. Redmond so she might be better able to see just what exactly had happened to him.

With her initial shock at the recognition of him, she had missed the extent of his injuries. His eye was already turning black, while a slight bit of blood oozed from his nose, signaling that he had likely taken a beating. She wondered at the extent of injuries to his body but was most worried about his lack of consciousness. Gently feeling around his scalp, she discovered a particularly large bump on the side of his head, and she hissed through her teeth. From its position, it was most likely that he had fallen back upon the hard ground beneath him. The injury was certainly concerning, for there was honestly not much she could do but hope that it would heal in time without any lingering effects.

She found her knife, having no choice but to cut through his jacket and shirt, despite the fact that she was aware his clothing would have cost more than she had likely ever held in her hand at one time.

His chest was red, with a few scratches and newly forming bruises upon it, but there was one particularly deep gash that worried her.

Sarah filled a bucket of water, found clean rags and her basket of herbs, and cleaned his wounds before searching for the loosestrife in her bag. She had recently picked it up at the marketplace, as it had just begun to grow for the season on riverbanks throughout England, and she was pleased that she had not yet dried it. Everything worked much better fresh, she found, but supplies were limited here in London. She could hardly wait until she was back in a place where she could forage for her own herbs.

Sarah tore the yellowish-green leaves from the brown, hairy stalk, and bruised them slightly before pounding them to extract the juice. She applied it around Mr. Redmond's cuts and scrapes, hoping it would do its job and stop the bleeding, allowing her to clean and close up the wounds as quickly as possible. She spread the liquid over the deep gash, a smaller amount on some of the smaller scratches. Taking prepared strips of linen, she wrapped them over the wounds.

After that, there was not much more she could do but hope he soon woke up. In the morning, she would have to find a way to contact his family — she was sure they would be sick with worry over his whereabouts. Sarah found her one extra blanket in the cabinet near her bed, stretching it over him, tucking the edges around him. She hated to leave him on the floor, but she currently didn't have much choice. In the morning, if he was awake and allowed it, she could ask just who she should contact in order to return him home. If not, she supposed she would send a messenger to Elizabeth or Phoebe, for they would surely know to whom to reach out.

She wondered what had happened to him. He must have been attacked, perhaps by thieves in the street. She tiptoed back over to him, feeling as though she were violating him as she reached into the pocket of his jacket, only to find that he still carried coins on him. Strange. What kind of attack was this, that he hadn't been robbed, and, in fact, had been left on her doorstep? Many of her neighbors were aware that she was a healer of sorts, but why bring David, the son of an earl, to her? She had no idea, but it worried her.

Sarah sighed and, looking out the window to find no hint of sun on the horizon, she decided she had better sleep a couple of more hours herself before she would wake up and see to her patient once more.

* * *

DAVID SLOWLY AWOKE as light began to filter through his eyelids. He was never much of an early riser, but something tugged at him, something he couldn't ignore. He began to sit up but nearly bellowed aloud as pain sliced through his brain, particularly when he attempted to open his eyes. And then his chest began to ache something fierce. As slowly as he could, he pushed himself up on his elbows and opened his eyes a crack to determine exactly where he was.

He was within a boarding room of some type, and though not a particularly extravagant one, it was clean, at least. His heart hammered hard beneath the ache in his chest as he wondered just exactly whose room he was in. His mind searched the past frantically as he tried to recall just what had happened that would cause him to be here.

Before anything came to him, however, he heard a soft rustle from across the room, and his eyes came to rest on the bed — upon which lay a form. The small, dirty window didn't emit much light, so it was difficult to tell who was upon it, and David wasn't sure he wanted to know. Perhaps he could leave before the person awoke. He swore to himself he wouldn't have another drink for the longest time. Clarence had told him to keep his wits about him, and currently, last night remained blurred in his mind.

He tried to stand but found he couldn't make it to much more than a crawl, not with the way his head pounded and his chest burned. He put a hand upon it, finding that it had been wrapped — which meant that, at least, whoever was with him had cared enough to see that he didn't expire from his injuries.

David tried to move to the door, but it seemed the more he moved, the farther away it became. Finally, he collapsed to the floor, his efforts useless.

He heard movement behind him but couldn't look, his eyes seemingly sewn shut as his head pounded with his exertion.

He forced himself to move to his back and crack open his eyes, an involuntary groan escaping as he did so. But if he was going to encounter whoever approached, he refused to do so with his back to the person.

A face appeared, blurred, the back of it surrounded by a halo of light. Despite the fact he could hardly see, somehow he sensed that there was no threat to him, that he had nothing to fear.

And then everything went dark once more.

* * *

WAS he attempting to run from her? Sarah had no idea just what threat he assumed she posed, but then, she wasn't entirely sure of his current state of mind after the injury he had sustained. Now the fool was once again passed out at her feet, and she simply left him where he was, in the entryway of the room, as she inspected the bandages upon his bare chest, though she did place a pillow behind his head and returned the blanket to him.

The deep wound was rather ghastly, and Sarah wished she had aromatic vinegar, which would be much more effective in preventing it from festering. She supposed his family would likely call a physician once he returned home, which somewhat worried her. There were some physicians who were knowledgeable and she had seen produce effective results, but in her experience, most treatments they performed actually led to further distress of the patient.

Her task complete, she sat back on her heels and stared down at Mr. Redmond, for he actually looked quite peaceful in repose, the lines of his face smoothed, his nose slightly crooked, she realized with a smile, his full lips ever so slightly parted. His sandy hair had a small smattering of blood within it, and she stood to wet a cloth to wash some of it out.

As she returned, she attempted to keep herself from staring down at his chest. She should only be assessing him as someone who required treatment from her. And yet, she couldn't help what seemed to be a few extra beats of her heart as she stared at the smooth chest in front of her, now marred by the bandages. He had the slightest dusting of blond hair upon the top of it, and her fingers itched to trace it.

Then there was his abdomen, in which were finely cut muscles that tapered down to a vee where the top of his breeches rested. He was not the first man she had seen in such a state of undress, for she had previously tended patients with similarly placed wounds, but she could admit that never before had she felt such emotions stirred within her at seeing a half-naked body before her.

As she wiped the dried blood from his hair, Sarah supposed this was why he had the reputation he did — and, if she were to guess, what had led to his current state of injury. She shook her head at both her thoughts and her reaction to him, and was just about to stand to wash out her cloth when his hand shot up as his eyes opened, and he gripped her wrist tightly.

"Just what," he said, his words guttural, as though it took great effort to speak them, "do you think you are doing?"

CHAPTER 5

*D*avid shouldn't be here. As far as he could tell, he
and this woman were alone in what appeared to
be rented rooms a far cry from his own, and if he could rely
on his own sight, then it seemed it was the lovely and apparently innocent Sarah Jones crouching beside him. But
perhaps it was just his imagination playing tricks on him, for
she couldn't actually be here with him — could she?

And how the hell had he gotten here?

"I am seeing to your injuries," she said crisply, "And I
would appreciate it if you would release me."

He nodded, though the effort caused pain to shoot
through his temple and begin to throb within his skull once
more.

"My apologies," he muttered as he did as she asked, and
she blessedly returned moments later with a glass of water,
which he took eagerly, as it seemed that someone had
stabbed his throat as well as his body.

He closed his eyes for a moment at the thought as finally,
the events of the previous evening came rushing back to him,
and he cringed as he felt the pain anew. When he eventually

opened his eyes once more, he couldn't help but acknowledge the contrast of the scene last night with what appeared before him now.

Miss Jones sat upon a bed in front of him. Despite the fact she wore nothing but a wrapper over what he assumed was a nightrail, she looked nothing but proper, her legs crossed at the ankles and her hands folded within her lap. The only true sign of dishabille was her bare toes peeking out from beneath the bottom hem of her blue wrapper, which looked as though it had once been a rather brilliant color but had now faded.

"How did I get here? And where are we?" He asked aloud, and she regarded him calmly as she answered his questions in her gentle, flat voice.

"This is where I live. I would ask that you please not share the location or my situation with others, however. There are many people, particularly within this neighborhood, who are aware of my skills as a healer. I have no knowledge of how you came to be here, as I simply responded to a knock at my door in the middle of the night, likely the early hours of the morning when it was still dark. There you were, with injuries that you have likely already ascertained for yourself — wounds to your head and torso. I would hazard a guess that you took a decent beating, hitting your head when you fell upon the ground. The gash within your chest looks to be from a knife or sword, although you are lucky that it isn't any deeper than it is. Still, I am worried about it festering, depending upon the weapon used against you."

David furrowed his brow as she spoke, for her words were measured, emotionless. He had not encountered many women in his life who would see such injuries before them and lack any particular reaction.

"How does a woman such as you become a healer?" he asked, to which she smiled.

"That is a story for another day," she said softly. "But rest

43

assured you are in good hands. Now, tell me, Mr. Redmond, how did you find yourself in such a predicament?"

He sighed, lifting a hand to run it through his hair, only to find it wet. That's right — she had been washing his hair. Why?

"It was bloody," she said now, as though she could hear his thoughts, and he sighed again. He supposed if she had treated him, she deserved to know the truth.

"I was at a club," he said. "The Red Lion. There wasn't anything particularly remarkable about the night. I played a bit of faro, lost a few games, won a few, likely came out about even. I saw some friends, had a drink or two... and then decided to return home."

If there was something remarkable, that was it — he had rebuffed the flirtations of the working women, and he couldn't determine just what had caused him to do so. It was as though suddenly their faces had been too painted, their bodices too low, their dresses too garish. Which was ridiculous. He had been attracted to these women with no qualms for so long — why was anything different right now?

He refused to believe it had to do with this woman sitting in front of him. He was not a man who pursued innocent women, for he knew they would not be content with a simple liaison. No, she would be looking for a man who would commit to her, could provide for her — the type of man she deserved. Not someone like him.

He must have been tired — that was it. Which would also explain how he had been taken so off guard.

"I departed the club and asked for my carriage to be brought around," he continued, closing his eyes as he pictured it once more. "They surprised me, taking me off guard. One held my arms behind me, the other used his fists to 'Teach me a lesson,' I believe is how he phrased it."

"Did you know him?" she asked.

"I did not. He was only the man who had been hired, not the one who desired to see me in such a state."

"Do you know who that would be?"

"I do."

He didn't want to continue, didn't want to sully this room, this woman, with any further discussion of what he had done or why the man was interested in seeing to his demise. He could sense, however, that Miss Jones was waiting for him to finish the story.

"It was Lord Houghton."

"Lord Houghton…" she repeated, nibbling her lip as she thought on the name, and he noted when recognition dawned. She was the type of woman who easily shared her thoughts and feelings, for her expressions were vivid. Her brown eyes, which were warm and comforting, widened. "He is a proud man. Rather… stern."

"Yes, that would be the proper way to term it," he murmured.

"What did you do?" she asked, but then saw the disapproval in her eyes and realized she likely already had a fairly good inkling of just what he had done to deserve such treatment. At first, he felt ashamed at his actions, but before he refused to allow such emotion, he became indignant to the fact that she would feel she had the right to judge him. He knew nothing of her life — how could she sit there and suggest that he might be at fault with his own actions?

"His wife was… taken with me," he said finally, unable to admit to anything further, and she nodded, as though her suspicions were confirmed, and he opened his mouth to ask her just why she thought she could judge him so, but then promptly closed it. For that would hardly be fair. She had obviously spent some time caring for him, and that was no way to repay her. He was relieved when she did not pursue his story further.

"I shall have someone send for your family," she said. "I would go myself but I'm not sure I should leave you for any great length of time. What is the address of your home?"

"No," David said immediately. "My family cannot come here, cannot see me like this."

"You need help," she insisted, but he shook his head, so vigorously that he winced.

"If my father became aware of my current state, he would lose the tiniest bit of respect that he still holds for me. My mother would be similarly disappointed."

"Do you have any siblings?"

"My brother, but I'd prefer he not be aware of this."

"All right," she said slowly. "What about the Duke? Or perhaps Lord Berkley?"

He could summon them, and he had no doubt that they would come to his aid. But when he thought of the lives they were currently living, the contentment they had found and their continued suggestion that he settle down himself, he had no desire to prove them right.

"I'd prefer not to bring them into this."

She raised her hands, sighing in exasperation.

"Do you have a valet? A trusted servant?"

"I have a valet and servant in one, but I cannot say he is trusted — except by my father," David said, aware that Hampton would immediately send word to his father about his latest deeds. "If you would be so kind as to summon a hack, I will find myself room at an inn until I am recovered enough to return to my own rooms so that I am not questioned by anyone."

"Absolutely not!" she exclaimed, and he shrank back ever so slightly, stunned at how much conviction she held within her tone. "I cannot allow you to be alone like this. Your head injury needs to be observed, and your wound addressed. As it is, I am fearful that it might not heal as it should. I do not currently have what I need to treat it properly, so I made do with what I have."

"Can you find what you are searching for?"

"I would have to ask around, as I am sure it is available somewhere within London; however, it can be mighty expensive, and I haven't the means to purchase it."

Once again, David was intrigued by who she was and just how a woman who attended all matter of social events with every level of the nobility could be living in such a place with apparently so little funds at her disposal.

Suddenly the fact that she was sitting there, judging him, when he knew nothing about her or what had brought her to her current place in life, rankled him. He was tired of others thinking him less than worthy simply because he enjoyed life — what else was he supposed to do? He had nothing but time on his hands with no real purpose to fill it.

"Find what you need and I'll pay for it," he said, a bit more harshly than he meant to. "You believe I deserved this."

She sat up straighter at that. "I make no judgments," she said with a shake of her head. "People come to me requiring various treatments, and I only ask for the circumstances in order to ascertain how to best treat their injuries. For example, in your case, I am now aware that you were injured with a blade that is likely quite unclean, which I believe cause greater concern."

Sarah rose. "Well. I will dress and be off to find what you need. You must, however, promise not to try to escape again untreated. While you are more than welcome to leave at any time, of course, I would far prefer that you would do so accompanied by another who can ensure that you do not pass out in the middle of the street and find yourself back on my doorstep. It is already mid-day, so I should not be long."

He saluted her as one would within the army, and he caught her attempt to hide her smile as she swept across the room, moving a privacy screen between them.

David swallowed. Was she going to dress within the same room as him, where he lay with half his body exposed? It was not as though he was modest, but despite his injuries, he was still a man, and she a woman to whom he couldn't deny he was inexplicably attracted.

He watched her from the corner of his eye as she crossed beyond the screen, opened a wardrobe, and selected a practical muslin gown of a drab gray. Why did she own such a dress? It was more of what one might find on a woman of middle class. But then... here she apparently lived. She hurried behind the screen, and David couldn't help but listen to her movements, identifying each rustle or slip of fabric with her current action — her wrapper removed, followed by her nightrail, both tossed over the top of the screen.

She must be standing there naked, he realized, and he felt his pulse quicken as he tried to keep the image from his mind, but he couldn't help but picture what she must look like. He wondered if her soft, creamy skin was freckled anywhere besides her nose. She was compact, he thought, remembering their dance together. And despite the softness of her looks, he sensed she held strength within her, in both the physical sense as well as her own power.

He heard another rustle of fabric and pictured her clothing herself in her chemise and gown. Would she wear stays? His fingers itched as he imagined untying the laces as quickly as she did them up.

David cursed his thoughts, attempting to dismiss them before she came out and found him in such a state. He sat up slowly and inched his way across the room to sit up against a wall. He had just finagled himself into a somewhat comfortable position when she emerged from the screen, her hair now pulled back behind her head in a loose chignon.

"You've been busy," Sarah acknowledged. "Now then, let's get you in bed, and then off I'll go."

Her words sent heat coursing through him once more, and all he could do was stare at her.

CHAPTER 6

Sarah had nearly sighed aloud with exasperation when she emerged from behind the privacy screen. Mr. Redmond was sitting back against the wall, having obviously expended a great deal of effort to find his way there, when she was only going to help him into the bed anyway.

"What did you say?" he asked now, his eyes wide as though she had said something to completely shock him.

"I said, 'Let's get you into bed,'" she repeated, placing her nightrail and wrapper in the wardrobe before walking over to him, sitting behind him and lacing an arm around his back. He stilled at her action, and a tremor ran through her at the contact of their skin. She closed her eyes. She was a healer, and she was being ridiculous to think of anything besides this man's health.

"Come," she said, standing with him, and she could tell he was attempting to keep his weight from her as he reluctantly stood, and together they walked toward the bed.

"I'm fine," he insisted, waving away her help. While Sarah didn't believe him and was aware that it was likely primarily pride at stake here, she released him, and he nearly fell onto the bed. That head injury bothered her, but she was well aware there wasn't much that could be done besides be grateful that, at the moment, he remained conscious.

"There's a bottle beside the bed," she said. "If you find yourself in too much pain, take a spoonful, but no more. I'll return shortly, and will bring with me some sustenance for you as well."

Satisfied that she had done all she could for now, she made for the door but stopped when she heard him speak behind her.

"You know, if you wanted me in your bed..." he said, causing Sarah to whirl around.

"I did not—" she began, ready to defend herself, but then she saw the grin on his face and knew he was teasing her. So here was the charm she had been warned about. She was pleased to see it emerge, for it meant his head would likely be fine.

"From what I have heard, Mr. Redmond," she quipped, "It would take hardly any effort at all."

On that note, without providing him a moment within which he could offer a retort, she let herself out the door, laughing as she began walking down the Cheapside street.

* * *

DAVID COULDN'T HELP but chuckle at the cheeky woman. She was certainly an enigma. On the surface, she was quiet, gentle, and unassuming. How many times had he likely passed her by at a social event and not even taken note? Yet now that he had, he could hardly think of any other woman. She had a quiet strength about her, and it seemed a sense of humor as well. She attended social events of the *ton*, and yet apparently lived here, in these dingy rented rooms. He wasn't entirely sure where they were, but from the bustle of noise outside the door and the bells of what sounded like St. Paul's in the distance, if he had to guess they were in Cheapside, which was respectable enough — better than some of the other options, at least, though far from the world in which he had been raised.

And she was a healer, which made no sense to him at all. He had heard of midwives and the sort, but most of the people he knew preferred to see physicians. How in the world would she have picked up her knowledge?

Now that she had departed, his distraction gone, he found that the pain became much worse. He eyed the brown bottle beside the bed, not entirely sure he trusted it. His hesitation increased when he opened it and smelled the contents, which nearly caused him to gag. That, however, caused his chest to ache, and so he finally submitted and took a spoonful of what he determined was laudanum, washing it down with the rest of the water in the glass beside him.

The last thing he could recall until he woke sometime later was the image of a shotgun propped against the wall beside him. He had stared at it curiously, until his eyelids closed despite his best efforts and he fell into a dreamless sleep.

The opening of the door woke him, and when he sat up in bed, he could see Miss Jones struggling to open the exterior door while carrying apparently heavy baskets. He attempted to leap up to help her, but his body seemed to be holding him back.

"Stay where you are," she commanded, shutting the door behind her. "Thankfully, I found what I needed."

She worked quickly, efficiently, storing what she needed and preparing her potions on the table in the middle of the room.

"You're a witch," he said before thinking about what he was saying, hoping she wasn't insulted. She turned with one eyebrow quirked.

"I have been called that before," she said. "My mother received far worse by others — until they found themselves in need of her skills."

"She was a healer as well?" he asked as Sarah approached the bed, her arms full of nasty smelling paste. Why did it all have to be so putrid?

"She was," she said softly, and David sensed her mother had passed, so he said nothing further on the subject, for the moment at least. Miss Jones set everything she required on the small table beside the bed, before leaning over him and beginning to remove a couple of bandages.

Despite the smell of the potion she had placed next to him — which contained a great deal of vinegar, if he was not mistaken — when she leaned over him, he could smell her as well, as a tendril of escaped hair tickled his nose, her fresh scent of orange and lavender filling his nostrils. It reminded him of Clarence's warning to stay away from her — which made him laugh. Of all the doorsteps in all of London, hers was the one he had ended up on, and in the sorriest state of affairs.

"Are you not concerned about your reputation?" he asked suddenly, then, and she began to shake her head, but before she could say anything she bit her lip, concern filling her eyes as she stared down at him.

"Damn it," she muttered, the curse surprising him, though he was more focused on the fact that she was staring at his open wound.

"Something troubling you?" he asked, purposefully keeping his tone light.

"This wound... it's not looking as healthy as I'd like," she said. "Hopefully I'm not too late and can, at the very least, keep it from festering."

"I'm sure it's fine," he said, as much for his own peace of mind, but she shook her head, picking up the bottle she had mixed.

"This might hurt," she said, and seconds later was pouring the contents of it on the wound, causing him to cry out in shock at the pain it caused. "I'm sorry," she said, pressing a cloth hard upon it. "But it will be far better than a worrying infection."

He nodded, attempting to find his breath, but his lungs appeared to have been melted by the vinegar potion she poured on him.

Thankfully she soon packed a clean cloth, wet with likely some other concoction, upon the wound, and then covered it with yet another bandage.

"Sleep," she decreed, and despite his best efforts not to, he did as she commanded.

SARAH WAS WORRIED. This entire situation was now completely out of her control. Not only was an unattached man, a renowned rake at that, asleep in her bed, but he had a concerning wound and a head injury. They were treatable, but she was unsure if she should do as he wished, or if she should go ahead and contact someone. She would normally tell Elizabeth or Phoebe of such a thing, but they, of course, would tell their husbands, whom Mr. Redmond had expressly decided he did want to be aware of this situation. Were Julia here, she would speak to her, but she was with her husband, a jockey, on a racetrack somewhere else in England.

Sarah stared down at Mr. Redmond now, who was sleeping once more. She began to clean up behind her as she determined her next course of action. Once he awoke, she would convince him that he must, at the very least, contact his family to put them at peace that all was well. Were they not worried regarding his whereabouts?

He stirred in his sleep, and Sarah placed a hand against his forehead, finding it warm. She frowned, wet a cloth, and sat next to him, attempting to ignore the feel of his slightly heated skin through the muslin of her dress as she accidentally slumped against him on the uneven mattress. She lifted a hand to bring the cloth to his forehead, but as she did so she gasped when he reached out, grasping her wrist in a strong grip. Before she knew what was happening, his other arm wrapped around back, pulled her in close, and her lips were pressed against his.

Sarah was so shocked she had no idea how to respond. She should likely push away from him, but his lips upon hers were exactly what her body yearned for, as he expertly kissed her, coaxing her mouth open before she even knew what he was doing. His tongue teased hers, and with a groan Sarah gave in, responding to him in equal measure. Then his hand left her wrist, running down her back to cup the curve of her hip, and reason flooded in through Sarah's consciousness. She pushed back away from him, stepping away from the bed so quickly she nearly stumbled.

This was a patient. A man who was slightly feverish and not in his right mind. She had taken advantage of the situation, spending far too much time admiring him and enjoying his closeness, and now guilt rushed through her. She took one breath, then another, and then turned to the door. She needed a walk, some time out of this room and away from the man who wouldn't leave her thoughts.

* * *

DAVID SMILED when he heard the door close behind her. He wasn't sure what had caused him to kiss her like that — he knew he shouldn't have, that this was a woman who would never be more than an acquaintance, and was now his healer. He had awoken to her light touch upon his forehead, and then she had leaned over him, her bosom so close to his face, her scent filling his nostrils, and there was nothing in the world that could have kept him from knowing what those lush pink lips upon his would feel like. So he had taken what not only wasn't his, but also what he had no right to even ask for. The problem? Now that he had a taste, he yearned for more, and he wasn't sure any other flavor could ever satisfy him.

It was no use — he had to get out of here. For if he stayed, he was liable to seduce her, and that would certainly make a mess of things, especially after all she had done for him. Were it not for her, who knows where he would have ended up last night?

Despite the pain in his chest and the sore bruises that covered him, David looked around the room for the remainder of his clothing, finally finding it in one corner. It looked to have been washed, but there were still blood stains upon it that would likely never come out, and as he lifted the shirt, he noted that it had been cut clear through to the bottom. Well, it was of no use. There was nothing else in this room for him to wear but Sarah's dresses, and he couldn't walk through the streets of London completely shirtless. He gingerly donned his destroyed garment, finding that dressing took far longer than he could ever have imagined.

He eased himself to the edge of the bed, pleased to find he could stand, and shuffled to the door, unsure of just how he would find his way home with no carriage or money, and then nearly fell back to the ground, where he had spent far too much time as of late. For there, in front of him in the corridor, was Miss Jones, standing with her hands on her hips and a stern expression on her face.

"David Redmond," she said, "Whatever do you think you are doing out of bed?"

CHAPTER 7

A short walk around the neighborhood had thankfully cleared Sarah's thoughts. The kiss never should have happened and was clearly just a feverish mind assuming she was someone else. Sarah returned to her rooms at a good clip, now determined to ignore the fact that the kiss had even happened, for Mr. Redmond likely would have no idea of what had occurred. Instead, her fresh outlook provided space to consider how she should treat his injuries. He should be well soon, and then he would leave and she could continue her quest, and all would be as it was.

Then she had opened the door and was shocked to find him standing there awaiting her. The man should hardly have been able to get out of bed, let alone dress and determine that he was fit enough to leave.

"I ah… thought I'd take a walk myself," he said with a shrug. "It's a bit stuffy in here."

Sarah nodded slowly. "That it is, Mr. Redmond." She sighed. "If you are so insistent, then I will accompany you, and we will go for a few minutes. If you feel a moment of weariness, we return. Is that fair?"

"Very well," he said, with a half-grin. "I shall obey your command."

"You will if you want to get well," she said sternly. "Follow me."

They passed the small door to the left where she stored and prepared her food. Sarah walked across the bedroom to her wardrobe, rummaging through a bottom drawer for the man's shirt she had stored. She had a few items on hand, in case of such situations.

"Here," she said, holding it out to him, refusing to look at his bare chest peeking out between the two halves of his torn linen. "It is not nearly as fine as your own, but at least it is still in one piece."

She locked the door behind them and held out her arm. He hesitated, but she insisted, and he finally took it, though she could tell he was attempting to resist from leaning on her.

"So tell me," he said, looking around them at the neighborhood as they emerged from the alleyway in a slow shuffle. Sarah's building was fairly small and away from the busier street, but not far from her were similar lodging residences, as well as storefronts and markets offering a variety of wares. "How is it that you have come to stay in such... accommodations by yourself? I would suspect it of a young man, perhaps, but a lady?"

Sarah knew the question would be coming, and she had prepared for it.

"I am in London visiting family," she said. "Lady Alexander has been kind enough to act as my chaperone, but unfortunately she does not have the capacity for me to stay within her residence. Therefore, I found my own lodgings."

David looked at her out of the corner of his eye, and she could sense his confusion. She knew it was not an altogether commonplace situation, yet how else was she supposed to explain?

"As a healer, I must be close to those who need me," she said. "And I find that this is a neighborhood which bridges those who would come to a healer instead of a physician, and yet is not too threatening a place. It has worked well for me, I must say."

"But you are alone," he stated, and she nodded, for she couldn't very well deny it.

"What if," he continued, "The night I was placed upon your doorstep, I was someone else — someone who desired to take advantage of you?"

"I don't suppose there are many who would do so," she murmured.

"Whyever not?" he demanded, and she could see that he was actually concerned now. "You are a beautiful woman and one who must return to her lodgings late at night in fine gowns. You could not be more attractive to those who would be looking to steal from you or... more."

Sarah swallowed hard. "Thank you for the compliment, Mr. Redmond," she said, though she knew he was simply being kind. She had seen the women he preferred, and she was far plainer than the lot of them. "However, I am well able to defend myself."

"Are you telling me that you know how to fire the shotgun that sits in the corner of your rooms?"

"I do," she said indignantly in response to his incredulous expression.

"And how long would it take you to prepare the shotgun?" he asked, his eyebrows raising. "Longer, I'm sure, than it might be for someone to break into your door."

"I have other weapons," she retorted.

He shook his head. "Is there really no one who can watch over you? I had thought Lady Alexander was a relative? Have you no other family to rely upon while you search for the rest?"

"My mother has passed," she said quietly. "I have no siblings of whom I am aware. Lady Alexander has been kind, but she is unable to provide me any more support than she already does."

"I am sorry to hear of your mother," he said quietly. "What of your father?"

Sarah took a breath. She hadn't intended to tell him of this, and in fact, she still hesitated to do so. But she had never been the type of person to whom dishonesty came naturally, and she was growing tired of living a lie. What was the worst that could happen now — she would be found out and have to return home to America? She was on the verge of doing so anyway.

Somehow, despite his reputation, she had a feeling that she could trust David Redmond. She was keeping his secret — he must do the same for her. Perhaps he could even help. Although if Elizabeth's husband hadn't been able to provide any assistance, she wasn't sure anymore if there was any who could. She took a breath.

"My father is a lord," she said, then bit her lip. "I just don't know which one."

"Pardon me?" he said, his eyebrows rising in surprise.

"I don't know who my father is," she said without meeting his eyes, but then forced herself to lift them. She had no reason to be ashamed — her mother had always been sure to tell her of that. It was not as though Sarah had asked to be born to a woman alone in the world. Which she certainly wasn't. Sarah was proud of her mother and all that she had accomplished, despite the circumstances she had found herself in.

"I received a letter suggesting that I should find him, telling me that he was an English lord. I hesitated, but in the end, decided to do what I could to find him. Not because I want anything from him. I just... felt a need to know who he is."

She sighed, bringing a hand to her temple. "It's been a long search now, and I feel that I am no closer than I ever have been to finding him."

Mr. Redmond simply stared at her as though she had told him she came from another world — which, she supposed, she did.

"Please, Mr. Redmond, I beg of you — do not tell anyone else of this?" she asked. "I am invited to society events due to my association with Lady Alexander. Most assume, as you did, that I am a member of her family, and while I have never outright lied, I am ashamed to say that I have allowed the untruth to continue. However, I know not what else to do for if all knew the truth I would no longer be invited to the very events where my father might be found."

He slowly nodded and cleared his throat.

"I must say, this is certainly the revelation," he marveled. "Clarence knows all of this, does he not?"

"Most of it," she said, then looked at him more shrewdly, wondering how much Elizabeth's husband had shared with him, if he was truly as surprised as he acted upon her confessions.

"Well, then, you have the best man on your side, that is for certain," he said. "I have never seen Clarence fail in anything."

That bolstered her spirits, though Sarah refused to raise her hopes. In all honesty, she was beginning to feel more than homesick — for America, yes, but also for the opportunity to live in nature once more, to be surrounded by the fields and forests where she could forage for the very things that allowed her to aid others. She missed being awakened by the birds seeming to call her name, by the sun streaming in from a window that was left open to the natural light and views outside her window. None of that could be found in London, and certainly not anywhere near her rooms. She was fortunate that she had made wonderful friends, but beyond that, she had no idea how her stay here would have been bearable.

Not that she was going to tell Mr. Redmond any of that. She had shared enough.

"You are here, then — alone?" he asked, raising an eyebrow at her, the expression one that could have been suggestive, had she not known better.

"I am," she said warily.

"Cheapside may not be the most dangerous of neighborhoods," he said slowly, as though he were contemplating her situation quite seriously. "But it still concerns me to think of you here by yourself, particularly when you will open your door to seemingly anyone."

"I knew who you were!"

"Yes, but did you know it was me at first?"

When she said nothing, he continued.

"You did not. What if I was feigning sleep, and then rolled over to take you by knifepoint once you opened your door to me? What then? No, you cannot continue to stay here alone."

Sarah crossed her arms over her chest. Who did he think he was, that he could make proclamations about what she could and couldn't do?

"While I appreciate your concern, I do as I please, Mr. Redmond."

"So I am supposed to walk out that door, return to my own home, and forget that you are here alone, at risk? I think not."

He was becoming as angry as she, though why, she had no idea.

"I have been just fine for the past nearly three years, and I will continue to be fine in the future."

He was shaking his head. "I have heard of many midwives and the like who have been taken advantage of. I will not allow that to happen to you."

"Why?" she questioned. "Why do you care?"

"I just… do," was his response, as he looked away from her, not meeting her eye. "Can you not stay with the Duchess of Clarence, or perhaps Lady Berkley?"

"They have both been kind enough to offer me residence, but people come here for me to treat them, and I do not want to be far from them, in order that I might continue my work."

"Is there no one else who can look after them?" he asked as though he already knew the answer, and she shrugged.

"I suppose there is, yes," she said. "However, if I had not the purpose to help these people, then I would lose all reason to remain in England and would leave entirely. I promised myself three years to see this through, and I have nearly completed my timeline. Upon that, I will be returning home."

"Which would be?"

Sarah opened her mouth to tell him, but then shut it just as quickly, using their return to her rooms as an excuse to give herself time to think of what she should say. She couldn't explain why, but suddenly she feared what it would mean were she to tell him. Would he think less of her? She was aware of what some English felt about America, though that shouldn't worry her. And yet, his opinion seemed to matter to her.

"Far from here," she finally settled on, allowing him to think what he chose as she turned the lock and opened the door for him.

"Very well," he said, apparently having decided upon something himself. "If you do not wish to move, then I shall have to stay here with you."

"Pardon me?" It was Sarah's turn to exclaim. "You cannot stay *here*!"

"Whyever not?"

"You have a life — a family! You cannot leave it all to act as my protector. Besides that, were anyone to ever find out…"

Sarah shook her head, not believing that he could even suggest such a thing.

"I have already been here for two days and no one is the wiser. Who would ever determine such a thing? No one will be overly concerned about my whereabouts — trust me. My valet will think that I— ah, have found other lodgings for a time."

That he was staying with a mistress, no doubt, which Sarah determined she would never, ever become, despite how drawn to him she was.

"You cannot stay," she repeated.

"Then find somewhere else to live," he said nonchalantly, and she dug her nails into her palms. He irked her to no end.

She reached out a hand to feel his forehead once more, hoping that if she focused on his treatment, she might forget about him as a man. He was still warm, but certainly no hotter than before.

"You seem to be getting much better," she said. "Though I would like to keep an eye on that wound for one more night — one more only — if you will stay?"

"A beautiful woman asks me to stay with her another night?" he asked with a cheeky grin, and she would have swatted him were she not afraid of injuring him any further. "Of course I will."

"Very well," she said, though she was somewhat worried about what that might mean. "For tonight only."

Luckily, he did not seem inclined to try anything further, and he fell into sleep quite easily, as she had thought he might with the medication she had given him for pain, as well as his body's requirement for sleep as it healed.

She made sure to dress before he woke this time, and resolved to maintain formality as they parted that morning.

"Time to go!" she said cheerily once he rose. "Return to your own home and give your family some peace by allowing them to be aware that no harm has come to you. I shall be fine. You take care of yourself."

She turned to her small table and began preparing a couple of small vials for him.

"If you choose to see a physician, then so be it. Otherwise, ensure you change your bandages. I've included more potion for the pain."

She pointed to one vial, then the next.

"The other is to apply to your wound when you change your bandage, which you must do — often. Ensure that your hands, or those of your valet, are clean when you do so."

She put both vials into his hand, his warm fingers closing over hers for a few seconds before she could pull them away.

Neither of them said anything for a moment, until finally he cleared his throat.

"Clean hands?"

"Yes," she said with a nod. "My mother always told me it helps in recovery. I have no idea why."

"Interesting," he murmured. "Well, fortunately I will return here and you can see to me yourself later on, to ensure that I have followed your instructions accordingly."

"You do not need to return," she said. "I have lived here on my own in perfect safety for quite some time now. Nothing has changed."

"On that, you are wrong," he returned, holding up a finger. "For what has changed is that I now know you are here alone, and I could not sleep well at night knowing that you were here in danger."

"I'm not in any dang—" she tried to protest, but he cut her off.

"I will be back," he promised, and she warily watched him leave, wondering if he would be true to his word — and whether or not she wanted him to be.

CHAPTER 8

When David pushed open the door to his lodgings, Hampton was sitting upon a chair, darning a sock. He looked up and then rose as David entered, nodding to him with only the words, "Good morning, Mr. Redmond."

"Good morning?" David said with some shock. "That is all you have to say?"

"Is there another matter to which I must attend?" Hampton asked as David practically stumbled into the room.

"Ah, if you could go pay the hack I hired to convey me here, I would most appreciate it."

Hampton nodded, finding the petty cash David kept nearby and leaving to pay the man.

David could hardly believe it. He had been gone a few days now, and his one servant did not seem to think it a noteworthy event? Sure, there had been times in days gone by where he had spent most of his nights with a mistress of one sort of another, but never had he simply been gone for both days and nights without warning.

Hampton returned and resumed his duties as David stared down at him.

"Did my parents inquire about me?"

"I am sorry, Mr. Redmond, but in what regard?"

"About my whereabouts," David said, attempting to hold onto his patience. "You do realize I have not been home now for two nights?"

"Ah, yes, Mr. Redmond," Hampton said, then looked up at him conspiratorially. "I assumed you were… with company. But to answer your question, no, your parents have not inquired about you."

"Has… anyone else?"

"No, Mr. Redmond."

David sat heavily upon the chair next to Hampton, who hurriedly collected his work and moved into his own sitting area. David rubbed at his temple. Not one person had worried about where he might have been. It made him feel slightly sick to his stomach.

Was there really no one who cared enough about him to wonder as to his whereabouts? Or was it simply that his own usual habits were so careless that no one questioned the fact he had been out of touch for more than a couple of days?

The fact was, no matter the reason, he had no one close enough in his life to take any notice. It shouldn't bother him. This was how he wanted to live, was it not? Unencumbered, without having to answer to anyone? And yet… somehow it left him feeling altogether alone.

He reflected on the two days and nights he had spent with Miss Jones, though much of it had been rather a blur, and the first night abbreviated. She had been concerned for him, taking note of his continued whereabouts, ensuring that he recovered. While clearly, she was doing so because he was a man in need of medical care, at the same time, he could admit that it was… comforting, in a way, to have someone there looking after him. He sighed. His injury was causing him to go soft in the head.

David knew he did have some manner of wits about him, however, for another thought that wouldn't leave his mind was the feeling of Miss Sarah Jones' lips upon his. He couldn't pinpoint just what it was about her that called to him. She did not seem to have any feminine wiles, no powers of seduction, practiced ploys, or artful methods of making herself up in order to catch the eye of a gentleman. Those were the women he typically pursued, for then he had far less fear of them asking for anything in return from him.

Miss Jones was the type of woman he avoided — one who would only provide attention to a man she was interested in for more than a moment in time. She would be looking for commitment, for attachment.

Her soft vulnerability, however, combined with that surprising touch of inner strength, was more enticing than he cared to admit.

Then there was her story — so mysterious, and yet he had appreciated the fact that she had been honest with him. She was a lady of charade with her attempts to mask her true upbringing. If others within the *ton* found out she was actually the illegitimate daughter of a man within their set... there would be uproar, he was sure. He wondered what Lady Alexander had to gain from all of this. He reminded himself to ask Clarence what he thought of the fact that the woman had agreed to assist Miss Jones, and yet not completely support her nor look out for her best interests.

For how could one leave a woman like Miss Jones to fend for herself in the middle of London? It was unheard of — and now left him with the responsibility to ensure she was safe. For he couldn't very well leave her to her own defenses now that he knew that truth of her situation, could he? She had likely saved his life. At the very least, he could protect her.

He took a deep breath. What scared him the most was the fact that looking out for her wasn't the upsetting prospect he would have thought it to be.

* * *

SARAH FINISHED CLEANING HER ROOMS, then placed her hands on her hips as she looked about her. It was strange, really, how Mr. Redmond had been within her chamber but two days and now it felt slightly bereft here without him.

The truth was, she didn't often treat her patients within her rooms — she usually went to wherever they needed her help. This had been quite an unconventional situation. The memory of their kiss swirled around her mind, and she shook her head in annoyance. It had been an accident. One that he was likely not even aware of. Why this dratted man was getting into her head, she had no idea, but she had to put an end to this, or she would be in trouble. For not only had she no time for a dalliance, which is all there would ever be between them, but she also had greater matters to attend to.

At that moment, a knock on her door revealed a messenger, and Sarah smiled at the boy, giving him a coin and sending him on his way before she opened the note, revealing it to be from Lady Alexander, telling her of a party that evening. It was rather short notice, but it was at the home of the Earl of Torrington — a man who remained on her list as one that could potentially be for whom she was searching.

She would go, she decided, though she wasn't sure she could stomach many more of these events. She hated carrying on the lie of who she was, where she had come from, and she no longer wanted to impose on Lady Alexander. She was losing heart in her quest, beginning to question why she had ever come here in the first place. Did it really matter who her father was, or whether she had any other family?

But it did, came the quiet reminder from a corner of her heart. For she had no one else in the world. She did have her friends, true — and what great friends they had become. But they were growing their own families now, and while she knew they would always be there for her in whatever capacity she required, she longed for a greater tie to someone else.

She walked over to her wardrobe with some determination. Which tired dress she would wear tonight, she had no idea. She had only a few that remained fashionable, and even then, she was sure they had been seen far too often. She stroked her hand over the silver one, her favorite, and decided one more wear wouldn't hurt. Had Mr. Redmond seen her in it before?

Enough, Sarah, she scolded herself. It didn't matter what Mr. Redmond thought or had seen. He had already seen her in her nightrail and wrapper, for goodness sake! Surely he would hardly notice if she wore the same dress twice.

As she pulled the dress out, she realized that she had assumed he would be present tonight, though in his current state she would actually advise him *not* to attend, were she asked. Yet she hoped he wouldn't heed such advice. For the truth was, she wanted to see him again. And she wasn't sure what to do about such a thought.

* * *

SARAH's first question was answered when she walked into the home of the Earl and Countess of Torrington later that evening. The house was spectacular, the Countess obviously taking great care in the upkeep of her home. Everything seemed to be gilded and painted in magnificent fashion, clearly aimed to impress — and impress it did, with its Egyptian flavor and spacious, connecting rooms. Sarah wondered what their country estate must look like if this was their London home.

"Do not crane your neck so," Lady Alexander admonished from beside her, and Sarah turned and smiled ever so slightly at her, vowing not to do so any longer. Lady Alexander had been kind to her ever since they had met, though her tone could come off as rather harsh. Sarah was aware that she said such things for no reason other than to assist her in fitting in with the noble set.

And there he was — Mr. Redmond. He was rather pale and his eyes seemed hallowed, one blackened, and as he shocked Sarah by walking straight toward her, his steps somewhat sloppy, Sarah found herself admonishing him as a nervous wife would her husband.

"Mr. Redmond, I hardly think you are fit for a party," she said, her hands on her hips, as Lady Alexander stared at the two of them, her features composed yet her eyes flitting between the two of them in her confusion.

"Perhaps not," he agreed as he lifted his drink to her in a salute. "But I have been restored to rights well enough that I am already tired of my own company."

"Are you... not well, Mr. Redmond?" Lady Alexander asked, finding her voice, and Mr. Redmond turned to her as though he had just noticed her presence.

"I had a bit of an accident the other day," he explained. "I find I am now feeling a great deal better."

"Very good," she said, then gestured to Sarah. "And you are acquainted with Miss Jones after your dance last week?"

"Of course. I have had the pleasure of meeting Miss Jones through mutual good friends," he said with a smile that was, of course, meant to charm Lady Alexander. "And here they come now. If you will excuse me. A dance later, Miss Jones?"

Sarah could only nod as she watched him stride over to the Duke of Clarence, and she turned to find Lady Alexander's shrewd gaze upon her.

"What was that about?"

"He was being friendly, I suppose," Sarah said, trying to shrug off Mr. Redmond's attention.

"How were you aware that he had been involved in an accident?" Lady Alexander asked, and Sarah stilled for a moment.

"The Duchess of Clarence informed me of it," she finally said. She had never shared with Lady Alexander her abilities as a healer. She felt the woman might disdain her endeavors, telling her that she must stop before being found out by anyone within the nobility. If she ever discovered that Sarah had actually treated one of her own station, Sarah knew Lady Alexander would be more than scandalized.

"Well, please be careful of the man," Lady Alexander murmured. "I know he is a charming one, but it is well known that his affairs are not kept particularly discreet and that he has no interest in actually committing to any one woman."

"Yes, I am aware," Sarah said. "I will be on my guard, Lady Alexander. Thank you."

And at that, Lady Alexander nodded, stared at her for a moment as though assessing the truth of her words, and then continued on her way, leaving Sarah alone with jumbled thoughts — and finally, the realization that if she wanted to do a further search of the Earl's past, there would be no better time to do so than now.

CHAPTER 9

*D*avid kept an interested eye on the innocent Sarah Jones. She looked lovely tonight, dressed in an ethereal silver gown that shimmered when she walked. He wondered where she had found the money to dress in such a fashion. Surely not from the patients who appeared at her doorstep, for he doubted many of them could pay anything near what would keep her in fine fashions.

Wherever her funds came from, she clearly wasn't spending it on her lodgings.

As Lady Alexander walked away from her, David watched the woman shrewdly. She had married well, he knew, but had been widowed some years ago, with no children to speak of. Miss Jones seemed grateful to her, but David couldn't help his own bitterness that she would leave Sarah to fend for herself in potential danger when she would have more than enough room in her own home to house her apparent charge.

It was all quite bizarre, he thought, as he tapped a hand against his leg. David had been raised in every sense of propriety, and though he often shirked what he knew to be morally right, he had never strayed far from what was appropriate in the eyes of society.

Miss Jones broke most conventions, though she was rather silent about it, which his own mother would appreciate.

He watched her now look around the room somewhat... furtively, almost, as though determining whether or not she was being watched. Then with a slow swish of her silver silk, she turned and made her way to the corridor leading out of the large drawing room, which tonight was serving as a mock ballroom. Where was she going? She had just arrived.

David knew he was being somewhat obsessive, but he couldn't help the curiosity this woman created in him. Where *was* she going? He set his drink down on a side table and followed her, nodding to acquaintances as he made his way through the room, uncaring whether he seemed rude to not stop and have any further discussions, as he didn't want to lose her. He stepped into the empty corridor just as he saw her ahead of him, noting the shimmering gown and the soft cinnamon of her hair slipping through a door near the end of the hall.

He followed as silently as he could. David hardly wanted to admit it, even to himself, but he was well-versed in the art of stealth from sneaking out of a few homes and establishments in his time.

Miss Jones had left the door to the room she had entered ajar, and David followed behind, peeking in through the crack. This looked to be the Earl's office, and she was now sitting behind the desk, rifling through loose pieces of paper on the tabletop before opening the top drawer.

David thought back to her story. Was she actually looking for proof that the man might be her father? He had no idea how she thought she might find such a thing by looking through the man's desk. She bent down, attempting to open one of the solid mahogany drawers, but it must have been locked, for she grunted in her attempt to do so.

He nearly laughed, but then he heard footsteps from behind him — firm footsteps that seemed to be well aware of their destination, and a quick look revealed the Earl himself walking down the hall.

David slipped into the room, shutting the door behind him quietly as he did, but from the gasp that echoed around the room, he had clearly startled Miss Jones. She sat up quickly, bumping her head on the top of the desk as she did so, emitting a quiet yet audible yelp.

Hearing the footsteps approaching on the other side of the door, David lunged toward her. With no time to explain, he grasped her by the waist, picked her up to swing her in front of the desk, and then set her down in front of him, wrapping his arms around her and taking her lips in a passionate kiss, practically bending her backward over the desk.

It was just in time too, for before Miss Jones had any time to react besides grasping the lapels of his jacket in order to help prevent herself from falling over, the door swung open behind him.

"I say!" came the shocked exclamation, and David lifted his head, though he kept his arms around Miss Jones in order to keep her from falling. He turned to look behind his shoulder, allowing a sheepish smile to cross his face.

"Lord Torrington!" he exclaimed. "How are you this evening?"

The Earl lifted an eyebrow. "I am well," he said slowly. "And just what do you think you are doing in my study, Redmond?"

David looked around him as though he were just realizing where he was.

"My deepest apologies, Torrington," he said. "I became

rather carried away, I'm afraid, and opened the first door I came to. Forgive me? And please," he lowered his voice, "You'll keep this between us, I hope? I wouldn't want the lady's reputation to be brought into question."

Torrington stood there for a moment, apparently caught between anger at finding them within his private area and understanding David's predicament.

Finally he sighed and waved a hand in the air.

"I'm not a gossip, Redmond, and therefore I will not be saying anything. Just keep out of my study, all right? Take your tryst elsewhere."

David nodded.

"Of course. My apologies once more."

He took Miss Jones' hand in his own, then led her out of the office. It was only when they were back in the corridor once more, the door shut behind them, that he risked a look at her face. Her eyes were wide, a hand pressed against her lips as she stared out in front of them.

When she eventually turned up to look at him, he was concerned about how she might react. Would she slap him for taking such liberties, or would she understand that he had only taken such action in order to keep her from being found out?

He waited for a moment, hesitant — typically he had full awareness that his affections were well received, but in this case...

Then she burst out into laughter.

He paused for a moment, surprised at her reaction, but then he began to chuckle himself, for her mirth was contagious.

"Thank you," she finally said. "That was quite close. Goodness, what would the Earl have thought if he had come into his study to find me going through his desk?"

"He would likely be wondering the same as I am — just why were you studying Lord Torrington's personal files?"

"And just why were you watching me do so?"

They stared at one another for a moment, not in any animosity, but in silent contemplation. She finally relented.

"I was looking for information — any hints that he might be the man I suppose him to be."

"Your father?"

"Yes."

"What were you thinking, that he would keep a record of your birth upon the top of his desk?"

He placed a hand on her back as they spoke, moving her away from the door and down the hallway. Opening another door, he found a small sitting room with a fire cheerily lit in the grate — a room that was quite obviously more welcoming to any guests of the party, unlike the Earl's unlit, dark, cold study.

They entered, and he gestured for her to take a seat on the sofa while he chose a chair across from her.

"Honestly, Mr. Redmond, I have no idea what I am doing any longer. I seem to have come to a complete stall in my search."

She looked so defeated that David longed to stand and take her in his arms once more. For the truth was, though their kiss had been brief and for a greater purpose, he could still feel her lips upon his, could taste the lemonade she had obviously just drank, and all that the kiss had succeeded in doing, besides masking her true actions, was stir his passion and leave him wanting more.

But now wasn't the time to attempt any more with her.

He tilted his head to the side as he contemplated her situation.

"I wonder," he murmured, "If you are taking the wrong direction in this."

"What do you mean?"

"You have been focused on determining who your father is, correct?"

She nodded.

"Have you not thought that perhaps the better option may be attempting to determine who wrote you the letter? This mysterious person obviously holds the answers to your questions. Why would he or she not provide them to you?"

"I have no idea," Miss Jones responded with a shrug of her shoulders. "Perhaps this is all some great farce."

"I doubt it," he said with a frown. "For what purpose would that serve? No, I believe there is some greater work at play, though what, I have no idea. Have you the letter still?"

She nodded. "In my rooms, yes."

"I will take a look at it this evening, then," he said, and she looked up at him, her eyes widening once more.

"You would like me to bring it to you?"

"No, you can show it to me when I come to your lodgings."

"And just why would you be returning once more, Mr. Redmond?

"Do you not recall me telling you I would return? I can hardly leave you alone, Miss Jones."

"I enjoy being alone, Mr. Redmond, and have been for some time."

"Nevertheless," he said, shaking his head. "No longer."

"But—"

"I will tell no one. Your reputation is safe with me."

At her quirked eyebrow, he laughed.

"All right, that is the first time I believe I've ever said that to a woman. But rest assured, I will tell no one of this arrangement."

"Will your family not notice when you are never home to sleep?"

He snorted and shook his head.

"I have my own lodgings, and my family didn't even notice I was gone for two days when you were caring for me," he said. "It seems, Miss Jones, that there is no one who cares more about my whereabouts and wellbeing than you currently do."

She wrinkled her nose, and David was well aware that she was likely reflecting on the fact that she didn't overly care, so what did that mean for everyone else?

"We will discuss this later, Mr. Redmond," she said instead, and he smiled, knowing that was as near to victory as she would apparently admit.

"Very well," he said, but then continued on another tack. "What about Lady Alexander?"

"What about her?"

"Have you thought about whether or not she might have a connection to the letter writer, your mother, or your father?"

"Oh no," she said, shaking her head. "I met Lady Alexander... at another point in time. She is unconnected to the whole of it."

He pursed his lips. "I am not so sure."

"I am."

"Very well," he said, not wanting to push her on this, but deciding he would look into it himself. "We best not remain ensconced in here for too long — who knows what others may think of us."

He winked at her, rose, and held out his hand to help her rise before leading her to the door.

Damn, Miss Jones. The more he tried to keep himself away, the closer he found himself to her.

CHAPTER 10

Sarah waited for the barrage of warnings from her friends, and she was not disappointed when they arrived at her side but moments later. She hadn't seen them at the party previously, but then Phoebe and Elizabeth usually arrived slightly later than many of the guests. Sarah was pleasantly surprised to find that even Julia was in attendance tonight. Eddie must have a race in London or some time away from the track.

"Do we even need to say anything?" Elizabeth asked as she approached and Sarah sighed, suggesting they sit around one of the provided tables before she began to tell pieces of the story — of Mr. Redmond appearing on her doorstep, her treatment of him, and what she had shared of her own life. Her friends looked surprised yet contemplative as she spoke.

"He may have a point," Phoebe mused, and Sarah furrowed her brows.

"About what?"

"Lady Alexander," she said. "I always have found it to be a rather interesting situation — that you would so coincidentally meet this woman who would agree to be your chaperone yet nothing more."

"She enjoys her privacy," Sarah said, defending Lady Alexander. "Besides, without her, I wouldn't even find myself at any such parties."

"Gabriel has been unable to find any untoward connections thus far," Elizabeth said, before catching Sarah's look. "I know, I know, you did not ask for him to look into anything regarding her. He was simply covering all possibilities. He was quite discreet, of that, I can promise you."

"Well, I must thank you all for your support, anyway," Sarah said, biting her lip before she felt a hand on her arm and looked over to Julia.

"I know I have not been around much, and for that, I apologize," she said, and Sarah waved away her words, knowing well that Julia's lifestyle did not allow for a great deal of time in London. "Please tell me if I am wrong about this; however, it seems that you and Mr. Redmond are somewhat... familiar with one another."

Familiar as in the fact they had slept in the same room for two nights, that she had treated his injuries while appreciating the beauty of his body, and that he had perused her person wearing nothing more than a nightrail and wrapper? That he had remained in the room while she had changed from said nightrail into her muslin dress, her nerves jumping at every touch of fabric as it brushed over her body?

"Not overly," Sarah answered, though she could feel warmth creeping up her cheeks. "We are acquainted, that is all."

Time to change the subject, she decided.

"Julia, Eddie used to ride for the Earl of Torrington, did he not?"

"He did," Julia confirmed. "That was when all of the

scandal occurred, however, and the Earl has not been around the race track often since that time."

"Ah, yes, that's right," she said, recalling now all that had happened last year, much of it involving Julia and Eddie. "My apologies, Julia, I have been far too caught up in my own concerns these days."

"It is nothing to worry yourself over," Julia said with a smile, a blonde curl falling over one of her blue eyes. "Now, what is your question?"

"Is Lord Torrington a good man? Has he been married long?"

"He proved himself to be somewhat dishonest, though, in the end, Eddie said he was more than contrite, which is something, I suppose. He did try to help Eddie when he became drawn into everything, although it was Lord Torrington's fault to begin with," Julia mused. "As for his marriage... I know he and the Countess are not overly close, but then who would be with a woman like that?"

"I am afraid I do not know her."

"She is the daughter of a marquess, and therefore feels herself above most others — and that attitude seems to extend to those who have married into a higher rank," Elizabeth said, with a glint in her violet eyes. "I tend to avoid her as I am able, though her husband is jovial enough."

"Interesting," Sarah mused, though what she was going to do with that information, she had no idea. So the Earl's wife was not particularly warm. What did that mean to her?

Sarah sighed, but then her attention was caught when a shadow fell over her lap. The women looked up to find four gentlemen awaiting their attention. Sarah could feel the stares of her friends, for while three of the men were their own husbands, Mr. Redmond was clearly awaiting her notice. It seemed no matter how she attempted to distance herself from the man, there he was, becoming part of her life one way or another.

"A waltz is beginning," he said, the slightest of smiles dancing around his lips, though Sarah realized it was somewhat hesitant, as though he was unsure of just how she would respond to him. "Dance with me?"

She bit her lip. She shouldn't. But as her friends drifted off to the dance floor themselves, she decided that she really had no choice.

"Very well," she said. "Let us waltz."

WHEN SARAH LET herself into her rooms hours later after being conveyed home by Lady Alexander's carriage, she took a moment to lean back against the door and compose herself. She shut her eyes as she allowed all of the emotions of the evening to finally sweep through her.

She was typically fairly adept at reading people, particularly their emotions and motivations behind their actions. But David Redmond remained a mystery.

From all she knew about him, he was a man who cared primarily for the pleasures of life, taking on little to no responsibility for anything else about him. So why did he seem to care so much about her current situation, be it her search for her father or the fact she lived here alone?

For the truth was, she was growing far too close to him. When he had held her in his arms throughout their waltz, it was difficult to ignore the feel of the muscles she had seen firsthand beneath his jacket, to not allow his scent of brandy and spicy cologne to invade her nostrils. When he spoke, his warm, soothing voice so close to her ear sent chills down her spine. And then there had been that kiss... she knew it was for no reason other than to hide her true purpose for sneaking around the Earl's study, but still, it had caused a reaction within her that had left her every nerve on edge throughout the rest of the night. It was as though she could sense him wherever he was within the room, notice his every movement, his every breath.

The worst of it all was that it wasn't just his physical presence nor her attraction to him that bothered her. That, she felt she could handle. It was the fact that she was beginning to enjoy the thought of having someone look out for her — a man who would care enough to worry that she was protected at night, who would help extricate her from what could have been a potentially disastrous situation, who would dance with her when she was the lone single woman within her circle of friends.

She had been told so much about him — the fact that he shirked responsibility, respectability. That he dallied with any woman with whom he had the opportunity to do so. It wasn't that she didn't know it to be true, for she had seen firsthand the result of one of his previous liaisons with a married woman. It was that he had shown her a completely different side, one of care and compassion, humor and charm.

Though that was likely what drew in other women as well, she thought with a rueful smile as she pushed away from the door to pull out her nightrail and begin preparing for bed.

She jumped slightly when she heard a knock on the door, and she fisted her pistol in her hand as she opened the door a crack. To her surprise, it was the very man who refused to leave her thoughts.

"What are you doing here?" she asked, opening the door wide to allow him entrance.

"I told you I would be here tonight," he said, shutting the

door behind him, still dressed in his evening clothes. "And here I am."

Sarah could hardly think when standing so close to him, so she stepped back and returned to her pile of clothing to tidy it up.

"As you didn't mention anything toward the end of the evening, I thought perhaps you had forgotten. Or had arranged for another… liaison, perhaps."

"Another liaison?" he asked, raising his eyebrows. "I promised you I would be here. And here I am."

"I never asked you to be!" she exclaimed in frustration, though she immediately regretted her words when she saw him take a step back as though she had hurt him.

"I'm sorry," she immediately said, though she had no idea how to explain that the reason she didn't want him close was that she couldn't handle the effect he had upon her, that she was worried she would lose more than just her reputation if someone were to find out about their current state of living. "I suppose I am just overwhelmed by everything, and I feel guilty about the fact that you are leaving your life to be here to protect me when I am perfectly fine and have been for months now."

"No need to worry about me," he said with a cheerful smile. "Though if you have an extra blanket, I will make my bed here on the floor by the door. And, perhaps, if you feel so inclined, I could move your dressing screen between us in order to provide you with more privacy?"

Sarah's heart began to beat faster at how considerate he was being. How was she supposed to merge the rake he was purported to be with the man before her now?

"Thank you," she said, her voice just above a whisper as she looked at him, standing now in his beautifully cut evening clothes, looking so out of place here where she currently called home. She cleared her throat. "While you are here, we should look at those wounds of yours. You may have made it through the evening, but I am still of the opinion that you should be resting and looking after yourself. I cannot say I am particularly pleased with your current appearance."

He grasped his chest as though she had wounded him once more.

"Your words hurt, my lady," he said, causing her to cringe, for one thing she was not was a lady.

"I only mean that you seem... pale, and tired," she said, softening her words with a smile. "It has not been long at all since you were injured. We must see if you have done any additional damage to yourself."

"Very well," he said with a nod. "Where would you like me?"

"On the bed, if you will," she said, wishing she had somewhere else she could attend to him. "You can remain seated, but will need to take off your jacket and waistcoat."

He nodded and did as she bid, though as he sat down he looked at her with a half-smile and a quick wink.

"You know if you wanted me in bed..."

She ignored him, though it made her heart glad to see that he was well enough to joke with her. It meant he was likely on the road to full health, though she couldn't help the warmth that filled her cheeks at his words. She decided it was best to change the subject.

"Did you see a physician?" she asked, as she busied herself by seeing to her supplies.

"I did not. I trust that your treatment is the best I could come by."

She laughed softly as he unbuttoned the top of his shirt to provide her access to the wound. At the very least, it looked as though he had changed the dressing, and she began to remove it, ignoring the heat of his skin upon her fingertips.

"You place a lot of trust in a woman you hardly know."

"I know enough," he said, his breath brushing her cheek, and Sarah attempted to take deep breaths to slow her racing heart. "You seem to enjoy caring for others and seek human affection over any other currency. You give of yourself and ask nothing in return. Anything provided to you results in more gratefulness than such small actions might deserve. You are a wonder, Miss Jones."

Sarah didn't know how to respond to that, so instead, she bent down to better observe his wound. It did look much improved, she was relieved to see. He had scared her there, with his brief feverish state, but it seemed she had been able to provide him what he needed to heal it just in time, for which she was more than glad.

"Have you been dizzy? Feeling faint?"

He snorted at that, but she eyed him with a look, and he shrugged a shoulder slightly.

"Not overly, as long as I sit for a spell every now and then."

She nodded and finished her dressing, smoothing a fresh bandage overtop. She was about to straighten when her eyes caught his. They were emerald green, and tonight they seemed much more vivid than usual. She wasn't sure if it was the dim light of the room or the fact that she was closer than she had any right to be, but they called to her in a way she couldn't explain.

Before she could even think of what she was doing, she laid her hands on his shoulders and her lips upon his.

CHAPTER 11

*D*avid nearly fell off the bed.

Of course, he had felt the tension simmering between them — it had been there throughout the entire evening, since he first kissed her in the library — but he had begun to wonder if it was all coming from him, and if she was completely oblivious to his body's humming desire for her.

Apparently not.

While it certainly wasn't the first time they had kissed, what completely shocked him was the fact that *she* was the aggressor.

Despite the worry that he would scare her away, he had to see her, to attempt to read what she was feeling. He pulled back from her ever so slightly, looking into her warm brown eyes, shocked by the pools of desire held within them. Their locked stare was nearly more intimate than the kiss itself.

The only sound in the room was the quick rasp of their intermingling breath, and now and then the crack of the fire she must have started in the grate before he arrived. He had hardly even noticed it when he entered.

He ran a hand over her hair, pulling out one pin and then another, until it was soft and flowing over her shoulders.

"You are so beautiful," he said, surprised at himself when his voice emerged as just above a whisper.

Her cheeks turned pink at that pronouncement.

He ran his hands down her arms, stopping when he came to her waist, feeling something hard and out of place.

"What is this?" he asked, and she blushed even deeper.

"Nothing," she said, beginning to squirm away from him.

He stilled her with a look, holding her tightly against him. Somehow her legs had come to wrap around his waist so that she was straddling him, and he had to take a deep breath to attempt to hold onto his control and not allow his desire to overcome all else. When he realized the object was beneath the fabric of her dress, he brought his hand to her ankle, then slowly began to trail his fingers up the smooth silk of her leg. He could see the pulse beating in her throat as his hand traveled over her calf, her thigh, and then finally came to her hip. Something was banded to her, something that fit quite delicately into his hand. It was—

"What are you doing with this?" he asked in shock as he unhooked the knife and slid it back down out of her skirts.

"You were worried about my protection, were you not?" she asked with a raised eyebrow. "Well, as you can see, I am more than capable of taking care of myself."

"How long would it take for you to get to that knife through all of those skirts?" he asked her.

"Would you like a demonstration?" she asked with a smile, and he swallowed hard.

"If you insist."

He regretted his words as she squirmed backward off of his lap until her feet were touching the floor once more. Then she proceeded to quickly lift the one side of her dress and reach her knife — now unsheathed — in less time than he could count to three.

"Impressive," he acknowledged.

"You see?" she said, flipping the knife in the air, panicking him, until she caught it neatly by the handle and he began to breathe once more. She looked across the room to the door, and after a moment in which she squinted one eye and took a deep breath, she threw the knife across the room, where it lodged itself perfectly between the door and its frame. David could only stare at her in shock.

"Who are you?" he asked incredulously, and she grinned.

"Who do you think I am, Mr. Redmond?"

"When I first met you, I thought you were a refined lady, related to Lady Alexander. Now... I have no idea."

She looked to the floor for a moment before returning her gaze to him.

"Are you disappointed?"

"Not at all," he said, not wanting to say anything further. For the truth was, far from being disappointed, he was in awe.

He avoided innocent women — which Miss Jones seemingly was — because he was always afraid they would fall for him and he would be forced to break off an attachment to them. But with her, the truth was that he was the one beginning to fall for her. It felt as though his heart was beating erratically in his chest, a feeling that he was quite unfamiliar with — and one he didn't overly appreciate.

When he looked up at her as she walked over to the door, dislodging her knife, he longed to draw her down to him, to kiss her once more. He yearned to feel her softness beneath him, to know what it would be like to have her curves under his hands, to run his fingers everywhere he could find that silky skin.

But if he did so, he knew that he wouldn't be able to stop

himself from going further, to the point where he would determine just what it felt like to be on top of her, within her. And then he would be exactly the man he was reputed to be, showing up at her rooms as her protector and then taking her to bed.

He wouldn't be that man. Not tonight.

She stood there in front of him, light from the fire glinting off the steel of the knife that she twirled in her fingers, her eyes shimmering and her hair flowing around her shoulders. She was an ethereal presence, both angel and warrior mixed together.

He glanced over at the shotgun in the corner before looking back at her, suddenly needing to know more of who she was, where she had come from, how she had come to be this woman she was today.

"Where did you learn to use a knife?" he asked, and she raised her gaze back to his as she bit her lip in hesitation.

"A friend," she said, and David nearly groaned in frustration as she continued to hide from him. She finally sighed as though she had come to a decision, one she was unhappy with. "When I grew up, we lived in a village where there were few children my age. He was the son of one of our neighbors. There wasn't much to do where we lived, and so he taught me skills with weapons that he had learned from his father."

"Did your mother care that you were learning such things?"

"No, she encouraged it," Miss Jones said with a soft smile in memory of her mother. "She felt it was important for me to be able to protect myself, particularly in case something ever happened to her. Which... it did, though fortunately I was already grown."

"What happened?" he asked softly, not wanting to pry, but sensing that she needed to speak of it. He hoped he wasn't overstepping, as he knew he was wont to do. Thankfully, she didn't seem to mind.

"She became ill," Miss Jones said, sitting down upon the one other small chair in the room. "We never entirely knew what it was. She was a healer herself, much more skilled than I, and even in her most lucid moments, she couldn't identify the illness. It was in her throat, her tonsils, chest pain… she had a persistent fever and finally everything just failed. I did what I could, but knew not how exactly to treat her, besides easing her pain as best I could."

She paused for a moment, rubbing her nose.

"I just wish I could have done something more to help her."

"If you were there with her," he said gently, wanting to go to her, but sensing he should stay where he was at the edge of the bed and give her some space, "I am sure that was most important to her."

"That's what she said," Miss Jones nodded.

"This search for your father…" he began, wishing desperately within himself for the ability to help her in some way but unsure exactly how to go about doing so, except perhaps, starting at the beginning. "Can I see the letter you mentioned?"

She nodded and walked over to a side table, finding the letter within a bag of her belongings. She passed it to him and he looked it over, but besides some spidery writing that suggested perhaps the writer was not someone who would have received a formal education, there was nothing else that provided him with any additional information.

"Perhaps I could better help you if you tell me of the relationship your parents had. How did they know one another? Why did it not work, Miss Jones?"

"Call me Sarah, please," she implored. "I believe we are far past formalities, seeing as you have already spent multiple nights sleeping in my room."

He chuckled, but nodded.

"Very well. I would prefer David, as it were."

She smiled. "Very well, David."

He loved the sound of his given name on her lips. Few ever used it, and the familiarity caused him to feel that, for once, someone was close enough to him to have cause to use it.

"As for my parents," she said slowly. "To be honest, I do not know much. My mother hardly ever spoke of my father. She said it was too painful. From what I know, he was far above her in station. She was the daughter of a healer in the village near his family's estate — as for where that was, I know you will ask and I sincerely have no idea. She never told me the name of it. He was the eldest son of a lord. From the way she did speak of him, I gathered that they were deeply in love — or, at least, she loved him very much. His father forbade their marriage, telling his son that he would lose everything if he chose my mother. He was torn. She didn't allow him to make the choice, but left, not wanting to tear his entire family apart."

"But in doing so," he said, not wanting to offend her or her mother but unable to withhold his thoughts, "She tore apart your own family."

Sarah sniffed, and it broke David's heart that he had caused her pain to resurface. But if she wanted to determine the truth, she would have to face this.

"She thought she did what was best," she said with a shrug as she blinked away tears that welled up within her eyes. "I just wish she had given me more in terms of memories... and family."

David couldn't keep himself away from her any longer. He crossed the room, scooped her up in his arms, and sat her down upon his lap. He held her against him, stroking her hair as she finally allowed the tears to fall. He felt like a monster that he had caused such pain to come to the surface, but as she clutched the lapels of his jacket, he hoped that, at the very least, she could find some healing, giving some of her pain to him so that he could turn it into something positive.

He had a purpose now — to help her find what she was searching for. He could think of no greater result than bringing her peace.

"If the man turns out to be…" he wasn't sure how to properly say it, but he was fearful that Sarah's father would reject her, especially if he had found his way to another family, another life.

"If it turns out that he wants nothing to do with me?"

That wasn't how he would have put it, but she had obviously determined that this was a possible outcome.

"I suppose you could say it that way," he said slowly.

"I am not naive, David," she said. "I am aware that this is likely the most probable outcome. And in that case… then so be it. I will have, at the very least, attempted to find him, to determine that familial connection. If he doesn't want it, then I will return home and put this all behind me."

He nodded, though the thought of her leaving created an ache within his heart.

"And just where, exactly, would home be?"

CHAPTER 12

*S*arah took a slow breath. What would he think of her, once she shared her home, her upbringing? She shouldn't care. If he chose to leave, then so be it — nothing would have changed in her life.

Except she knew that was a lie. For in truth, everything had changed. She just didn't want to admit it.

"America."

His eyes widened as he sat back in the chair.

"You traveled here all the way from America?"

"I did. My mother had it much more difficult, however, finding her way there as an expectant mother, giving birth in a cabin in the woods."

"You are not from one of the cities there, then?"

"No," Sarah shook her head. "Mother had never lived in a city before, and she had no wish to begin to do so in America. We were close enough to Baltimore that we could travel there when needed, but for the most part, we lived in a small village within nature." She smiled softly in memory. "I loved it."

"And now you are in the midst of London," he mused.

"Yes," she said tersely. "It is… different."

"You hate it," he observed, causing her to laugh slightly.

"I do," she said. "I really do. Thankfully I have found people I am close with, who feel like family."

"Your friends."

"Yes," she confirmed. "They truly are wonderful. Though they have families of their own now."

"They would still miss you if you left," he said, and only then did she notice he was softly stroking her arm, his bare fingertips upon her skin.

Suddenly the intimacy of the two of them here together came rushing in. The fact that he cared enough to comfort her, to hold her, to allow her emotions to come to the surface caused the connection between them to feel closer than any physical act ever could. Though now she could hardly deny her yearning to act upon all that she was feeling toward him.

She had already kissed him once, however, and he had pulled back, more interested in her knife than anything else. The next time they came together, it would have to be of his choosing. For she had doubted he felt much toward her besides gratitude, and she had no wish to be rejected or, even worse, pitied.

And the fact he had promised to help her… she didn't want to get her hopes up, but then, she also wasn't going to turn away his offer, that was for certain.

Sarah reluctantly pushed herself off of his lap and stood in front of him.

"I find myself rather tired tonight," she said, though she forced a smile on her face. "I'm going to prepare to retire. I'll fetch some blankets for you."

She hated to end this moment between the two of them, but she also needed the space.

But as she removed her wrapper behind the privacy screen between them and lay down for the night, having

David just steps away, beyond the screen, allowed her to feel safe, secure, and cared for. She slept better that night than she had ever since arriving in London.

* * *

IT WAS INTERESTING, David mused as his carriage came to a stop in front of his parents' Mayfair home, how one could become so used to such routine. And surprising how it could begin to feel so natural, particularly for a man who had always rather enjoyed the newness each day could bring.

He would have thought that he would miss the carousing each night, but in fact, he began to look forward to darkness because it meant that he had the opportunity to see Sarah once more. Familiar with one another now, there was an unspoken intimacy between them after the night she had shared all with him, but one that they had made an unspoken agreement to ignore. For his part, he was too worried that if he took another step toward the *physical* intimacy that he knew they could share, it would break everything else that had been growing between them.

For while he had known many women in a sexual way, he had never before experienced such an intense emotional connection.

And it scared him.

He had no idea how to react to it, what it could mean for the future, or how he could protect himself from becoming hurt. One thing Sarah seemed adamant on was leaving. To return to America. He wasn't sure how he could handle never seeing her again, particularly if the relationship they currently held developed any further.

Now and again he would arrive at her rooms to find that she was out with a patient, though she always left him a note so that he wouldn't worry. The odd time when she was summoned to an emergency while he was there, he insisted on accompanying her, watching her while she tended to those who required her attention. Typically they were minor ailments, and he found he enjoyed watching her work, seeing the way she interacted with everyone from children to the elderly. She took payment when her patients could afford it, waived it when they couldn't. He had tried to pay her a few times himself, but she had refused, saying that his protection, as unwanted as it was, was payment enough.

His daylight hours were spent helping her in the search for her father. He questioned her as much as he could to help him in his quest. So far he had determined that her mother had grown up in a village where there were nearby church bells and fields of bluebells. Because that could be so many places in England, it would be difficult to pinpoint a location simply with that information.

He had attempted to put off tonight's dinner for as long as possible. His parents had been pushing for him to join them for some time now, and finally, he had run out of excuses. That, and Sarah continued to gently remind him that he was lucky to have family. He tried not to balk at her words. He knew she didn't have family of her own, and he couldn't help that he didn't like the guilt she unknowingly poured upon him at the fact that his parents were alive and well, yet he hardly ever saw them.

His parents' butler greeted him with the slightest bit of a smile, and David continued into the drawing room, where his parents, his brother, and his sister-in-law awaited.

In addition to three other people he had never seen before.

"Ah, David, I am so glad you arrived on time," his mother said, all smiles as she came over to greet him. She leaned in to kiss his cheek, pausing for a moment before pulling away as she whispered in his ear, "Be cordial if you please."

"Come, son," his father said, beckoning him over. "There are a few people we would like you to meet."

Warily, David approached, though manners engrained on him since youth forced a smile upon his face.

"Lord and Lady Buckworth, I am pleased to introduce my son, Mr. David Redmond."

The couple, his parents' age, seemed kind enough as they greeted him.

"This is our daughter, Lady Georgina," Lord Buckworth introduced the young woman, who rose from the chesterfield to incline her head to David.

David smiled, though his chest began to ache at the introduction. This had been prepared ahead of time. His parents had purposefully not told him who else would be in attendance, for then they knew he would never have come. Why did they care so much as to whether he married or not? He was not yet thirty — nor was he the firstborn. He had plenty of time to settle down.

The poor girl, young and innocent, looked up at him with a hesitant expression.

"Where do you call home?" David asked the family. "I must admit I do not believe I have seen you in London before."

"We typically remain in Bath," Lord Buckworth said. "However, your father and I are old friends from youth."

David nodded, though he could not remember his father mentioning such a man. He wondered if his father had to search beyond London in order to find someone who had not heard of his son's reputation, who would be willing to sacrifice his daughter to a man such as himself.

"London is wonderful," Lady Georgina said, a polite, practiced smile on her face. "I have most enjoyed it."

All David could think of was Sarah and her own response to London, so unlike Lady Georgina's. Unless Lady Georgina was only saying so in order to maintain polite conversation. It was often difficult to know in such situations.

Dinner proceeded in a civil fashion. David was, of course, seated next to Lady Georgina, but she hardly spoke a word to him, despite his attempts to draw her out into conversation. She refused to meet his eye, her gaze remaining on her plate, or straight ahead, as though she was listening with rapt attention to all that David's parents and her own had to say.

When David caught his brother's eye, Franklin only gave him a slight shrug, telling him in an unspoken way that he had no prior knowledge of this ploy of their parents, that he had just appeared for dinner himself. David believed him — his brother had no reason to lie, nor even to care whether or not David married.

After the Buckworths finally departed for the evening, David stood with his arms crossed, waiting for his parents' explanation of tonight's arrangement. They did not disappoint.

"So," his mother said as she re-entered the drawing room after seeing out the Buckworths, a smile on her face, her hands clasped in front of her, "What did you think of Lady Georgina?"

"I think," David said carefully, "That she is a lovely woman, who does not deserve the likes of me."

"Oh, David," his mother admonished. "You are the son of an earl! Yes, you are the second son, but do not allow that to discourage you."

David rolled his eyes.

"It is not my station in life to which I am referring, Mother," he said. "But I have to tell you that I feel nothing for her but pity, that she was thrust into this situation, believing that something might come out of this meeting between the two of us."

"Are you suggesting that nothing will?" his father asked

now, standing before David, making him feel as though he were eight years old once more, having just been caught in an act of naughtiness, such as placing a mouse in the bed of the butler — something he *had* done a time or two. "I will have you know that I went to a great deal of trouble in order for the Buckworths to not only agree to have dinner with us but to be interested in a potential match between you and their daughter!"

"I am sorry you did so, Father," David said sincerely. "Had you but asked me, I would have told you that I had no wish for such a match."

"Neither did your brother," his father thundered, and David saw Franklin flinch across the room as he reached over and took the hand of his wife. "And that seemed to have turned out just fine!"

"There is no need to involve Franklin nor Andrea," David said, attempting to keep his voice calm, as Sarah always did when she was faced with a volatile situation while in the midst of her work. It always seemed to help her to diffuse the situation. "Why did you not tell me of tonight's arrangement?"

"Because you never would have come," his mother huffed.

"You are correct," David said with a nod. "I have no wish to ruin the life of that woman. For she could hardly speak to me at dinner. How would a marriage then proceed? We would live separate lives, I am sure, and neither of us would ever be happy. She seems lovely. I am simply not the man for her."

"You are going to base that supposition off of one conversation?" his father asked, raising an eyebrow.

"If I had said otherwise — that I *would* marry her after one conversation — then you would likely be more than happy to agree," David pointed out, to which his father did not respond, telling David that he was correct in his assessment.

He thought of his first conversation with Sarah. It had been one that intrigued him. Had anyone asked him at the time, *there* was a woman he would be interested in getting to know better, though he would never admit to marriage, as that was stretching things a little too far.

"Please do not encourage the poor woman or her family," he said with a sigh, rubbing the bridge of his nose, as he felt the disapproving stares of his parents and the sympathetic glances of his brother and his wife.

"What do you suppose you are going to do?" his father asked, standing before him, attempting to intimidate David with his full height of authority. "Spend the rest of your life, until you are an old man, chasing women and gambling away all of your money? Money which comes from an allowance that I generously supply you?"

David typically enjoyed throwing his lifestyle back in the face of his parents, for he was aware that while they were disappointed in him, they were equally disappointed in themselves for allowing him to become the man that he was.

But tonight... it was as though something had changed. He was actually regretting the fact that they disapproved of the man he had become. He felt the urge to prove to them that he was more than the rake all thought him to be.

"It is not that I do not want to marry the woman because I do not desire to be married," he began. "I can tell you that the two of us will not suit. The woman barely speaks. I have no wish for a wife who would meekly do whatever I say."

"I hardly see the issue with that," his father said dryly, causing his mother to look over at her husband with a glance that was not particularly friendly, for she was far from a mild-mannered woman, though the two of them still seemed to get along just fine. "I am simply saying that I am sure she will come around in time," he amended.

"Lady Georgina is a lovely young girl," his mother said.

"Perhaps you are right. Perhaps it is best that you do not sully her reputation as well by joining her name to yours."

David rose, not allowing his family to see how much his mother's words had hurt. But they did cut deeply. He hadn't been aware of just how much his family felt they were suffering from the choices he was making.

"I apologize for any hardship I have caused you." He turned and looked meaningfully at his brother, the one person to whom he truly meant his apology. "All of you. I will strive to do better. But I will not marry that woman simply because you, Father, choose it to be so."

"I hardly see the issue with marrying a woman of your father's choosing," his mother said, changing her tone slightly, as though she felt that he might be convinced by a different approach. "Franklin did, and is he not happy now?"

A pained expression crossed Franklin's face for a moment, and David knew he was torn between being the dutiful son and loyal to his brother.

"It is true," Franklin said slowly, after a brief glance at his wife. "Lady Georgina could be a good match for you, David, if you consider the possibility."

"I appreciate the thought, Franklin, but it will not work."

"I know you think she will not suit, but perhaps try once more—"

"I cannot."

His family looked on at him in silence now. David knew he likely sounded unreasonable — for what harm could one more meeting with the woman bring?

"False expectations," he finally said, in an attempt to convince both himself and his family. "I do not want her to think that there could be more between us."

In fact, perhaps he would have to call upon Lady Georgina herself to acknowledge that there would be

ELLIE ST. CLAIR

nothing between them, to ensure that she didn't raise her hopes for a marriage that may never occur.

"No," his father said dryly. "It wouldn't do for anyone to imagine that David Redmond, son of the Earl of Brentford, could possibly be mistaken for a man who might try for some semblance of respectability."

David refused to look any longer at his father, whose words hurt more than he wanted to admit.

"I will leave you now," he said, as he suddenly longed to be home with Sarah, a longing which scared him but which he nonetheless could not deny. "Goodnight."

CHAPTER 13

*A*fter such an evening, David could hardly wait for some peace. While he more than enjoyed conversing with Sarah, she seemed to sense precisely when he needed quiet and was perfectly happy to sit in his company in harmonious silence.

As he walked up to the door to her rooms, however, his footsteps changed from a walk to a run when he heard screaming from within. His heart began to beat in a rapid staccato as he couldn't keep his mind from racing toward the worst of possible scenarios that could have happened to her if someone had forced his way within, or if she had been injured while tending to another.

He tried the latch of the door, relief flooding through him when he found it unlocked, and he threw the door open, only to stand there in shock at the scene before him.

For there on the bed was a woman, writhing in pain, with Sarah sitting on a small stool at the end of the bed in front of her.

"Emily, I know it's early, but whether you are ready or not, this baby is coming," Sarah said, her voice soothing even now as she looked back over her shoulder to see David standing in the doorway, though she simply nodded at him in greeting before turning her attention over to the laboring woman in front of her. "Where is your husband?"

"He's working," the woman managed. "That's why I came to you myself. I had no one to send to ask you to come to me."

"You were smart to do so," Sarah said, "For you would not have wanted to do this alone."

David began backing out of the door, knowing this was not a place for a man to be — nor did he have any desire to be present for a birth.

"David!" Sarah called, halting him. "I'll need a bit of help here."

He swallowed hard. What help could *he* possibly be? However, he couldn't find it in himself to deny her, and he took a step back slowly into the room.

"What do you need?" he asked, and Sarah stood, placing a wet cloth gently over the woman's forehead before walking over to him.

"We'll need some boiling water, hot cloths, and a clean blanket," she said. "And then, do you think you could go fetch her husband?"

Go fetch? David paused for a moment at her words, as he was certainly no one's dog or errand boy. But as he looked down at her wide, pleading eyes, he once again found himself doing her bidding.

"Where is he?" he asked as he followed after her to the wardrobe, holding out his arms for the towels she placed within them.

"Emily, where does your husband work?"

"He pours drinks," she said between gasps, "At The Red Lion."

"Ah, David knows where that is," Sarah asked, looking

over to him, and David slowly nodded, wishing that he hadn't had to share his previous association with the establishment. At least there was no issue now in finding his way there.

"I do," he said.

"His name is Billy," Emily said, and David nodded as he filled the kettle and placed it over the fire in order to set it to boiling.

"Are you going to be all right here?" he asked Sarah, and she nodded.

"Go."

He did as she said, thankful to simply be out of the room for the rest of the process, and headed to his old haunt.

* * *

DAVID WAS GREETED as though he were a forgotten friend when he entered through the doors of the gambling hell. The man at the door gave him a slap on the back, while he received more than one sultry wink and suggestive nod to the back rooms from the barmaids who passed by — women who were, in all actuality, far more than barmaids.

He nodded to them all in greeting but no inkling of temptation for gambling and women surfaced. Instead, he forged his way through the crowd to the back of the hell, where he found men pouring drinks.

When he asked for "Billy?" he received a stare from a man he had never before seen.

"This," said John, the man next to him and a longtime fixture at the establishment, "Is Mr. David Redmond."

David felt slightly uncomfortable at the fact that a man who worked in a gambling hell would think him to be so important as to introduce him in such a way. But he pushed away the thought, for there were far more important aspects to discuss.

"Billy, you have to come with me," he said, and the man frowned at him as he pushed his long black hair out of his eyes.

"I just began this job, I cannot—"

"Your wife is giving birth to her babe."

"What?" the man's confused look turned into one of astonishment. "It's too early, she cannot—"

"She is," David confirmed, and then the man turned to have a quick word with John, who waved him away. Billy followed after David and as they hurried out of the building and down the street, Billy began firing questions at David.

"How did this happen? How do you know about it? What am I supposed to do?"

"I was sent by the woman who is helping her give birth," he said, answering the man's questions as quickly as he could, knowing that if he were in the same position, he would only be placated by receiving all the knowledge he could of the circumstance. "I have no idea how it happened, nor do I know what you are supposed to do. I've actually never been anywhere near a birthing situation before."

David was well aware that most women would probably cringe at the "birthing situation" being referred to as such, but he knew absolutely nothing ng to do with matters of a woman's health.

They came up to Sarah's lodgings, and David hesitated. As far as he was aware, men stayed far from the birth until well after the baby was born. Were things different where Sarah was from? Were they different even within classes other than his own? Never before had he any interest in asking such a thing of anyone.

His thoughts were interrupted, however, when a noise from within answered their question of what to do now.

Billy jumped when he heard the cry, and David knocked quickly on the door, knowing it would be locked as he had ensured it was so when he left.

The crying became louder as footsteps approached, and the next thing he knew, Sarah was standing on the other side of the door, a wide smile on her face and a babe in her arms.

David stood there transfixed at the sight in front of him. She looked exhausted, her hair falling in tendrils out of the chignon on the back of her head, the old dress she wore stained, black circles under her eyes due to the late hour.

And to him, she had never been more beautiful.

"My God," Billy said with a cry, and as he stepped past David and into the room, Sarah gently handed him the baby. He looked frantically around the room for a moment, but when he saw his wife was upon the bed, completely well, though obviously exhausted, he rushed in toward her and took a seat next to her on the mattress. As the three of them sat there, a new family bonding, Sarah stepped outside of the door, shutting it behind her as the two of them stood now in the night air.

"That was… fast?" David said, as he had never actually known a woman who had given birth, but from what he had heard, it typically took much longer.

"It was," she affirmed, the smile remaining on her face. "But Emily did so wonderfully."

"The babe is well?"

Sarah nodded. "Emily must have been farther along than she thought. It happens. It is difficult to know for sure."

David was silent for a moment as he contemplated Sarah. He had seen her within many different situations now, and never before had she seemed so true to herself, so content.

"You love this," he commented, crossing his arms as he leaned back against the door.

"I do," she affirmed.

"How many times have you done this, helped a woman give birth?"

She leaned against the brick wall adjoining the door, leaving a foot between them as she stared up into the starry night, a sliver of it visible through the thick swell of buildings around them.

"Perhaps... fifteen or so?"

"Fifteen?" he repeated incredulously. "Have they all gone well?"

"No," she said, her eyes remaining on the sky, melancholy crossing her face. "But most have, thank goodness."

"Those women are lucky to have had you," he said softly, and she smiled in return at him.

"That's kind of you to say."

"It's the truth," he said. "I saw you in there, with her, with the babe. Besides your skills, you are calm, considerate of the patient's feelings. If I were to ever give birth, I would want you there."

She laughed at that, which warmed his soul as it stripped the despondency from her countenance.

"I would insist on being there, if that was ever the case, to see how such a thing could ever occur."

They stood there, smiling at one another and saying not a word, until the door behind them opened to reveal Billy, a wide smile still stretched across his face.

"Miss Jones? Emily says she's feeling well, though a mite tired. I think it best we return to our own home now."

"She is welcome to sleep here," Sarah said, but Billy was already shaking his head.

"We cannot put you out any longer and we live not far. Besides, it will be good for us to be home with Sarah."

"With... Sarah?"

Billy grinned as he opened the door wider for the two of them to return to the room.

"We named her after you," Emily said from the bed, and Sarah only nodded, leading David to believe that tears likely filled her eyes.

"That is altogether lovely, though unnecessary," she finally said, her words somewhat choked.

"I shudder to think of what could have happened had I been on my own," Emily said with the slightest of smiles. "It wasn't the easiest of births, was it?"

"You did well, Emily. Your baby was a bit stubborn, but you were so strong."

"Thank you."

"We will be back to pay you, I promise," Billy said earnestly. "I just began at the club and in due time, I'm sure I will—"

"It's fine," Sarah said, shaking her head, and when Billy began to protest, she held up a hand.

"No, please. You have a family to support now. I do not need it."

"I will make it up to you, Miss Jones, I promise."

Sarah held the baby one last time, making cooing noises that David would have thought would bother him but instead were causing all kinds of warm feelings within his heart, as Billy helped Emily to the door.

"Here," David said, helplessness overcoming him as he attempted to be of some use. "I will call a hack for you."

"We are not far—"

"I insist," he said. "I will pay for it, as my gift to you in celebration of your new joy."

"We appreciate it, very much," Billy said with a smile. "Next time you're at The Red Lion, your drinks are on me."

"Very well," David agreed, sensing the man needed to somewhat repay them in order to keep his honor and pride intact. "I will take you up on that."

After hailing the hack and helping the family on board,

Sarah and David stood at the doorway together like proud parents themselves as they watched Billy, Emily, and little Sarah depart.

David looked down to see tears within Sarah's eyes.

"Are you all right?"

"I think so," she sniffed. "It's just such a miracle. I know that sounds trite, but it's true."

He nodded slowly. "And all was fine?"

"Are you sure you want to know further details?"

"Sure," he said with a shrug, though he wasn't entirely sure that he did.

"The cord was wrapped around the baby's neck during delivery, but I managed to free it. Thank goodness."

David wasn't entirely sure of what she was speaking, but it sounded dangerous, and he was once more impressed with Sarah's skill, as well as the calm she had maintained.

She walked over to a chair and sat down upon it as though she was suddenly overcome by all that had occurred.

"What time is it?" she asked, clearly having completely lost track.

"It's late," David replied. "After midnight, for certain. You best get some rest."

He looked over to the bed in its current state of disarray.

"Sit. I'll clean up the bed for you."

"Absolutely not. I will—"

He turned and quelled her with a look.

"Let me do this for you — please?"

Then he turned back around before she could see the panic on his face due to the sight in front of him, took a deep breath, and proceeded to strip a bed to replace it with clean linens for the first time in his life.

CHAPTER 14

*T*hrough tired eyes, Sarah watched as David stood before her bed, staring down upon it as though it were a puzzle waiting to be solved. She was well aware that he had likely never changed bed linens before, and most assuredly not those that were completely soiled.

"Are you sure—" she began to call out, but he held up a hand to stop her words as he went to work.

Sarah leaned her chin upon her fist as her eyes began to close, but she couldn't keep from watching the scene in front of her. From all she knew of David Redmond, he should be the last person on earth not only keeping her company in her rooms each night — with nothing asked in return — but also doing her bidding during a birthing, and now actually cleaning up afterward. Who was this man?

One thing was for certain — she could no longer deny the rush of emotion coursing through her as he worked in front of her. He had stripped off his jacket and waistcoat so that he was now down to his linen shirt, and she could see his lean muscle stretch the fabric of it, while his breeches molded perfectly over the back of his legs when he bent down. He was a fine specimen of a man, there was no doubt about it, and she longed to see him in his true form once more.

It was then she began to hear his mutterings, and she realized he was giving himself some instruction — or perhaps arguing with himself over the next step to take in the procedure he was currently undertaking.

She began to laugh, though silently, for she knew he might take that as an insult and she was actually impressed that he was performing a task she knew would be far beneath him. It was strange, how a person could be known by one reputation but then act in a completely different manner.

When he turned to ask where the new linens might be and she pointed them out, she was sure to hide her mirth. And when he finally finished in making up the bed, he turned, throwing his arms out in a flourish. Sarah had never in her life had to work so hard to maintain control over her emotions as she did when she received a good look at the bed. It was the untidiest, most terrible bed-making she had ever seen in her life, but at least it was clean. And he was so incredibly proud of his efforts, she could do nothing but fix a thankful smile on her face and stand as she walked over to him.

"Thank you," she said, and it seemed the most natural thing in the world to reach out and take his hands within hers. "You have been more than kind."

"You need someone to look after you," he said gruffly, causing a deep ache to begin in her chest. She had looked after herself for so very long, the thought of someone else doing so was almost too much to bear, for there was equally as great a chance that it would never actually come to be.

"I appreciate that, truly I do, but I am perfectly capable in looking out for myself," she said, and he tugged at her hands, forcing her to look up at him.

"No one is fine alone."

She realized then that he was talking not only of her but himself as well. She knew he had family here — in fact, that was where he had been this evening — but she was equally aware that they were not particularly close.

"How was dinner?" she asked, feeling as though she had taken all of his attention and not provided any back to him.

He shook his head. "I have no wish to speak of it at the moment."

"But—"

He lifted a hand and placed his finger upon her lips.

"Let's get you into bed," he said, releasing her hands, leaving her feeling bereft, as he pulled out the privacy screen for her.

"Change," he ordered, and only then did she realize she was still wearing the same clothes as she had for the past fair number of hours, and suddenly the thought of being rid of them was greater than any other longing currently within her. She did as he said, reveling in the feel of the loose fabric of her nightrail settling overtop her chemise. She pulled her wrapper around her and stepped out, her bare feet padding over the hardwood floor.

"Better?" she asked, stretching her arms wide, but then suddenly felt as though she were leaving herself rather too open and vulnerable as his green eyes seemed to darken, becoming somewhat smoky.

She swallowed, but before he said anything regarding her current state of dress, he turned away and began to roll out his blankets.

Sarah lay down under her own, but despite her exhaustion, she found that she could only stare at the ceiling, sleep eluding her, particularly after David blew out the lanterns and she could hear him rustling around in his own coverings.

Her mind began to war with her heart over what she should do, what she should say. For she knew that to become closer to him in any way would only endanger her heart all the more, and yet... did she not deserve one night to enjoy herself, to act upon the emotion coursing through her, that would not leave her be?

"David?" she finally whispered into the dark room. "Are you sleeping?"

"No," came his short, terse reply, and wondered if he was being surly because she had awoken him.

"Are you tired?"

"No, but you are," came his reply.

"Would you..." she began, but her voice was a soft whisper. "Would you come lie with me?"

The room went silent, and Sarah squeezed her eyes shut as his lack of response. Had she completely misread what she had assumed were signs of his attraction toward her? She was not particularly experienced nor skilled in matters of flirtation, that was for certain. Suddenly her entire body went warm at the embarrassment coursing through her.

"Please, forget I said anything," she said hurriedly. "I was only asking because—"

"Because..." he continued as her words died out, as she had no idea what excuse she could offer. Only, she then heard him push back his own coverings and walk toward her, the floorboards creaking under his footsteps. As he slowly sat down next to her on the bed, her body rolled toward his weight on the uneven mattress.

"Because I am lonely," she finished, and he stayed where he was, sitting upright next to her.

"I am happy to provide you company," he said. "Always. Is there anything of which you would like to speak?"

She shook her head, but then realized that he couldn't see her in the dim light, with only the slightest bit of embers from the fire remaining with the room.

"I actually have no wish to discuss anything," she said. "It is rather... I just want to be close. To you."

He bent down closer toward her. "Is it me you want, or are you lonely for any companionship?"

"Only yours," she whispered, and she could sense him hovering above her — so close, and yet the inch between them could have been a mile. Should she take this next step, knowing she could lose her heart in the process?

Her body decided for her, as she leaned up, meeting his lips, and the same shock that had coursed through her the previous times they had done so began once again. This kiss, however, was urgent, wanting, needing, a promise of more to come.

He bent over top of her, his elbows coming to rest on the pillow around her head, while she lifted her arms to encircle his neck, pulling him down even closer. She opened her mouth to him, shock coursing down to her very core when his tongue touched hers, expertly stroking, tasting, kneading. Oh, but this felt so right, their arms about each other, learning more of one another and all they held within.

"David," she breathed when he broke the connection, though only to place his lips on one of her temples, then the other, and finally on the tip of her nose before he began working his way down. She tilted her head to the side to allow him better access to her neck, and when he reached the high neckline of her nightrail, she impatiently tried to move the material out of the way to allow him better access. Frustrated when she couldn't do so, she removed her arms from his neck to reach down to pull the garment up over her head.

"Oh, Sarah," he said with a groan as she threw it on the floor. "You shouldn't have done that. For I'm not sure... I don't know if I can ever stop once we go any further."

"I don't want you to," she responded as she placed her arms

back around her neck, the truth coming out before she even had time to think of it, to process it. Sarah always reacted according to what she felt, not what she thought, and she knew now with all certainty that nothing would ever feel as imperative as being with David Redmond did at this moment.

"I want to know what it's like to feel you — all of you — to know you, inside and out," she said, and he brought his forehead down to hers, their noses against one another as he tensed.

"You do know what you are asking?" he said, his voice husky. "Once we do this… there is no going back."

"Then let's go forward," she said simply, not entirely knowing what she was saying, or of what was to come in their future, but needing this nevertheless.

Sarah could sense when he let go of whatever doubts were holding him back, and when he returned to her it was with an intense desire that nearly overwhelmed her with its passion. He kissed her with the urgency of a man starving for more, his raw, unbridled desire flowing from him into her, igniting her own passion for more.

"Please, David," she said, not wanting to beg, but needing him to understand that she wanted him, more than she had ever wanted anything before in her life. What was to come afterward, she had no idea. But one thing Sarah knew was that never before had anyone treated her with such care, provided her such protection, nor given up so much of himself for her.

As he kissed her now, he filled his hands with her breasts, and she nearly arched up off the bed when he brushed his thumbs over her nipples. She knew everything about anatomy, of course. But no one had ever taught nor prepared her for how it might feel when certain aspects of her were touched in the way David touched her now. And then, through the fabric of her thin chemise, he brought his mouth down to her, and she cried out aloud at the sensations that rushed through her.

Suddenly she needed to feel his skin upon hers, to know what it would feel like for that light dusting of hair to brush up against her chest. She brought her hands to the buttons of his shirt, urgently pushing them through the loops. He made no move to help her but allowed her hands to go to work, until she was lifting the hem of his shirt, and he finally assisted her by drawing it up overhead, her chemise soon following suit.

When he came back down to her, Sarah could sense that he was holding back, but she wanted more, needed to feel his weight upon her.

"You won't hurt me," she whispered, knowing within her heart that the words were true. And then she could tell when he stopped thinking but gave into the emotions as well, for their kisses and their touches became all the more intense. His fingers ran down her body, over her ribcage, encircling her waist, before cupping her hip and then moving even lower still. She opened for him without even thinking, and when he found the place where she particularly longed for him, she groaned aloud. All of the sensations he was causing within her, from the warmth upon her breast to the smooth strokes of his fingertips, caused a release unlike anything she could ever describe to course through her, tremors rolling from their beginning point throughout her entire body.

And still, she needed more.

He was lying beside her now, still holding himself up and away from her. She reached out to find he still wore his breeches, though there was certainly a strain at the fall. She loosened the fastenings, and through ragged breathing, he managed, "Are you sure, love?"

"Yes," she moaned, never surer of anything in her entire life. He helped her with the breeches, springing free as he rid himself of them. He hesitated for only a moment before entering her, and together they gasped at the perfection of coming together.

The pain she had been expecting lasted for but a moment, and soon she was urging him on to move within her. Sarah knew everything about the act, but certainly not how exquisite the sensations with a man could be — or perhaps it was just *this* man. Of that, she wasn't entirely sure.

"I cannot hold back much longer," he said, his breath heavy.

All she could say was, "Then don't," and he freed himself from her before he finished. Sarah hadn't even thought of such a thing, so hazy her mind had been amidst their passion.

Spent, they lay beside one another as they caught their breath. David reached an arm out around her, pulling her in close. As Sarah lay her head upon his bare chest, she wanted to stay awake, to revel in this moment and all that had just happened, but before another thought could flow through her mind, her eyes closed and she fell fast asleep.

CHAPTER 15

*D*avid had been with many women before. Too many, he could admit even to himself. But it had always been for his own satisfaction. Not that he didn't take their own into consideration. He had just never, in his life, woken up with a woman in the same bed. In his arms. And worried about how she had felt about their time together.

He bent his head to Sarah's hair, closing his eyes within it, smelling the lemony freshness of her, feeling the tickle of its softness upon his face. The thing about it was, there was no other woman like her. Certainly not within England, which was why, he supposed, he had had to wait for one from America to find him.

Was she a woman with whom he could spend the rest of his life? For the first time ever, the notion of such a thing didn't cause panic to race through him. He was still uneasy, yes, for he wondered if his current infatuation with her was something that could last forever. He was hard-pressed to consider that it could, but then the thought of her leaving, of being without her... was also more than he could bear.

He lay there, staring up at the stained ceiling above him,

visible through the dim light filtering through the clouded window. He chuckled to himself at the thought of bringing her home to meet his parents, wondering just what his father would say if he told him that he had, finally, found a woman to call his own — a woman with no title but that of an illegitimate birth, who was a healer from the Americas and currently living within leased rooms in Cheapside as she passed herself off as family of the nobility.

The explanation, even within his own head, sounded far worse than it actually was. Sarah was simply trying to find family, to find a connection, and she was doing the best she could within those circumstances.

She stirred on his chest, and instead of his typical rush to escape as fast as he possibly could, for the first time, David was looking forward to waking up with the woman who slept so soundly upon him.

Sarah blinked a few times as she pushed herself up from his chest, as though she wondered just what her head lay upon.

"Good morning," he said, and she looked up at him in a daze.

"Good morning," she responded, looking positively angelic with her hair in a halo around her head. "I'm sorry I fell asleep so quickly."

"It's fine," he said with a smile. "I'm glad you did. You were exhausted."

"Yes, well..." her cheeks turned bright pink as she smiled at him, a smile that brought him incredible satisfaction.

"Are you feeling well?"

"I am," she said, and he wondered if her blush could deepen any further. "Thank you, for last night. For your help and for... for everything."

"It was my pleasure," he said with a grin, and she finally

laughed, though he could tell she was not quite as uninhibited in the light of day.

"It looks quite bright out," she said, though how she could tell through that excuse for a window, he had no idea, but then, she had far more experience within this room than he did.

"I should probably be going," he said, though he wanted nothing more than to stay where he was, to make love to her once again. Would she welcome it? If he returned here tonight, what should he expect? But he couldn't very well stay here all day, for then what would that mean for the two of them?

Everything he had ever thought about himself, about relationships, was in question now, all because of this woman. His desire to please her, to protect her, shocked him to his very core.

"I will help you find your father, Sarah," he promised her as she moved off his chest to lie on the bed next to him. "I can promise you that."

He continued to talk as he walked about the room, collecting his clothing and dressing to return home.

"I've narrowed down the areas of where his estate could be to a few within the country, based on what your mother told you of nearby fields and forests and what was growing. However, it is still quite a wide range of locations. I'm going to speak with Clarence today. I thought perhaps if we put our minds together, we might come up with additional ideas on where would be best to next search."

He walked over to the basin in the corner, pouring water from the pail next to it into the bowl before splashing it upon his face to revive himself. He would change once more after he returned to his own rooms, but he needed to be somewhat respectable in case he encountered anyone he knew along the way.

He picked up the towel beside the bowl, wiped off his face, and then was about to replace it when something caught his eye. It was a ring, sitting within a dish beside the basin. He reached out, picking it up and turning it over between his fingers as he noted the crest within the black setting.

"What is this?" he asked, turning to show Sarah at what he was looking.

"It's my ring," she said, her face closing as she sat up in bed, drawing the sheet around herself, though he would have dearly liked to have seen what she looked like in the light of day. "My mother gave it to me. I believe it might have been my father's."

"Sarah!" he exclaimed. "This could be exactly what we are looking for — something to lead us to the man. Did you not think that this would be something of significance?"

She shrugged a delicate shoulder, though her eyes hardened ever so slightly at his admonishment and she looked down for a moment.

"I suppose I was being foolish. I just thought... if you knew I held onto such a thing, from a man who doesn't even know I exist, you may think it silly. Besides, it's just an insignificant design. Probably some trinket he gave my mother. I doubt it is actually worth anything."

"This is more than a design," he said, staring at it once more. "This is a family crest. This, Sarah, could be the answer. Can I hold onto it while I look further into it?" At her furrowed brow, he continued, "I promise I shall return it."

"Of course," she said, and he palmed it in his hand before slipping it onto his own finger, excited now to finally have a lead. He would share it with Clarence, he decided. Surely he would have some idea of to whom it belonged.

"I should be going, then," he said, though he made no

move toward the door, torn between needing to leave and the longing to stay here, with her, all day.

"Good day, David."

After a moment of hesitation, he strode over to the bed, cupped a hand around the back of her head, and then kissed her long and hard, an unspoken reminder to her of all that had occurred between them the previous night, and a promise of what was to come.

For now that he had a taste of her, he didn't think he would ever be satisfied with anything else. Though a part of him was aware that a woman like Sarah would expect more than a simple tryst between the two of them.

Could he make that leap? He had never thought it so before. But, perhaps, with her — perhaps he could.

SARAH REMAINED WHERE SHE WAS, trapped in her current position as she had no wish to reveal herself in the light of day, as she watched David walk out the door with one last glance over his shoulder toward her. She forced a smile onto her face and gave him a little wave to reassure him that she would be fine until his return.

The moment he shut the door and his footsteps retreated beyond it, she threw herself backward on the bed and flung an arm over her eyes.

What had she done?

She had made love with Mr. David Redmond, the greatest rake in all of England, according to most within the noble set. If that had been all, however, she might not be so worried. For the fact was, it was the most indescribable, enjoyable moment of her life.

No, the problem was much more than that they had physically come together. It was that the connection she had been beginning to feel for him, the deep attachment that she had been determined to avoid, was now tightening, pulling them even closer together.

Sarah felt tears begin to prick her eyes at the hopelessness of the situation. What was she to do now? Continue to allow him into her bed, to the point where she would fall hopelessly in love with him? And then what? For surely she was not the type of woman he would ever marry. A man like David Redmond may not hold a title, but he remained the son of the Earl of Brentford, and was the closest of friends with a duke and a marquess, for goodness sake. He would not marry the illegitimate daughter of a nobleman, who had grown up in the wilds of America.

Besides that, even if he did go against what would surely be his parents' wishes, how was she ever to trust him? He may be committed to her for now, but at some point, once he felt he had returned the favor of saving his life, he would find something new — perhaps even *someone* new — to catch his interest, and she would truly be left alone once more.

When he came back tonight, would he expect the same from her once more? At the thought of it, Sarah felt a shiver run through her, and instead of it being one of chagrin, it was actually the thrill of anticipation. She must remember, however, that besides all of that, she had no wish to remain here, in London, for any longer than she had to. And if she were to stay here for David, then this would become her home. And that thought made her feel like one of the caged animals she had once seen when a strange act had made its way through London.

She must give up on all of this, she determined, and leave any thoughts of her father or David behind while she returned home. If David found nothing came of the crest upon the ring — and she truly didn't believe anything would

— then she would be gone. It was the only way she could survive.

* * *

SARAH'S IDEA TO return as soon as possible, however, was soon thwarted by one simple invitation.

She was walking through Hyde Park with her friends, a circumstance that had now become rather rare, though at one point in time had been a familiar weekly occurrence.

Despite the fact that these women were the closest people in the world to her, Sarah's heart was beating quickly as she continued to review the words in her mind — the words that would allow them to know that while she appreciated their friendship so very, very much, and would cherish it for the rest of her life, she was returning home. To America. To the familiar. And escaping all that London held.

Just as she took a breath, however, Phoebe began to speak.

"With the Season now coming to a close, we will be returning to the country," she said, which at first strengthened Sarah's resolve to leave. If her friends were no longer within London, as they had their own lives and their own schedules, then they truly would hardly even miss her. "We would love nothing more than for all of you to join us for a week!"

Sarah honed in on her words as Elizabeth and Julia enthusiastically agreed.

"It is the one weekend of the entire racing season that I do not believe we are otherwise occupied," Julia said. "We would love to join you, I am sure, though I will speak with Eddie first."

"As would we," Elizabeth said with a warm smile. "In fact, I believe this is the first time in a long while that the four of us might be able to find time to be together, what with our schedules and time with the children."

Sarah continued to look forward, her denial prepared, but it wouldn't seem to cross her lips.

"Sarah, you will come, will you not?" Phoebe asked once more, and Sarah played with the ribbon that was tied around the waist of her dress.

"I…" she looked around at the three of them, at the expectant smiles on their faces and thought of the promise of a wonderful time together ahead. "Very well," she replied in a rush, considering that perhaps she could have one more enjoyable weekend with them. "For a short time."

"Any time that works for you," Phoebe said, and Sarah swallowed. She should have said no, should have left England completely, but at the very least they would be heading out to the country, where the air was cleaner and the surroundings, while likely perfectly manicured landscapes, might offer a sense of home.

Sarah nodded, and Phoebe clapped her hands together once excitedly.

"Very good," she said. "I shall see you all there in a week's time."

What she was to do until then, Sarah had no idea.

CHAPTER 16

*D*avid's horse trotted along beside those of the three other men — Clarence, Berkley, and Eddie Francis, the jockey who had captured Lady Julia's heart. Their coming together had been quite the unusual situation, but then, it had all seemed to work out well for them and even Julia's parents hadn't seemed particularly displeased by their daughter's marriage.

David welcomed the warm sun upon his face, the fresh air of the countryside filling and renewing him. Some time out of the city — that was what he needed. Perhaps Sarah's words were having an effect on him.

He hadn't spent much time in the past few years at any of his parents' estates. Of course, he would attend the odd weekend party or visit them for a short while each summer, but he always felt rather... alone when he was there, despite what family may have accompanied him.

He glanced over at the carriage trundling along beside them, which held the women. He smiled at the thought of the four women and the four men who were traveling together — three couples married, leaving him and Sarah.

His smile fell somewhat, however, when he thought of the strain that had formed within their relationship over the past week. Not so much a strain, perhaps, but... distance that he would have thought had been bridged since their night together.

Clarence glanced over at him, perceptive to David's countenance, which was currently aimed toward the said carriage.

"Does something — or someone — have you down, friend?" he asked drolly, with a smile that only turned up one side of his lips, and David straightened.

"Not entirely," he answered, not wanting to lie but also not exactly keen on sharing his state of emotions with his friend.

"She must be different, this one," Berkley chimed in, "For I have never known a woman to affect you before, Redmond."

"I am not affected," he defended himself, and Berkley chuckled.

"'Tis nothing to be ashamed of," the blond man said, shaking his head. "We've all been there before. Miss Jones is a lovely one."

"I do hope," Clarence said, his expression now serious as he glanced over at David, "That you have done nothing to compromise one of the closest friends of my wife."

David shifted uncomfortably in his saddle, as he was unable to meet the Duke's eye. He wasn't sure Clarence would accept the explanation that they had each been willing partners, that Sarah had asked it of him, and that it had been about more than just the coming together of their bodies.

He opened his mouth to refute their words and defend himself, but as he did so he realized that he was, in fact, lost, having no idea what direction to now take when it came to his relationship with Sarah Jones. These three men had found happiness — perhaps they could help guide him.

"I was under the impression that perhaps she and I were entering into an... understanding with one another," he said, not missing Clarence's perceptive glance. "However, it appears I must have been mistaken as she has been rather cold for the past week or so."

"She's distancing herself from you," Eddie said, and David started for a moment, nearly forgetting the man who had been riding along silently beside them, listening to their conversation. "No insult meant, Redmond, but..."

He trailed off as though unsure of whether or not it was his place to say anything, but Clarence took pity on him, obviously much more at ease in saying exactly what he thought to David.

"Why would she *not* be worried about what it could mean to become close to you, what with the company you keep?"

"I have not kept such company lately," David muttered, and Clarence chuckled.

"Even so," he acknowledged. "Just what do you think my wife is telling her about you within that carriage right now?"

David rubbed at his temple. He had never thought he would have any reason to regret the life of pleasure he had been living, but apparently, he was very, very wrong.

"Whatever she feels, I did promise to help her," he said, needing to speak of something else.

"With finding her father," Clarence confirmed, and David nodded. At the knowing gazes of the other men, David knew that they were all aware of the situation. "I have been doing my best to determine his identity for some time now, but with the lack of information..." Clarence continued, clearly unsure of himself now as well.

David nodded. He knew that Clarence was the best help Sarah could find. The man seemed to know everything about everyone. And yet the thought of the Duke being the one to aid her in her quest caused a fit of odd jealousy to begin to flare within him — despite the fact that the man was happily married to one of Sarah's closest friends.

He pushed aside the irrational emotion to address the issue at hand.

"I have something now — something that might help," David said, shifting the reins into one hand as he reached into his inside jacket pocket and pulled out the ring. He passed it over to Clarence, taking care not to drop it between them.

"It's a family crest," Clarence said, raising his eyebrows, somewhat incredulous. "Where did you find this?"

David's cheeks warmed for a moment as he realized he could not entirely tell the truth — that he had found it near the washbasin in Sarah's rooms when he was dressing one morning.

"Miss Jones had it on her person," he finally managed. "I saw it upon her finger — her thumb I suppose — and asked her where she had gotten such a thing. She told me her mother had given it to her, that it had been her father's previously."

"Why did she not think to give this to me earlier?"

"She thought it was nothing but an insignificant trinket," David said, repeating her words. "Do you recognize it?"

"No," Clarence shook his head before showing it to Berkley, who also had no recognition of the ring. "However, we can look further into it — unfortunately likely not until we return back to London."

"Very well," David said, nodding his head.

A few hours later, they finally arrived at Berkley's estate and the ladies emerged from the carriage, looking pleased to finally be out amidst the fresh air.

"We should have ridden ourselves," Julia grumbled, though her countenance turned much more pleasant as they entered the grand estate through the front entrance, which was surrounded by columns reminiscent of Greece. The entrance hall where they congregated as the servants greeted them and took their bags was a mint green with cream wainscotting. A large fireplace was surrounded by busts of Roman figurines, the pattern which was echoed within the ceiling.

"My great-grandparents were slightly overzealous," Berkley said with a bit of a shrug in reference to his ancestors who David knew had built the estate years prior in order to impress their guests — and impress it did.

David attempted to capture Sarah's attention, but it was no use. She was purposefully ignoring him, he knew, and yet he had no idea what he was to do about it.

SARAH HAD NEVER BEFORE BEEN to Berkley's estate. In fact, she had never been to any English estate before. She had been outside of London, sure, but only to Bath and Newmarket. This... it was like she was returning to her forests, albeit much more manicured ones. As they walked up the drive, she stopped for a moment, closing her eyes and taking a deep breath of the sweet smelling air. She could sense David's attention upon her, but she resisted looking at him, despite the fact that every fiber in her being was urging her to do so.

Since the day they had made love with one another, she had managed to keep from doing so again. Most often she feigned sleep before he returned to her rooms, and the one night he had caught her awake, she made the excuse of feeling as though she was coming down with an illness.

He never asked her to do anything again, never pushed her, never attempted a thing. But he was making it clear that he would appreciate some intimacy — not sexual, but rather, emotional, which was much more dangerous, and the very reason she was staying away.

For it was not that she did not want to make love with him again. Oh no, every part of her body was yearning to do so. It was that she knew if she did, it would only make it that much more difficult when the time came for them to separate.

"I will escort you to your rooms, Miss Jones," the housekeeper said, interrupting her reverie. Sarah noted David watched the direction in which they walked quite closely, but finally they were in a place where he would not be required to guard her nightly. In fact, Lady Alexander was due to arrive the next day, along with other guests of the house party. She had agreed that it was fine for Sarah to travel with three married companions, despite the fact that there would be a single man within their party — for what could happen in one night?

Sarah was certainly not inclined to tell her.

She thought back to her conversation with her friends within the carriage.

"You must tell us," Phoebe had demanded, "What has occurred between you and Mr. Redmond. For clearly, there is something amiss."

"Perhaps," Sarah had said with a nod of her head. She hadn't planned on telling them the entirety of her current relationship with David, but she also wasn't about to lie to the three women in front of her.

"You are aware that Mr. Redmond was left at my door quite injured, and that I treated him and told him a bit of my situation. What I didn't tell you is that once he was well, Mr. Redmond decided that my safety was an issue. He did not feel that I should be staying alone in my rooms."

"He's quite right regarding the fact that you should never have been alone," Elizabeth agreed with a nod, but then went silent to allow Sarah time to continue on with her story.

"So he decided that he would stay with me each night."

136

Three shocked faces had stared back at her, her words quelling them all into silence. In fact, had the carriage not begun to rock slightly back and forth, she was not sure any of them ever would have ever moved again.

"David Redmond... has been staying with you every night?" Elizabeth asked, obviously attempting to mask her disapproval.

"He has been altogether a gentleman," Sarah said, feeling the need to defend him, for, in all actuality, he had been. "In fact, he insisted on making himself a bed on the floor, and has even proven himself useful when I have been treating others who have come to me for help."

Julia smiled at the story. Elizabeth continued to look slightly concerned and Phoebe studied her contemplatively, as though she knew there was more to this.

"Nothing has ever happened between the two of you?"

Sarah's cheeks became so hot she knew they must have turned a bright red. But if she couldn't tell these women about what had happened between the two of them, who could she speak to?

"About a week ago," she began slowly, "We had a moment in which we were so close — as close as two people can be. We... acted upon it. But—" she added quickly before any of them could say anything, "—It was completely my choice. He could not have been more concerned, more understanding, more questioning about whether or not that was what I truly wanted."

Phoebe reached across the seat to place a hand on her knee reassuringly.

"Afterward, did you regret it, or were you happy that all had occurred?"

Sarah sighed. She wasn't much for dramatics, but then, if ever a situation called for them, it was this one.

"Both, in equal measure, I suppose," she said, raising a

hand in the air helplessly. "It honestly seemed as though it was one of the best things to ever happen to me. Had you asked me that night, right afterward, I would have told you that it was the best decision I had ever made in my entire life. Nothing before had ever felt so right, so fitting, as to lie in his arms after coming together. I'm not a fool — I know that I am certainly far from the first woman he has ever been with, and yet it seemed to me to be more than simply a physical joining, but that somehow our hearts, our souls spoke to one another."

She paused, deep in thought, until Julia nudged her with a gentle, "But..."

"But then I woke up the next morning. He was readying himself for the day. I looked over at him and thought, 'This is not my life. This will never be my life, waking up in the morning with a man such as David Redmond.' And therefore what I had just not only allowed to occur but had asked for could not have been a worse decision, for all it did was cause my attachment to him to grow even deeper."

They were all silent for a moment, contemplating her dilemma, until at last, Elizabeth broke the silence, shocking them all with her words.

"Are you sure it has to be that way — that the two of you might not find a way to be together?"

At their three incredulous faces, she shrugged.

"I am capable of having a heart, you know," Elizabeth said, raising an eyebrow. "And I am well aware that people can change. I would never before have suggested that Sarah and Mr. Redmond pursue a greater acquaintance, however... I could have been wrong."

"No," Sarah said, shaking her head. "His father is an earl. I am illegitimate."

"Eddie and I made it work," Julia said softly.

"This is different," Sarah said resolutely. "Besides that,

once my quest is over — either through resolution or by my own choosing — I will be returning to America."

"Oh, please say that isn't true," said Phoebe with a hand on her arm.

But Sarah shook her head. "I must go back. It's where I belong."

The words now resonated within her mind as she placed her small valise within the extravagant guest room. She had been telling herself for some time that there was nowhere else for her but America. So why did the words no longer feel altogether true?

CHAPTER 17

*D*avid was determined to find time alone with Sarah — particularly before Lady Alexander arrived to join them. How he was going to do so, however, he had no idea, for she was always so closely surrounded by the three other women.

They were all wonderful women, of course, but at the moment he wished they were anywhere but here.

He knew he was acting like a young lad in the first blushes of love in the way he had to convince himself not to stare at her throughout dinner. Afterward, as he and the other gentlemen shared a cigar and a glass of port as they enjoyed their last night in some solitude before the house party would expand, he had to force himself to concentrate on what the rest of them were speaking of as his thoughts continued to drift back toward Sarah, their night together, and what type of future could await them — if any.

He sighed as the gentlemen then moved to the drawing room. It was an impressive estate, each room painted in a different, rich color, with inlaid gold tying the various rooms together. Gold picture frames and accents were interspersed everywhere from the furniture to the crown molding.

And yet he would be just as happy to be back in Sarah's small lodging, as long as it would mean the two of them could have some time alone. He should have woken her up one night this week to speak further. But every time he was tempted to do so, she always looked so perfect that he couldn't bring himself to wake her from sleep. He attempted to catch her attention throughout her current conversation in order to speak with her, but she refused to look at him, purposefully seeming to avoid him. Which left him alone, unsatisfied, and completely awake later that night.

After tossing around for what seemed like hours, he decided he could no longer simply lie there staring into the darkness of night. David finally threw back the covers and made his way down the grand staircase, walking on his toes so as not to make a sound and wake the rest of the house. Where he was going, he had no idea, but he felt trapped within his chamber. He was so used to coming and going from his own boarding room whenever he pleased at whatever time of day or night that he was feeling altogether restless at the thought of staying in one place, particularly when the woman he needed to speak with so very badly was sleeping somewhere within this estate.

The truth was if he knew where exactly she was, he would have no qualms about searching for her and speaking to her within her rooms. But with his luck, he would find himself in the bedroom of another and would spend the rest of the weekend here apologizing.

Following along the corridor, David looked within one room and then the next of the ground floor, holding his candle out in front of him to determine each room's contents. When he finally came across the room he was looking for, he entered the library to search the shelves for something that would put him to sleep.

It wasn't the largest library he had ever seen, but the shelves were tall, and when he found his way amongst them, he was pleased to see that some of the titles were of interest — one about Captain Cook's voyages, and there was Henry Fielding's *Tom Jones,* though he had read it before. The key was to find something that was interesting, but not interesting enough to keep him awake throughout the night. He wondered what Berkley would say were he to go through all of the candles provided to his chamber in one night.

David set his lantern upon one of the shelves above him, where it cast enough light but was not near enough to any books that it may catch them aflame, and he began to wander further down the bookshelves.

David ran his finger over a few titles, struggling now in the dimmer light to make out what they read. He pulled one out for a better look, but not finding anything of interest, he flicked his gaze back up to the shelf in order to return it to its place. But what he saw nearly made his heart stop. For it was another pair of eyes peering back at him.

* * *

SARAH WASN'T sure what roused her from sleep. In fact, as she began to return to consciousness, she became aware of the ache in her back, the crick in her neck, and the chill that had entered her bones.

Where was she?

She looked around her at the darkness, the furniture only slightly illuminated by the moonlight filtering in through the windows. Ah, yes. She was in the library at the Marquess of Berkley's estate. Unable to sleep, she had left her room and began to wander, only to find herself in here. Lord Berkley had an interesting array of books, and Sarah had been delighted to discover a volume on the foliage to be found within the area.

The information, however, was primarily relegated to characteristics that would identify such flora and fauna and their scent — which Sarah did not find particularly helpful, and soon enough she was asleep in her chair, her candle, she now realized, melted to nothing beside her. When she had initially entered the room, a warm fire had remained in the hearth, but it had now fallen to near embers.

Her senses came suddenly alert as she realized she was not alone. She heard the fall of a footstep somewhere within the room, and a flicker of light caught her eye from amongst the shelves. She knew she was being foolish, that she should just call out, but instead, she began to tiptoe across the room to determine just who had joined her.

Seeing the candle's flame, she peeked through the shelf, planning on walking around to greet the newcomer once she determined his or her identity, but then suddenly another pair of eyes met hers, and she stumbled backward in surprise, her head banging into the shelf behind her.

She was still rubbing it, trying to ignore the sting of tears that threatened, when warm, strong hands encircled her arms.

"Are you all right?"

She looked up into David's eyes, and a feeling of safety and security rushed through her.

She was all right because she was here — with him. Which was exactly why she had been determined to stay away for so long.

"I'm fine," she said instead, stepping away from him, putting some space between them. "I should have told you I was in here but I was unsure who had joined me. My apologies."

"This is a welcome surprise," he said with a soft smile. "I have been trying to get you alone for some time now, but you keep avoiding me."

"Not on purpose," she lied, looking down at her hands, and he put a finger underneath her chin and lifted her face up to look at his.

"Why will you not speak to me?" he asked softly.

"Because…" she looked around, as though she would find something that would prevent her from having to answer this question. "Because you scare me."

"I *scare* you?" he asked, raising an eyebrow. "I cannot say any woman has ever said such a thing to me before."

"Well, I am not like other women," she said resolutely, attempting to ignore the jealousy that filled her at the mention of such women.

"You certainly are not," he acknowledged, though the way he said it, she wasn't sure whether she should feel complimented or insulted. He reached out and took her hand in his, and only then did she notice that he was in his nightwear, a gold wrapper pulled tightly around him.

"You match the house," she murmured before she even realized what she was saying, and he laughed.

"I suppose I do. It is rather gaudy, isn't it?"

"Your wrapper or the house?"

"Both."

It was her turn to laugh. If nothing else, David certainly knew how to bring humor to every situation. "The house is beautiful, but it is slightly ostentatious, yes. I must admit that I am still becoming used to such surroundings, having grown up in a one-bedroom cabin."

David reached a hand out, taking her bare fingers within his, and she wanted to pull her hand back at the tremors that ran through her from his touch. Before she could do so, however, he began to caress them, and it was so lovely she allowed herself to relax into it for a moment.

"None of this can compare to your own beauty."

"Stop," she whispered, not wanting to hear his contrived words, but he tugged slightly on her hand to capture her attention once more.

"I am serious," he said, punctuating each word in emphasis. "You possess a natural beauty that I have never seen in any other before."

"Is that a line?" she asked, raising an eyebrow. "One you use on all of your women?"

"I have no other women," he said, and when she looked up at him, it seemed as though his words were genuine. Sarah bit her lip. She should run from this room, leaving him and his words of love behind her. But instead, when he stroked her cheek with his fingertips until he cupped her face, she looked up at him, met his eyes, and gave in to the kiss he offered. The moment his lips touched hers, her body began to quicken, responding to him, and she wrapped her arms around his neck as his came around her back.

Was it ridiculous to feel as though she was coming home? His hard, strong body against hers almost felt like a symbol of reassurance, a pillar of strength — a reminder that she no longer had to feel completely alone, but that he was here for her and she could face whatever approached with someone by her side to support her.

One of his arms moved down to come underneath her knees, lifting her up in his arms, and he carried her over through the shelves to the large leather library chairs where she had been sitting but moments before. He sat down upon it, lifting her so that she was upon his lap. When one of his hands dug into her hair, which flowed around her shoulders, she felt tingles from his touch, which then ran down her spine.

This would be the last time with him, she promised herself, the vow only increasing the intensity of her kiss. The last time she would give herself to him, take all that he had to offer her.

So she was shocked when he broke their kiss and rested his forehead against hers, their breath intermingling.

"You should be sleeping," he said as he kissed her forehead and then drew her head against his chest. She leaned into him, taking his warmth and comfort.

"I should be — and so should you," she said, and he chuckled.

"Very true," he said. "I find it difficult to sleep in a new place."

"You never seemed to have any issue in my rooms," she said, smiling into his chest. "Your snores certainly proved otherwise."

He laughed then, a true, hearty laugh, one she enjoyed listening to.

"I do not snore."

"You do."

"You wound me, Sarah," he said, with a hand against his chest in mock pain, but then shook his head as he turned serious. "Would you like an escort back to your room?"

"I shouldn't," she said, pushing away from his chest and sitting up now. "Someone could see us."

"I shall be most discreet," he responded, his hand now molding over his heart in a promise, and she sighed and smiled.

"Very well," she said. "Though then, of course, you will know where to find me in the future."

"You have determined my ulterior motives all too well," he said with a feigned sigh, and she laughed but then stood, holding her hand out to him.

"Come," she said, and he followed along beside her, one

arm on the small of her back. It felt altogether too right, but as much as she knew she should put some space between them, she was enjoying the feeling of it more than she wanted to admit.

"Where to, my lady?" he asked with a smile, and she shook her head and scolded him.

"I am not a lady."

"You are, in all the ways that matter," he said breezily.

She knew he said the words with levity, yet they warmed Sarah right through, with even the possibility that he could see her in such a way. She caught him looking over at her, but she ducked her head to hide what she was sure were pink cheeks.

"So tell me," she said as they climbed the stairs, "Did you find what you were looking for upon Lord Berkley's shelves?"

"Not quite," he said with a sigh, "For I was seeking a book of sonnets with which to woo you."

"You were not!" she said with a laugh, and then looked at him with a more serious gaze. "Besides, I'm sure you already have all the lines."

"Not for a woman like you, I don't," he said, shaking his head with a sigh, and then gestured down the corridor when they reached the landing. "Which direction shall we take?"

"This way," she pointed. "And hush, now. We do not need the entire house to assume we are having some late night liaison."

"Oh, are we not?"

"No," she said in whispered tones, swatting at him. "I should, in fact, be returning to my rooms *alone*."

"I am escorting you like any gentleman would," he said, and she rolled her eyes at him, and then held a finger up to her lips when she heard voices from within one of the rooms they were passing.

He said nothing until she stopped in front of her doorway.

"Here I am," she said, suddenly feeling quite awkward, unsure of whether or not to invite him in. She knew she shouldn't and yet…

"Goodnight," he said, making the decision for her, and leaned in to place his lips upon hers. The kiss couldn't be called chaste, for he lingered far too long and tasted her ever so slightly, but it was a promise of more to come.

When David pulled back, his eyes were dark and hungry, but all he did was smile, nod, and take his leave.

CHAPTER 18

*D*avid awoke the next day with a renewed sense of purpose. While they had hardly spoken of anything of consequence, his interlude with Sarah last night had been one that reassured him, providing him with a sense that everything would be all right between them, would it not? She had joked with him, had laughed with him, and surely there was nothing that they could not overcome together.

He was well aware that she had desired him as much as he did her, but as much as he wanted to make love to her again — whether within the library or upon the return to her rooms — he had settled with a brief kiss goodnight. He was worried about giving her the impression that all he wanted from her was to come together physically once more. Then there was, of course, the potential of being discovered, but that he was willing to risk.

The entirety of what he truly did want in the future remained slightly out of his grasp, but it was becoming clearer to him the more time he spent together with her. He had no wish to rush into anything, however, for the last thing he wanted was to hurt this woman if he decided that a future together was not what he desired.

The gentlemen were to take part in a hunt that afternoon upon the arrival of others within the party, which David welcomed as he had always loved a good chase.

He followed Berkley out to the stables to prepare his mount, Francis and Clarence among them as well.

"You are in good spirits today," Clarence commented, and David nodded.

"It's a beautiful day and we are off on a hunt — what else could a man want?"

He noted Berkley and Clarence exchange a look, but he chose to ignore it.

"Say," Francis said, calling David's attention to him, for the man didn't typically say much amongst their company. "The ring you're wearing — is that the one you were discussing yesterday? The one belonging to Miss Jones?"

"It is," he affirmed, though he felt somewhat ridiculous at actually wearing the thing. He was worried, however, that he would otherwise lose it, which he was loathe to do after promising its safe return.

Francis surprised him by reaching out and taking his wrist, stepping closer to take a better look at the ring.

"I've seen this crest before," he murmured, causing the other three men to stop mid-step upon the grass halfway between the house and the stables and stare at him.

"You have?" David asked. "Where?"

"That's the problem — I'm not entirely sure," Francis said with a frown. "Permit me some time to think on it?"

"Of course," David said, and then, hoping to prompt the man's memory, continued. "Where would you have seen noble family crests?"

"Redmond," Clarence chastised with a disapproving stare and David quickly altered his words.

"I mean no offense, Francis. I am asking simply to try to help determine to whom this might belong."

"It's fine," Francis said with a wave of his hand. "However, I actually see more crests than you might think, upon jockeys' silks, horses' tack, or documents regarding the pedigrees. This one seems familiar. I just have to think about it. I'm sorry."

"No need to apologize," David said, though he impatiently wished he could shake the information out of the man. "It's more than we had to go on before."

Francis nodded, the contemplation remaining on his face, and David could only hope that his memory would prove useful.

* * *

So David was pleasantly surprised when, at a stop on the hunt much later that day, Francis pulled him aside.

"I think I've remembered," he said, and David couldn't recall the last time he had experienced such anticipation for another man's words.

"Yes?" he asked eagerly.

"I cannot be entirely sure, but you are aware that I rode for a time for the Earl of Torrington?"

David certainly did remember due to the scandal that had surrounded Lord Torrington's prized mount. But that was another story.

"I've seen Torrington's crest, and this is not it," he said with a frown, and Francis nodded.

"Correct. I would have known Torrington's crest immediately, having worn it for so long. But if I recall, his interest in racing was passed down from his mother's family, not his father's. While I must be honest in that often crests can look rather similar to me, I believe I saw that one in particular on some of the tack within his stables."

"Are you sure?" David asked, excitement filling him at finally having found a lead, and Francis lifted one corner of his mouth as he shrugged.

"I cannot be entirely sure," Francis said, "But I have my suspicions."

"I can make some discreet inquiries as to Torrington's past," Clarence said from behind David, and before David could open his mouth to object, to tell him that he could do so himself, Clarence held up a hand.

"I understand you would like to do so yourself, but you must understand, Redmond, that you are not exactly…"

He paused for a moment, looking up to the sky as if the right word would fall down upon him, and David chuckled ruefully. "Discreet? I only want to get to the heart of the matter."

"What are you going to do, walk up to the man and ask him if, around twenty or so years ago, he had an affair with a woman who then walked out of his life forever? And that you are asking because he now may have a daughter with whom you are rather enamored?" Clarence shook his head. "Allow me to determine what I can."

"Very well," David said, tapping his hand against his leg, realizing he didn't have many other choices but to accept the help. "Keep me apprised of what you find out."

* * *

SARAH WAS CONTEMPLATING how lovely it was to take tea out of doors. She had never been one who enjoyed the process of simply sitting and doing nothing but sipping from her cup, though she enjoyed the opportunity to converse with her friends. This was certainly better than being ensconced in a drawing room, though it did seem rather unnatural for servants to have to carry everything out of doors in order to serve them.

She had just lifted a pastry to her lips when there was a loud commotion from the bottom of the hill beneath them. The back of Lord Berkley's estate overlooked the valleys below, where the woodland was thick and the men were currently hunting.

They all looked up to see a horse thundering up the hill toward them, others beginning to climb the rise from far behind, moving slightly slower.

Eddie was the first rider, the fastest of them all, of course, being a jockey, his horse a former racer. He dismounted before the horse had even stopped running, a display that would have properly impressed Sarah were she not so worried about just why he had needed to race back to the house so quickly.

"We must send for a physician," he said, his breath coming in great huffs. "Lord Upwell has been shot."

"Shot?" Phoebe gasped as they all stared at him in shock.

"An accident," Eddie said, "But dangerous all the same. We believe the bullet went into his shoulder. Where is the closest physician? In the meantime, Miss Jones, are you able to help him?"

Eddie needn't have even asked. Sarah was already standing and determining exactly what she needed to treat a gunshot wound. Nearly before Eddie had even finished speaking, she was already beginning to provide orders.

"Phoebe, can you help — or arrange for help? I need clean linens, my bag from my chambers, and a bowl of boiling water. To which bedroom will you take him?"

Phoebe went to work as quickly as Sarah, and before long she had some of her servants beginning to prepare in the man's bedchamber, as she too helped herself. Sarah honestly had no idea who he was, but when he was settled upon the bed, she saw he was an older gentleman, who had likely traveled here with Lady Alexander's party. He was groaning in pain as he clasped his hand around the top of his left arm, where Sarah saw a bullet was still embedded. She took a deep breath. Bullet wounds could be difficult cases. Sometimes they came out easily, without causing any further issues, and all was fine. Other times, it could be extremely difficult to find the bullet and could have lingering effects. It was why limbs were often amputated during combat.

"Can I help you?" Elizabeth asked, coming to her side, and Sarah nodded. Of anyone, Elizabeth was the least likely to lose her head in a traumatic situation. Sarah had no idea how she would respond to the bloody mess that could ensue, but then, if there was ever anyone she would trust to handle all that came her way, it would be Elizabeth.

Sarah located her bag, looking through it until she found what she was looking for. First, a powder she had made of Cleavers. She had trouble, at first, determining which English plants would substitute for those she had used in America, but Sarah had found enough women in London to advise her.

After convincing Lord Upwell to remove his hand from where it clutched the wound, Sarah cut off his jacket and shirt at the shoulder and tied a long piece of fabric she had ripped from a towel around the top of his arm. She then sprinkled the powder over the wound, which she hoped would staunch the bleeding. Sarah found another jar and passed it to Elizabeth.

"Give him some laudanum, will you?"

Elizabeth complied despite the man's attempt to refuse, and he finally took a spoonful.

"Is the boiling water here?" Sarah asked, and when Elizabeth answered affirmatively, Sarah found her long instruments, which she would use to try to pinch the bullet, and placed them in the water.

"What are you doing?" Elizabeth asked, and Sarah turned to find her friend watching her quizzically. Sarah shrugged.

"My mother always told me that anything touching the interior of the body should be put in boiling water first. She never determined exactly why, but it had been taught to her by another, who was convinced it prevented infection from settling in. To this day, I am not entirely certain if she was correct, but I'm not about to test otherwise right now."

Elizabeth seemed interested in asking more, but their patient groaned and so they turned their attention back to him. Sarah took out the long metal pincers and looked at Lord Upwell's face to see if the laudanum had begun to take effect. She figured not entirely, but she didn't want to wait any longer.

The bleeding had mostly stopped, thank goodness, and she dabbed at the wound with a wet towel to clean away any blood so she could see what was beneath. He gave a slight yelp at her touch, and she cringed when she brought the pincers to the arm.

She paused.

"Elizabeth, can you please ask one of the gentlemen to come in here?"

Elizabeth, though not one to typically follow orders, seemed to understand the importance of the request and she complied, coming back in moments with her husband in tow.

"What do you need?" he asked, and Sarah bit her lip for a moment in contemplation. Should she really be asking a duke to assist her in this? But, then, she supposed, Elizabeth was a duchess and Sarah hadn't thought at all about any issues in asking her.

"Just hold him down," Sarah said.

"Hold him down?" the Duke repeated her words as he looked down at the man for a moment as if contemplating whether or not to comply, but then Elizabeth nudged him and he braced his hands upon Lord Upwell's shoulders.

"Here we go," Sarah said, taking a deep breath then looked over to the Duke of Clarence, nodded, and began to search for the bullet as efficiently as she could.

Lord Upwell bucked up off the table, but Sarah breathed deeply, ignoring him for a quick moment as she found what she was looking for, pinched it, and slid it out quickly.

"You found it?" Clarence asked incredulously, and Sarah nodded. "I did."

Sarah cleaned the wound as best she could, before bandaging the arm and sitting back to survey her work.

"I'm impressed," Clarence said, just as the door opened and a man, who must have been the physician, walked through.

"How is he?" The physician asked, coming to the side of the bed, then saw that the wound was bandaged. "What have you done?" he asked, looking at Sarah with wide eyes.

"I've found the bullet and treated the wound," she said, turning from him and beginning to clean her instruments. "He will be fine."

"How can you be sure?" he asked, crossing his arms over his chest. "What training have you had?"

Sarah was well aware that most physicians did not respond well to women who were practiced in healing. She understood. Their type of training was vastly different than hers, which she had learned from her mother. Hers was a knowledge passed down through generations of other women.

Sarah had full confidence in her abilities and how she had treated the man, yet how was she supposed to best share that information with the physician standing in front of her?

Before she could say anything, however, the Duke stepped forward.

"Miss Jones has done an exemplary job, Doctor," he said. "I apologize that you have been summoned unnecessarily. If there is any reason for us to contact you once more, we certainly will do so. We will ensure you are paid well for your time."

And with that, the Duke was escorting him from the room, and Sarah let out a long sigh as she looked over at Elizabeth and then Phoebe, who had remained by the door, surveying the scene and prepared to offer any additional assistance.

"If only people would listen to me like that," Sarah said with a wry grin, and Elizabeth laughed.

"I would like to say it is all his title," she said with a bit of a shrug. "But it is practiced charm as well."

"Whatever it is, I could use some of it," Sarah said as she lifted her bag and went out to the hall to speak with Lady Upwell about her husband's prognosis.

* * *

DAVID HEARD all about Sarah's treatment of Lord Upwell's wound, though he certainly wasn't surprised, seeing how well she had treated his own injury. Most of the party were now much more intrigued in Miss Sarah Jones and her healing abilities — where had they come from and just how did she know how to treat Lord Upwell? For the man was out of bed and at dinner the very next day, shocking them all as he praised Sarah and her treatment of him.

The weekend at Berkley's house had been filled with hunting, drinks, musicales, and billiards. Yet David could think of nothing other than Sarah, and the mystery of her father.

Of course, it didn't help that everywhere he turned, there she was, just out of reach. Lady Alexander had arrived along with many of the other guests who had been invited, and the woman looked at him as though he were a jackal attempting to steal her beloved hare.

Why she cared, he had no idea. She clearly had no intention of helping Sarah beyond offering her the link to society. If Sarah mattered more to her than that, why did she not truly provide her with a home?

He attempted to work on that angle further one evening after the gentlemen rejoined the ladies in the drawing room.

"Lady Alexander," he said, taking a seat in the stiff-backed chair next to her. She always seemed to choose the most uncomfortable chair in the room, he noted. "How do you do this evening?"

"I am well," she said, eyeing him from the side without actually turning her head toward him, as though if she ignored him he would leave her be. David, however, was far more determined than that. He pasted his most charming smile on his face — one that had won many hearts — and continued in as friendly a manner as possible.

"I am certainly glad to hear it," he said. "Lord Berkley has a lovely home, does he not?"

"He does."

"How do you know the family?"

"I am here, Mr. Redmond, to chaperone Miss Jones, as you well know."

"Of course," he said, attempting to infuse all matter of warmth into his tone. "However, your families must surely have had many connections over the years, have they not?"

"As much connection as to any other noble family, Mr. Redmond."

David had never met an icier woman, and he wondered how Sarah spent any manner of time in her company.

"Yes, well," he said, clearing his throat, attempting another tactic. "It is kind of you to chaperone Miss Jones."

She finally turned her head to look at him, and he nearly recoiled at just how icy her eyes were; how she caused a chill to creep down his spine as though melted snow was running down it.

"How did you happen to meet?"

"It seems to me that you have come to know Miss Jones well enough to ask her that yourself, have you not?"

David raised an eyebrow at the woman, who was certainly attempting to match wits against him. What he had done to garner her ire, he had no idea, but it only served to interest him all the more about Lady Alexander's connection with Sarah. She cared enough to note the young woman's attachment to him, yet not enough to offer her a home while she was in England?

"She mentioned that she met you shortly before coming to London, though did not provide details as to where exactly that was."

"Then perhaps she would not like you to know."

"Perhaps," he said, now losing all facade of charm.

"Did you know of Miss Jones prior to meeting her?"

"I did not."

"I can see why you would want to help her, however," David continued. "She has quite the caring soul."

"That she does."

David had run out of questions to ask her. The woman had won this round, he decided.

"Well, Lady Alexander, it has been a pleasure."

She simply looked up at him with one eyebrow raised as he stood, telling him that it was not a pleasure — for either of them — but she had enough good English breeding within her to keep her from doing so.

"Good evening, Mr. Redmond. And do take care with my charge's reputation."

"Of course, Lady Alexander," he said with a true smile now. If there was one thing he could agree to, it was that. "Good evening."

CHAPTER 19

*S*arah finished brushing out her hair and stared at her reflection in the mirror. It had been some time since she could remember her skin being so pale, her freckles so pronounced. She knew that the color of her skin, normally much darker with the sun, was not fashionable with the English, particularly the set who she was finding herself amongst. Yet if anyone had asked her, she would say that she felt rather sallow, sickly looking almost, when she was so wan.

Ah well, she thought with a shrug. Soon it would no longer matter. She was moving toward the bed when a soft knock came at the door, and she padded over to see who would be here at such an hour. Her heart began to beat in a slightly irregular pattern as she had a feeling of who it might be. She should turn him away, tell him that he couldn't be here, that she needed time alone. She cracked open the door.

"Yes?"

Her voice came out in just over a whisper, and she couldn't help the smile that crossed her face. Only one thought entered her mind — she was losing her heart to this man.

David smiled at her in return, then slipped in through the crack in the door when she opened it a bit wider.

"I apologize," he said immediately as she shut the door behind him. "I did not mean to force myself into your room, but nor did I wish to loiter in the hallway outside the door, in case someone should get the wrong — well, I suppose, the right — idea about us."

She laughed then, pulling her wrapper tighter around her as she moved closer to the fire once more.

"Come sit," she beckoned, interested in his company if nothing else.

"I'll leave if you are tired," he offered, but she shook her head, and they each claimed one of the matching chairs in front of the fire. As she looked over at him, Sarah's every instinct was to sit in his lap and allow his arms to surround her and hold her close, but that, she knew, would be a mistake.

"I'm not sure that I should ever become accustomed to someone tending to my every need," she said, nodding toward the grate, in which a servant had come in to prepare the fire for her.

"And I would have difficulty living without a valet," he said with a bit of a rueful laugh, which then caused a moment of silence between them as they were both reminded of just what different worlds they were from.

David opened his mouth as though he were going to say something, but then closed it quickly once more. She looked at him quizzically, about to ask what was on his mind, but he began speaking before she could do so.

"What was your mother's name?" he asked, and Sarah started slightly in surprise.

"My mother?" she asked. "What makes you ask?"

Had he found something?

"I only determined that if I am going to be looking into who your father might be, I should likely know her name."

"Mary," she said softly, a smile covering her face as she said it.

"Mary Jones?"

"I assume so," Sarah said with a bit of a shrug. "Unless she changed her name upon departing England. I must admit that I have been unable to find any relation with such a name, but then, she could be from anywhere within England, and there are quite a few people with the surname of Jones."

"Thank you," he murmured. "I shall remember it."

"Will you tell me once you learn anything?" she asked, not wanting to be left out of this quest she had been embarking on by herself for so long. She appreciated David's help but would prefer that they work on this together, that he not simply take over from where she had left off. "Do you promise not to keep anything from me?"

For a moment she wondered if he was hesitating, but then she quickly shook the thought out of her mind as he spoke.

"Of course I will."

"Thank you. I saw you speaking with Lady Alexander this evening," she said, turning to him now and raising an eyebrow. She had, in fact, been quite interested in their conversation, though she had no desire to enter into it herself.

"She's an... interesting woman," he said, as though unsure of just how deep were Sarah's feelings toward her.

"She can be a bit cold, I know that," Sarah said, aware that Lady Alexander did not approve of David, and had not been shy about telling Sarah exactly how she felt. "But I owe her a great deal, and therefore cannot say anything against her."

"Tell me again how you came to be acquainted with her,"

he said, and Sarah inwardly sighed. She had no idea why this was relevant, but if it would placate him, then so be it.

"Lady Alexander and I were on the same ship to England. I was gifted a first class passenger berth, and she and I happened to be placed at the same table for dinner the first night. I didn't share much of myself, though she was interested in who I was, and concerned that I was alone. She said that a woman such as myself should not be sailing across the Atlantic Ocean without a proper chaperone. She had a maid with her, but besides that, she was alone as well. She suggested that we keep one another company for the remainder of the journey. By the time we arrived in England, I had shared with her much of my story, and when no one met me upon arrival, she offered to chaperone me as I searched for my father."

David nodded as she spoke.

"I must admit that I am having difficulty equating the woman of whom you describe with the one with whom I spoke tonight, but perhaps you bring out her better side," he said with a forced smile, and Sarah shook her head slightly.

"That is kind of you to say," she said, looking down, unable to meet the brilliant green of his eyes, which always drew her in and made her forget all thought. She had a difficult time accepting such praise of her character, for she saw no reason why he should feel the need to compliment her so. Was he playing a game with her?

"You are an astounding woman, Sarah Jones," David said, planting his feet firmly on the floor and leaning over to cup her face in his hands. "I am a better person for knowing you."

Warmth crept up her cheeks that had nothing to do with her proximity to the fire in front of her.

"I do not require your lines, David," she said, biting her lip, and he ran his thumb over where her tooth had left an indentation in the pink flesh.

"There are no lines with you, Sarah," he said. "Just truth."

She looked up at him then, shocked by the desperate plea in his eyes — for her to believe him? She wasn't entirely sure, but when he reached out a hand to her, she took it, allowing him to draw her to him. She rose from her chair, took a couple of hesitant steps forward, and then followed where his hand led her, to sit on his lap, where she had wanted to be since he had entered her room. He smoothed one of his hands over her hair, through the long strands to down her back, until it cupped her hip. His eyes searched hers, as though he was attempting to find answers to whatever questions remained unspoken in his mind.

She splayed her hands across his chest over that awful gold wrapper, allowing her gaze to follow her fingers rather than focus on his face, where she knew she would become lost. She slipped her hands within the lapels of the wrapper, shocked when her fingers found bare skin.

"No nightshirt?" she murmured, and he shook his head.

"I sleep without."

"Of course you do."

Despite the fact that they had been together before, that she had seen more of him than she had any other man, her heart was beating furiously. She had made a mistake once. Why was she doing so again?

Because her heart wanted nothing more than to be close to David, to be with him again. A place where she felt warm, safe, and loved. As much as her mind told her it would be wrong, her heart, her body, and her soul were crying out that this was not a mistake at all, but where she was supposed to be.

"We shouldn't do this," she said, not realizing until afterward that she had spoken the words aloud, and he caught her hands within his.

"Then I will leave you," he said without any hesitation. "I apologize. I simply… wanted to see you."

He brought his hands around her waist as though to lift her from him, but she stopped him, covering them with her own.

"We shouldn't. But I want to."

Then she leaned down, cupped his face within her hands, and kissed him.

She could feel stubble beneath her fingertips, so masculine, and yet, in a strange way, causing him to seem somewhat vulnerable.

He tasted so good, a mixture of brandy and… *heat,* she thought as a bolt of longing shot through her. She placed her hands on the arms of the chair, her feet on the floor, and without breaking contact with him, she encouraged him to rise from the chair, and he backed her up toward the bed.

This time, their movements were of two people who were that much more familiar with one another, as their bodies were aware of just how one another yearned to be treated. David had her undressed before she even realized it, and when she shyly attempted to dive beneath the covers, he shook his head, taking seconds to simply stare at her. It felt as though her whole body was on fire beneath his gaze, but she trusted him, allowing him to take his time. As he eyes roamed over her, a slow smile began to spread across his face. If she hadn't come to know him and his expressions as well as she did, she would have worried for a moment that he was laughing at her, but no — he was smiling in satisfaction.

"You are perfect," he said, running a hand over her skin, causing fire to trail in the wake of his fingers.

"I am far from perfect," she said with a bit of a self-conscious laugh. "I have scars."

"Show me."

She sat down on the bed then, pointing to the remnants of what had been a deep gash in her thumb.

"Here, I sliced through my finger while attempting to cut down a plant. My mother sewed it back together."

He took her hand within his, kissing her thumb as though that would complete the healing.

"Where else?"

She pointed to her shoulder, where a long pair of lines ran down a few inches.

"I had an encounter with a bear."

"What?" he exclaimed, his shock so acute she had to laugh.

"She was protecting her cubs," Sarah said with the shrug of that same shoulder, smiling as she remembered the incident, which seemed to confuse David. "She was injured, her paw caught in a trap. I freed it, and she returned to her cubs nearly immediately, but in the process, she lashed out in her pain and I caught a bit of it."

He shuddered, which she understood. Yet somehow, at the time, she hadn't been afraid. It was as though she understood where the bear was coming from — the need for protection, the vulnerability it felt, the concern over who Sarah was and what she had been doing.

"Any others?"

"Here," she pointed to her hipbone. "I fell on my own knife."

"You what?" he asked with eyes so wide she laughed again.

"You have lived quite the protected life, David Redmond, have you not?"

"I've spent plenty of time with a sword in my hand," he defended himself, but then with a look of chagrin, amended his statement. "I have also almost always been covered in full protection during such situations."

"Fencing, correct?" she asked, and he nodded.

"It seems somewhat inconsequential after all that you have faced."

At his look of embarrassment, it was her turn to tip her face back up to look at him.

"Not at all. I was never in any danger. My scars are a result of where I lived, what my day included. You should not be ashamed of not holding any."

"Well," he said, his charming smile returned, "Yours are beautiful."

"I would hardly call them such, but they tell a story, if nothing else," she said with a smile.

He leaned over her, reaching out to trace the scars on her shoulder with two fingers, then moved to the scar on her thumb, and finally to that over her hip. He followed his fingers with his lips, kissing his way over them, and Sarah nearly arched off the bed toward him.

He finally returned to her lips, the kiss beginning gently but then gradually building to one of need, demanding more — a demand which she eagerly returned.

It was as though they had known one another for years instead of just one occurrence, and when he found her, he easily entered her. They moved together as one, and when they each found their release, Sarah could have cried for the perfection that it was.

Only afterward, when they lay together, did she allow the tears to fall from her eyes, catching them before they hit his chest. She could stay like this, with him, forever, and yet *forever* was far from a reality for them.

How she was ever supposed to go back to life as it was before him, she had no idea.

CHAPTER 20

heir time at Berkley's estate passed far too quickly for David's liking. He was enjoying the brief respite from life within London. It caused him to sorely wish that he had a home of his own to which he could retreat. His father had more than one, of course, but none were truly home for David — just empty estates for David to pace around feeling as though he was imposing.

If he had the opportunity to take other people to such a home — one person in particular, as it happened — would it make all the difference?

After his night with Sarah, he had returned to her the next night, and she had been as eager as he was to be with one another once again. David had mixed emotions. She was the type of woman he felt it was wrong to take such actions with unless there was a promise of more between them, and yet he was unsure of how to put into words just what he was feeling — and would she be accepting of him? He hoped so, and he planned to tell her of all that was in his mind and in his heart once they returned to London.

Once he mounted his horse, Clarence joined him as they began the ride.

"Enjoy yourself, Redmond?" he asked, the quirk in his eyebrow indicating that he likely knew far more than he would ever put into words.

David simply nodded. He would not speak of his time with Sarah with anyone else — even a friend as good as Clarence. "I did."

"A respite from the city is always welcome. In fact, Elizabeth and I will be leaving for the country for a time. Which makes it all the more imperative that we come to some conclusion regarding Miss Jones' dilemma. I know my wife is of a mind to resolve what she can for the woman."

"As am I."

"Very good. Have you told her of our suspicions as of yet?"

"No," David shook his head. "She asked that I would keep her informed, and I must admit, I do feel a bit of a bounder not doing so, but what is the use in raising her hopes and expectations if it comes to nothing, and we determine that there is no chance of Torrington being named her father? Besides that, the man has a wife... how do you think he might react to claims of a potential illegitimate daughter? Sarah says that her mother and father were in love, and while I know she believes that to be the case, of course that is the story a mother would tell her child, would she not?"

"I agree with you," Clarence said. "Though I did discuss this with Elizabeth, and she is of the opinion that Miss Jones should know all that we do. However, further to our suspicions, I had a discussion with Lord St. Albans."

Julia's father had been among the guests who had joined them for a few days. He was a jovial gentleman, one who had been far more accepting of a son-in-law such as Eddie Francis than most in his position would have been.

"St. Albans and Torrington are near to the same age," Clarence continued. "The man also assured me he would keep my inquiries to himself, and I do believe him. There are few that would do so. But I digress. Placing Miss Jones' age at just around twenty, at the time shortly before her birth, Torrington was not married and was, in fact, living at home with his family and spending much time at their country estate. In all actuality, he could have very well become connected with a woman from the area. St. Albans also recalls a falling out between Torrington and his father around that time, and shortly afterward the man moved to London, where he spent all of his time until the death of his father. One would have to make inquiries around Torrington's country seat, which is near Salisbury, but it is seemingly far more likely that he could be the man you are looking for."

David let out a long, low whistle, startling his horse, who he had to quickly reassure to regain control.

"Torrington. I wonder what he would think of learning of a daughter."

"I suppose it depends on how close he was with the mother — whether he did actually want to remain with her, or if those are imaginings from a woman attempting to placate her child with a story of love," Clarence said, a sentiment with which David agreed.

"I suppose the best thing to do might be to simply talk to Torrington himself," David said. "He is a reasonable man, and I am sure with a few simple questions I can determine whether or not he is who we would be searching for. Once we are back in London, I will seek him out. And soon, well, soon we will know the truth."

The moment he said it, David was actually surprised by the panic that coursed through him at the thought of doing so. He should welcome the idea, for determining the identity of Sarah's father would bring a resolution to their search,

171

one which had been following her around for far too long now.

But when her quest was finished, there was a very good chance that she would leave London, leave England, leave — him. He attempted to imagine his life without her now, of going back to nights spent at seedy establishments, with women who meant nothing but company and a warm body. For he realized now why he had lived the way he had — he was seeking companionship, a connection that always remained out of his grasp due to his inability to commit to any one woman.

How very foolish he had been.

* * *

DESPITE HIS CONFLICTION, David resolutely walked up the steps of the Earl of Torrington's London manor that evening. While it was not exactly the hour for social callers, David knew that he couldn't go to Sarah once more this evening without answers, or a promise of what he had done in order to aid her. The moment they had returned to London, he had only briefly refreshed himself before calling his carriage to be ready for his visit.

When he knocked on the door of Torrington's town-house, the answering butler looked him up and down as though assessing his worthiness for entry.

"Yes?" The butler asked.

"I would like to see Lord Torrington, if possible," David replied. "Please tell him Mr. David Redmond, son of Lord of Brentford, is calling."

The butler allowed him entry but then held up a finger. "One moment, please."

David looked around him as he waited for the butler to return. The foyer was opulent, clearly meant to impress those who called upon the Earl and his Countess. David had only met the woman once or twice before, and received the impression that she was quite proud of her station in life.

As though she was aware of his thoughts, it was the Countess herself who joined him in the foyer a few minutes later. She was a tall woman and had retained her looks over the years. Dressed as though she was entertaining, she looked David up and down much as her butler had done.

"Mr. Redmond, what a surprise," she said, her tone making it clear that it was not a pleasant one. "Unfortunately, my husband is not here this evening. Is there anything with which I can assist you?"

David chuckled within his own mind as he considered what her reaction might be were he to tell her that he was here to ask her husband if he had ever known a woman by the name of Mary Jones, whether he had loved her and potentially could have produced a child with her some twenty years ago.

Of course, even he would never actually say such a thing, but it was interesting to contemplate.

"It is no urgent matter," he said with a smile. "I shall seek out your husband another time."

"I believe he can be found this evening at White's Gentlemen's Club," she said, as though she would rather not have an occasion to see David at her door again. "Goodnight, Mr. Redmond."

Well, that was easy enough.

"Goodnight."

"Oh," she said, halting him before he could depart. "I also have heard that congratulations might be in order fairly soon."

"Unfortunately, Lady Torrington, I know not what you mean," David said, wondering if she had mistaken him for his brother.

173

"I had the pleasure of tea with your mother a few days ago, and she told me that an announcement regarding your nuptials with Lady Georgina, daughter of Lord Buckworth, were likely very soon forthcoming."

David could only stare at the woman in shock. He had been quite clear with his parents that he had no wish to marry Lady Georgina, let alone court the idea. He had meant to speak with Lady Georgina himself to express this to her, but with everything he had been focused on in regard to Sarah and his visit to the country, it had completely left his mind.

"My mother is mistaken, Lady Torrington," he said, forcing a smile to his face so that she wouldn't see his anger. "I am sorry to have disturbed you this evening."

And with that, he left the manor, knowing as he did so that he had likely provided Lady Torrington with a most interesting piece of news to share with her friends. Never mind the matter. He would prefer that over allowing such a lie to continue.

Entering White's Gentlemen's Club was more like coming home than returning to the manor in which he had been raised. There was something comforting about the solid building on the corner of Bond and St. James Street, with its nondescript white exterior and the rich, warm interior.

The doorman greeted him by name, and David asked after Lord Torrington and whether he was within. The man shook his head, telling him that no, the Lord had been here but had quickly left with a few other gentlemen. David exhaled sharply, frustrated by his lack of progress in his search for the man. Why was everything such a struggle for him? He often wished life would come more easily, as it seemed to do for Clarence or even his own brother.

He was about to walk into the room when another gentleman passing by tapped him on the shoulder.

"Did you say you were looking for Torrington?"

"I am, yes."

"He left to The Red Lion. You could likely find him there."

"Thank you very much."

The Red Lion. Why did Torrington have to choose what had been one of David's favorite haunts? Never before would he think that a woman could potentially change his perspective, but he was shocked to find that he had no desire to visit the gaming hell once more.

Except that was where he would find Torrington, so there he would go.

CHAPTER 21

"*M*r. Redmond!"

David lifted a hand in greeting when Billy saw him from across the room. The man looked to be in good spirits, and David cut through the crowd to greet him.

"How is your babe?" he asked, and Billy's grin stretched even wider.

"Very well. Thank you again for your assistance."

"There is not much to thank me for," he said. "Miss Jones is the one who made it possible."

"That she did," Billy agreed, then paused for a moment in his work. "This is a rather impudent question, Mr. Redmond, but… is she your woman, Miss Jones?"

David had no idea how to answer that. Every part of him wanted to yell out that *yes, of course she was!* But he had made no declaration of such to her — yet — and he wasn't sure how it would help matters to say such a thing.

"I, ah… why do you ask?"

"Well, I have a friend who has seen her in the marketplace and has been asking about her. We weren't sure, however, where she stood. Is she to be yours? She's not from around these parts, as most of us are, so we weren't entirely sure of her station, either. What do you think, Mr. Redmond? Would she be amenable?"

David's body felt as though it was burning at the thought of another man interested in Sarah, of the idea of her entertaining thoughts for anyone but him. But he couldn't very well say that to Billy. The man was only trying to be helpful, and as he continued to look at him earnestly, David knew he must provide an answer.

"I think that's best a question for Miss Jones," he finally said quietly. "We are… friends, at the moment anyway."

Billy nodded, though he looked at David discerningly. "Very well, Mr. Redmond."

"Say, Billy, do you happen to know Lord Torrington?"

"I know who he is," Billy said, throwing the rag with which he had been drying a glass over his shoulder. "He's over there, across the room."

"Thank you very much," David said, rapping his knuckles once on the table in front of him before rising to find the Earl.

"Torrington," David greeted him, and the man looked up from his card game to determine who had been calling to him. "How do you do?"

"Just fine, but give me a moment to finish this hand," Torrington said, and David nodded. He was well aware that despite his father being an earl, he was below Torrington's station and had no right to request anything of him. Just a conversation, he reminded himself, though he was becoming slightly worried at what the man's reaction might be to his potential news.

David took a seat nearby, impatiently tapping his fingers upon the table in front of him — a motion which did not go unnoticed by Torrington, who looked up at him now and then with some exasperation. Finally, his hand finished, though it was quite obviously not the outcome he had been anticipating by the way he flung the cards down upon the table. David swallowed. This conversation likely would have been more palatable were the Earl in a better mood.

The man sat down at the table across from him.

"What is it, Redmond?" he asked as he lifted a hand in the air to signal one of the barmaids for a drink. "Are you here to plan more liaisons with young ladies in my study?"

Ah, yes. David had forgotten about that.

"I apologize for that once more, Lord Torrington. But I actually have a rather... strange question for you," David began. "You grew up in the Salisbury area of England, did you not?"

"For the most part," Torrington said, his voice on edge as he was obviously wary of the line of questioning David had embarked upon.

"At what age did you leave there for London?"

"It is still my home."

"Yes," David was blundering this. He rubbed a hand over his forehead. "When you were younger, however, was there a time when you left home for London?"

"We all did," Torrington said, clearly growing impatient. "For school, for the Season, whatever it may have been."

"Right, right," David said, attempting not to sigh aloud, deciding to try a different line of questioning. "Did you ever happen to know a woman by the name of Mary Jones?"

The Earl's entire face lost every bit of color at the mention of Sarah's mother's name.

"Why do you ask me such a thing?" he said, his words emotionless, though he couldn't hide the brief flicker of panic that crossed his face.

David was able to keep himself from smiling in victory.

"I have an acquaintance who had mentioned knowing the

woman. Told me she was from the area, and I thought perhaps you might have come across her."

"She was a healer," Torrington said gruffly. "We couldn't summon the physician in time for my mother, and therefore she came to help."

"I see," David said, his heart now pumping hard as he realized he had likely found the man Sarah was searching for. "Did you come to know her well?"

The Earl shifted uncomfortably in his seat. "Well enough I suppose. She was a village girl. Why do you want to know?" He looked up suddenly, his countenance changed from one of dismissal to one of interest. "Do you happen to know where she is?"

David shook his head slowly. He hadn't thought of this side of things. He had always assumed that the love was on Sarah's mother's side, that the Earl's interest would have been a fleeting one. And yet... he was in nearly the same position, and his interest in Sarah certainly didn't seem to be waning.

The only heart he had thought might be broken was Sarah's, but what if the Earl was still searching for his lost love?

"She, ah..." he cleared his throat when he noted Torrington's expectant expression. "She passed away a few years ago, I'm sorry to say."

"I see," Torrington said, dropping his eyes and hiding any further emotion. "Do you know anything about what happened to her?" He paused for a moment, as though realizing that he was showing far too much interest. "I ask as I'm sure her family would like to know. She had a sister. Though..."

He looked off into the distance, retreating into memories rather than remaining focused on David's presence. David took a deep breath. Did he tell the Earl? Or did he allow Sarah to meet the man first, and have her tell him herself?

He recalled her plan to meet him, to determine what kind of person her father was before revealing the truth. David drummed his fingertips on the table, for once thinking through every possible outcome of this situation. He longed to tell Torrington, to ensure that Sarah's news would be welcomed... and yet, he had made a promise, one he knew he must keep.

He took a deep breath.

"I shall tell my friend that indeed, you knew of Mary Jones. I, ah, heard she was rather lovely."

A faraway smile crossed Torrington's face.

"That she was. More than lovely," Torrington said, looking down at his hands now. "She was beautiful, to be sure, but she was also gentle and kind. And yet she possessed a strength unlike any I had ever seen before. The tallest and burliest of men did not have the inner strength my— Miss Jones did."

Miss Jones. David thought of his own Miss Jones and knew of what the man spoke, that was for sure.

He opened his mouth to thank Torrington, to ask if perhaps he might call upon him the next day, but just then a hand clamped over his shoulder.

"Redmond!" He turned to find an old acquaintance, Lord Hartley, standing behind him. "Good to see you, man. It's been a time, hasn't it? I was beginning to worry about you."

Not worried enough, however, to seek him out. There were few who would do such a thing.

David looked back to introduce Torrington to Hartley, but only then did he notice the man had disappeared. Strange.

"Not to worry," Hartley said, taking Torrington's seat. "Your secret is safe with me."

"My secret?"

"Of course! The fact you are here in this club when you are engaged to my cousin."

"Your cousin? But—"

"Were you not aware that Lady Georgina and I were cousins? Through our mothers, as it were. She has long been out of London, of course, as they spend most of their time in Bath. Not to worry, Redmond, I didn't say anything to the family of your… ah, preferences. You're a good man and was there ever another who would understand, it would be me."

"Yes, but," David desperately cut in, "We are *not* betrothed. Not at all! Our families had one dinner together. I know my parents would like to see me with her, but I… my affections are otherwise engaged."

Hartley's eyebrows shot up to nearly his hairline. "Well, well, that is an interesting tidbit of information. The reason, perhaps, I have not seen you around here? Tell me, Redmond, do any of these beauties catch your eye?"

David looked around. Truth be told, for once, he hadn't noticed any of the women who served both drinks as well as pleasures. He couldn't very well explain that to Hartley, however.

He sighed. He was well and truly sunk.

"Carolina over there — you know, the redhead? Well, of course, you know her — or have, a time or two before," Hartley chuckled. "She's been staring at you since the moment you walked in here. If you want one last chance to take her for a ride, determine if marriage is really what you want, your secret is safe with me."

David glanced over to where Lord Hartley pointed. Sure enough, there was Carolina, leaning over another gentleman to serve his drink, but her eyes were on David. She was a beauty, though in an entirely different way than Sarah. For so long, David had scoffed at his friends for deciding to spend the rest of their lives with one woman, and now here he was, contemplating very much the same. Could he do it as well? At the moment he was sure, but would that change? He was well aware of how fickle he was — one only needed to ask his parents, or even Hartley himself across the table here. He cursed as he tried to determine what it was he should be doing with his life. At the very least, there was one first step he must make.

"Listen, Hartley," he said. "I need to speak with Lady Georgina. Can you arrange it? Without our parents?"

"You're not planning any sort of secret liaison?" Hartley asked, narrowing his eyes, and David shook his head.

"Not at all. In fact, the exact opposite," he said. "I have no wish for her to be misled — by me or my family. I must tell her the truth of my feelings before this is taken too far."

"Very well," Hartley said with a shrug. "I'll send you a note once I have spoken with her. Good luck with your woman, Redmond."

"Thank you," David said, nodding. "I believe I do require it."

CHAPTER 22

*S*arah was long in bed by the time she heard the door to her chamber finally creak open. She had wondered if David was going to come. He hadn't said a word to her since they had left the Berkley estate. She had sat within the carriage with the other women. This time Lady Alexander accompanied them, so the conversation was rather stilted and the ride felt interminably long.

David had approached the carriage when they reached Lady Alexander's home in London, where she disembarked, but Sarah had seen the look that Lady Alexander sent his way, which halted his footsteps. The truth was, however, this was becoming rather ridiculous, his protection of her. How long did he plan to continue it for? At some point, there would have to be a stop to this charade. She felt like a bit of a harlot, allowing him to come to her bed when she knew that there was little chance of a future together. But she didn't seem to have it within her to push him away.

"Sarah?" She heard him say her name, just above a whisper, and she thought of feigning sleep once more, but that would have been the cowardly escape.

"I'm awake," she said, her voice echoing through the room. Only embers remained in the grate, so once David shut the door it was difficult to make him out in the dim light.

He came over and sat on the edge of the bed, though he made no move to reach out to her, for which she was grateful.

"Where have you been?" she asked to break the silence, but then quickly realized just how her words sounded. "Not that you need to explain yourself to me," she added in a rush. "I was only wondering. Curious. Creating conversation."

Since when had she not been able to put together a sentence?

"I, ah…" When he paused, her heart sunk. He had been with another woman. She should have expected it. She never should have imagined anything else. They had never declared themselves for one another, so why should he not seek out another? She had hoped that their time together would mean more, but— "I was at The Red Lion."

"I see."

"No, Sarah, you don't. It's not what you think. I didn't go there for other women or anything like that."

Sarah nodded, despite the fact he couldn't see her in the dark. Perhaps it was for the best he had been there. Perhaps now was the time to have the conversation that had long been awaiting them.

"It's understandable if you had," she said softly, not wanting him to know just how much it would actually hurt her. She had no wish to appear vulnerable to him, nor to anyone else.

"Why would I need to take another woman?" he asked, puzzlement filling his voice.

"It is not as though we are promised to one another," she

said, attempting to keep her voice practical. "And I will be leaving soon, so there is no reason to tie yourself to me."

"Sarah," his voice came out softly, near to a whisper. "Must you truly go?"

"When we were at Berkley's estate, I had the chance to go walking in the woods, to breathe in the fresh air around me. It's certainly different than home, but it reminded me of how alive I feel when I am outside of the city, away from all the poison that is in the air and within so many people. Not that there are not good people within London, for there certainly are, but it seems that danger is rife around every corner, no matter whether one is within a Mayfair ballroom or on a corner of St. Giles."

"Please tell me that you have never walked around St. Giles alone."

She didn't answer his question, for she knew he wouldn't like the answer — but she hadn't been about to turn away from someone in need just because they lived in the wrong part of London.

"Ah, Sarah, you will be the undoing of me," he said, and she nearly laughed at the despair in his voice, except for the fact that she wished it to be anything but true.

"I cannot remain here indefinitely. It would torture my soul, break my spirit."

Would she stay for him, if he asked her? Possibly. The thought tore her in half, but she couldn't deny that the thought of leaving him was as heartbreaking as the thought of remaining in London for the rest of her life.

But besides that, he didn't ask. She knew he wasn't a man that desired any type of settling down.

"Sarah…" he began, and she wanted to stop him, to tell him not to waste any words upon her, and yet she sensed that he had to say whatever it was that was building inside of him. "You know that you… mean much to me, do you not?"

She smiled, a sad smile, glad he couldn't see her face in the dark.

"I know you care for me, David, yes," she said. "I hope that I am more to you than other women you have... been with."

"Of course you are," he said, surging across the bed, groping in the dim light until he found her hands, then clasping them to him. "I do care about you, very much so."

Had they been words of love, then perhaps she would have considered telling him that if he wanted her to, she would stay. But he was the son of an earl, and she was... well, she was simply Miss Jones. She could never ask him to leave everything for her.

"I care about you as well," she said carefully. "And I will remember my time with you for the rest of my life."

She sensed rather than saw him recoil from her, and she immediately regretted her words. But her heart was already breaking, and she couldn't allow it to be affected by him any more than it already was.

"David—"

"It's fine. I understand," he said, his words short as he stood from the bed. Sarah could hear him pacing around the room.

"You do not have to stay here anymore."

The footfalls of his boots stopped, but he didn't respond to her words. Instead, he completely shocked her.

"I think I have found your father."

Sarah's heart, which had before seemed to be so sore within her chest, now felt as though it had completely stopped.

"You... what?"

"I am about as certain as can be without outright asking him. Your suspicions were correct. It is Lord Torrington."

Sarah could hear loud, rapid breathing, and she wondered

why David was so affected — until she realized that she was hearing herself.

"But how… why…?"

She hardly knew what she was asking, but David seemed to understand her question.

"It was the ring. I had it with me at Berkley's, and Francis recognized it from his days of riding for Torrington."

"But it's not the Torrington crest. I've seen that."

"No, it isn't. It's Torrington's mother's family's. They were the horse fanatics. Francis recalled seeing it on some of the tack in Torrington's stable."

She took in the information, silent for a moment as she reflected on all David had just told her. She hardly knew a thing about Lord Torrington and had spoken to his wife only a few times in the past. She was a rather cold woman, but then, the same could be said for Lady Alexander.

A thought then occurred to her.

"How long have you known of this? When did Eddie tell you?"

"The day of the hunt."

And at the end of that day, he had come to her chamber.

"Why did you not tell me?"

He sighed. "I could not be completely sure he was the man, and I did not want to raise your expectations. As it is, I… I have no idea how he might welcome the news."

"I have been aware of that since the moment I embarked upon this journey," she said, frustrated at the fact he would suppose he could make the decision for her, despite the fact she knew he was doing what he thought was best in looking out for her. She took a breath to release her impatience, recalling that he was doing far more than she had ever requested of him. "What has changed since that time?"

"I went to see Torrington."

"You did what?"

Sarah forgot her intention to not be upset with David, for the thought of anyone else speaking to the man about his potential to be her father irked her no end. "David, I appreciate all you have done, but I very much wanted to—"

"I never told him about you," he cut in, walking back over to stand closer to the bed. "I asked him only if he knew of your mother. I told him that your mother and I had a mutual acquaintance."

"And he believed that? He never questioned how you, the son of an earl, might know my mother, a healer from a village?"

"No, he said not a thing about it," David replied. "I think he was too overcome, to be honest with you. It seemed to me that he remembers your mother with a great deal of fondness."

Sarah could hear the incredulity in his tone as he said it, and uninvited bitterness began to rise within her.

"You did not think it possible that he actually felt anything for my mother, did you?" she asked, her voice soft instead of accusatory, sad that he would think such a thing, for if that was the case, then clearly the "care" he had for her was nothing more than what she had always assumed it to be.

"I don't know Sarah. I suppose I always had my doubts," he said with an exhale, and she cringed inwardly. He was not even aware of how alike the two situations were. "The story of your mother leaving... I have heard such tales before, however, usually the woman was forced out of the household, instead of leaving of her own accord. This is the world in which I was raised."

"So you thought that my mother was sent away by the family, and then she told me a different story, one in which my father loved her?"

"It's not like that," he said, frustration underlying his

words. "I wasn't sure what to think. But I was of the mind that either way, your mother would have told you the same story. What mother would tell her child that she hadn't been wanted, hadn't been loved by one of her parents?"

It seemed as though Sarah was floating away from her body as her limbs were like lead, her consciousness outside of herself. This was what she had been waiting for so long, and yet now that she was aware of all she had been searching for, it was overwhelming her in waves.

"Look, Sarah, I am sorry if that seemed rather heartless. I did not mean it to be that way. The truth is, your mother must have been a wonderful woman, for she raised you, and I've never met someone who has a kinder, lovelier heart than you."

Sarah heard David's words, but it was difficult to listen to exactly what he was saying. She pulled the blankets closer to her chest, as though if she hid away within them, she would forget all else.

"I think… I think I'm going to go to sleep," was all she said, and then suddenly David was over top of her, leaning against the bed.

"Are you all right?" he asked, and she could just make out the dim outline of his eyes in the dark.

"I'm fine," she said, turning away from him. She had no wish for him to see how affected she was, by both his words as well as the news he had shared. "We can discuss all of this further in the morning?"

"Very well," he said, though he remained by her side for a moment longer. "Goodnight, Sarah."

She said nothing but stared at the wall for a long while until she finally fell into an exhausted sleep.

CHAPTER 23

*W*hen David had imagined returning to Sarah and sharing the news of all he had discovered, the scene had certainly played out much differently than the reality. In his mind, he would share his news, she would fall into his arms with gratefulness, and then together they would celebrate completing her mission, and he would take her to see the Earl, where the father and daughter would be reunited while David looked on with satisfaction.

What he had not anticipated was blundering the delivery, accidentally insulting her mother, and listening to Sarah's detached response.

David was aware that Sarah was hurting and upset, though he had no idea for what reason, nor what he was supposed to do to help her. When it came to women, there were certain areas in which he was quite skilled — and proud of it. However, in others, such as a woman in tears, he was most decidedly at a loss.

He wished he could tell Sarah that everything would be fine, but unfortunately, that could prove to be a lie. For while Torrington may very well still hold a penchant in his heart for Mary Jones, in no way did that mean he would be open to the return of a daughter of whom he had never been aware.

And so it was that David found himself facing a sleepless night once more on the hard floor of Sarah's lodgings. What made it worse was that he could hear her uneven breathing, knew that she was restless herself, and yet it seemed that despite their proximity she could have been miles away from him.

He must have fallen asleep briefly at some point in time, for the next morning when he groggily awoke, he could already hear noises behind him telling him that Sarah was awake. He rose from his blankets, folded them carefully, and then waited for her to emerge from behind the privacy screen.

She was clearly engrossed in her thoughts as she stopped, startled when she saw him.

"Forget that I was here?" he asked with a forced grin to attempt to ease the tension from last night, and she self-consciously shook her head as she reached behind her to finish tying the muslin dress she wore. David had noted that she wore dresses of which the ties or buttons were large enough and easy enough to reach herself. She must have had them modified, for most dresses he was familiar with required a legion of maids — or some very deft fingers — to remove them.

"I'm sorry. I am distracted."

"Understandably," he nodded. "I can hardly imagine what you must be feeling at the moment."

They seemed like the proper words. He had attempted to determine his best response as he lay there, not sleeping, throughout the night.

"I suppose I am simply overwhelmed," she said, managing a small, clearly forced smile.

"Sarah," he said, "Whenever you would like to reach out

to Lord Torrington, please tell me and I will arrange for us to meet him. Would you prefer it to be soon?"

She stared at him for a moment, then shook her head. "I should speak to him myself."

David had thought that perhaps that would be her response, but he sorely wished it were otherwise. For he still worried about the man rejecting her, and he sensed a great need to be there for her if that happened, to comfort her, to protect her from someone who might not want her. Though how a man could be so foolish as to not want Sarah Jones in his life, David had no idea.

"Please, Sarah?" he asked again, not wanting to beg, but unsure of how else to convince her. "I promise you, I will say nothing after I introduce you. You can say whatever it is you wish to him, and I will remain only an observer. Would you allow me to do that for you, to be there for you?"

She paused for a moment, staring at him, and finally, she managed a quick nod.

"Very well," she said. "Could it be for tomorrow? I believe I need a day to determine exactly how to approach him."

"Of course," he said, relieved that she had agreed. "Tomorrow."

As he left, the word played around in his mind. Tomorrow. The day that all would be revealed to both Sarah and Torrington. But it would bring something else as well — the potential end to all that was between him and Sarah. She had always said that once she had determined her father's identity, she would leave England and return home. Even if, on the chance that the Earl accepted her, convinced her to stay and become part of his life, where would that leave David? He would no longer have any reason to be there for her every night, staying with her and protecting her. He could, of course, offer for her — the thought had been on his mind often enough. But all of her actions told him that she was not entirely interested in him the way he was in her.

Oh, he knew she did care for him, as she had told him, but he could not imagine going as far as to marry her if she did not feel the same for him as he did for her. The idea of marriage triggered a thought in his mind, and he realized that he had not yet followed through on his determination to put an end to this ridiculous rumor regarding marriage between him and Lady Georgina. Despite his uncertainty regarding Sarah, he wouldn't take Lady Georgina's hand as his second choice. It wasn't fair to her, and he would never be happy married to a woman not of his own choosing.

When he returned home, he found a note waiting from Lord Hartley, informing him that he had sent word to his cousin and she would be happy to receive him. David scribbled two notes for Hampton to deliver. One to Lord Torrington, requesting an audience for tomorrow, and another to Lady Georgina, informing her that he would call upon her this afternoon.

Then he would pay a visit to his parents — but that would be a surprise.

* * *

SARAH HATED LYING TO DAVID. But he had been so insistent on accompanying her to Lord Torrington's, she knew he wouldn't relent until she had promised they would go together.

It was not that she didn't appreciate all that he had done for her, including his willingness to support her when she met — confronted? — her potential father. It was only that this was something she felt she had to do on her own. She and David had become rather attached, and Sarah had no idea how much was due to the fact that he felt indebted to her for saving his life, and how much it was because he "cared" about her.

He already protected her every single night, but her meeting with the Earl was something she could handle. She had survived living on her own in the wilds of America. She had crossed an ocean. She had navigated the social scene that was London's nobility. She could confront one man.

As she walked through Cheapside to Mayfair, her cheeks warmed as she recalled the Earl entering his study while she and David had been inside. She didn't think Lord Torrington had even looked at her, and she wondered now at what would have happened if he had actually caught her within his desk, going through his belongings.

Would she have told him who she was? Would he have realized, right then, that he was her father?

Her long walk complete, Sarah stood in front of Lord Torrington's London manor, looking up at the building on St. James Street, its front facade covered in dark stucco, sash windows rising with the building and surrounding the brown paneled door with the fanlight atop.

She had been inside before, of course, but never with such a purpose in mind. Sarah patted her hair, wishing she had put more thought into the fact that an hour's walk would leave her looking disheveled. There was nothing to be done about that now, however. Sarah took a deep breath and walked up to the door, her knock being answered in moments by a tall, disapproving butler.

"Good afternoon," she said. "Is Lord Torrington available to callers?"

The man furrowed his brow as he looked at her.

"Do you mean Lady Torrington?"

Oh, goodness. She hadn't even thought of the fact that Lady Torrington might insist on being in the room when she spoke to the Earl.

"No, I do mean Lord Torrington. I would like to speak with him alone."

"May I please provide your name?"

"Of course," she said hurriedly. "I have no calling card, unfortunately, but it is Miss Jones. Miss Sarah Jones."

"Very good," he said. "Please follow me."

She nodded, her heart slamming against her ribs as she entered the drawing room after him. It was an elegant room, though not one Sarah would describe as comfortable. Egyptian gods and goddesses looked down upon her from where they were painted in a border near the ceiling. Additional sculptures stood upon the mantel over the grate, while the chairs were not at all plush, but ornately carved in exquisite, intricate motifs. It seemed everything within the room was gilded, with the walls painted a brilliant red. The butler held out an arm in front of him, and Sarah followed his outstretched hand into the room, taking a seat on the settee facing the door. She took a deep breath, managing a smile for the butler who remained watching her.

"Please wait one moment," he said, before shutting the door behind him, leaving Sarah alone with her thoughts. She continued to repeat to herself the words she had been practicing since the day she found out that she might have a father, particularly an English nobleman. She would maintain calm, ensure that he understood she was asking nothing of him but a family connection.

The doorknob began to turn, and Sarah jumped to her feet in anticipation of the man, but instead, a woman filled the doorway.

She was slightly over average height, her hair still a deep chestnut despite the fact that she was old enough to be Sarah's mother. She was beautiful, made even more so by apparent enhancements such as the slightest hint of red on her lips, which would have been nearly imperceptible but for the fact that Sarah was well aware of the various ingredients used for lip pomades here in England.

The woman's hair was intricately styled, as though she were hosting another gathering that very evening. She wore a long, deep purple gown that Sarah was sure was of the latest fashion. Her face, while beautiful, was now marred by a deep frown.

This was Lady Torrington, Sarah recalled. She had to admit that she had not paid the woman any particular attention before. How Sarah was now supposed to explain her presence here, she had no idea, though she wondered from the chill emanating from the woman as to whether she had some suspicion as to Sarah's identity — though how that could be, she had no idea.

"Miss Jones," Lady Torrington said, as she seemed to practically float into the room. "My butler tells me you wish to see my husband."

"Ah, yes, that is correct," Sarah said, folding her hands over one another as she attempted to retain her calm.

"Unfortunately, he is not currently in residence," Lady Torrington said, standing across the table from Sarah and motioning for her to resume her seat. Sarah did so, though she had to attempt not to fidget as she had no idea what she was supposed to say to the woman. *I'm here to tell your husband that I may be his illegitimate daughter?* In her initial research of the man, she knew that he had not been married at the time she was born, so at the very least, she was not the result of an extramarital affair.

"I will return at another time," Sarah said, beginning to rise once more, but Lady Torrington held out a hand, motioning for her to remain seated.

"This is not the first time I have heard the name of Miss Jones."

"No?" Sarah asked, surprised.

"No," the woman said, a cold smile crossing her face. "One remembers the name of the harlot who attempted to capture my husband's affections."

Sarah could feel all the warmth drain out of her face.

"Excuse me?" she whispered.

"My husband and I have no secrets, Miss Jones," Lady Torrington continued. "And, in fact, when he became aware that you might call upon him, he asked that I handle this entire…" she waved a hand in front of her as though Sarah was a pest who required exterminating and Sarah bristled. "Situation."

"What is it you believe you know about me, Lady Torrington?" Sarah asked, willing her voice to remain steady.

"You look like her," the woman said, not answering the question, but instead narrowing her eyes at Sarah as she studied her. "I found you familiar to me the moment I first saw you with Lady Alexander. Of course, I will never forget the woman who attempted to steal my husband away."

"My mother never did anything to steal your husband," Sarah responded, insulted that the Countess would think to even say such a thing. "I believe I was born before you were married."

"Perhaps," Lady Torrington said with a shrug. "But I was always intended for Lord Torrington, since we were children. Men like to have their fun, I realize that. As you must be aware of as well, if you are so *interested* in Mr. Redmond, who seems to be willing to do whatever it takes to find himself in your bed at the moment. But know this, Miss Jones, a man will go back to where he belongs every time, once he has had his fun. My husband certainly did."

"My mother left of her own will," Sarah said, wincing when she finally noticed how hard she was squeezing together the hands in her lap.

Lady Torrington snorted. "Of course she would have told

you that. No, the truth was, while the Earl certainly couldn't order her away, my husband — then the apparent heir — told her the reality of the matter. That she had been an amusing dalliance, but that was all she would ever be. That he was to marry another. I do hope you understand that, Miss Jones. Which also means that my husband wants nothing to do with you. He is aware that you might exist, and he would prefer that all remains as it is."

Sarah swallowed the sob of despair that rose in her throat at the woman's words.

"I want nothing from you — or from him," Sarah said, refusing to allow her voice to waver. "I only desired the opportunity to come to know the man who might prove to be my father."

"He is *not* your father," Lady Torrington said, rising above Sarah now. "Legitimate children are only through marriage. You are nothing more than a by-blow. One he would prefer remained far from his life. He has no desire to acknowledge an illegitimate daughter. Return home, Miss Jones, to wherever you came from."

Sarah rose herself, though she didn't yet walk to the door.

"I wish to hear these words from Lord Torrington himself."

"Not every wish comes true, darling," the Countess said with an icy countenance. "You of anyone should know that. Do not return here. And tell your Mr. Redmond that he should desist in his quest to help you. It is beneath him."

Not caring about being rude — for this woman had far surpassed such a thing herself — Sarah refused to look at her any longer but strode past her toward the door before the tears that threatened began to rain. She would not give this woman the satisfaction of seeing such a thing.

"You will never compare to a woman like Lady Georgina."

Keep walking, Sarah, she told herself, well aware this

woman was only trying to goad her into a reaction. But Sarah had always been the curious sort — far too much for her own good.

She reached the door, had her hand on the handle — but then she turned around.

"Who is Lady Georgina?"

"Why, your Mr. Redmond's betrothed," the woman said with a satisfied smile. "Lady Georgina, daughter of Lord and Lady Buckworth of Bath. They are in London for a time in order to finalize this arrangement. Surely Mr. Redmond didn't neglect to inform you of the fact? Oh... I see perhaps he did. My sincerest apologies, Miss Jones. And best of luck."

CHAPTER 24

*D*avid was well aware of how important it was that he see Lady Georgina and explain to her the truth of the situation. Yet, as he ascended the stairs of the London manor where she could be found, part of him — the cowardly side — prayed she would not be in residence. It would only delay the inevitable, of course, and yet David had been so ill-equipped to handle Sarah's tears, he could hardly imagine how he might react to those of a woman with whom he did not feel nearly as comfortable.

But if Sarah could travel halfway around the world to speak the truth to a man who she knew would more than likely reject her, he could certainly be honest with a woman regarding how he felt, could he not?

When David knocked on the door of the manor, a housekeeper or maid — he couldn't be sure which — opened the door, affirming that yes, Lady Georgina was in, and she and her mother were accepting callers and expecting him.

Ah, yes, Lady Buckworth. Of course, she would be within as well, despite Hartley's promise to arrange everything otherwise. David steeled his resolve as the housekeeper led him into the sitting room, despite how much he longed to turn and run away as fast as he could.

"Mr. Redmond!" Lady Buckworth said, standing, though David didn't miss the look of panic that filled Lady Georgina's eyes. What was that about? "How lovely it is for you to call upon us today."

David managed a smile for her, though he kept his eyes on Lady Georgina. The girl — for she seemed much more girl than woman — was nearly shaking. Whatever could be the matter?

"Yes, well, it is far past time that I came to call," he said, taking a seat once the women did. He looked around him, noting that his mother would certainly not approve of the sitting room. It was clean, but the furniture was worn, and if he wasn't mistaken, the chesterfield upon which he sat was from the previous century.

He was aware that the Buckworths were renting the manor, but he wondered at their current state of finances.

"I actually came to speak with Lady Georgina," he said to Lady Buckworth in what he hoped was a firm yet polite tone.

"Of course," she said graciously. "Lady Georgina would be happy to speak with you." She stared pointedly at her daughter but did not move.

"I know it is rather untoward, but I was wondering if it might be possible for me to speak with her alone."

Lady Buckworth raised her eyebrows.

"I am sorry, Mr. Redmond, but you must realize that I could never allow such a thing."

It was the answer he had been expecting, but he had wanted to try nonetheless.

"Very well," he said, clearing his throat as he stopped himself from wiping his palms, which had begun to sweat, on his pants. "It seems there has been a misunderstanding."

"Oh?" Lady Buckworth said, and David gritted his teeth,

as he really wished the woman would allow her daughter to speak.

"I have heard a rumor lately — one that involves the two of us," he said, speaking now only to Lady Georgina. Lady Buckworth may remain, but that wouldn't stop him from having his discussion with her daughter instead. "The rumor claims that we are to be married."

Lady Georgina refused to meet his eye, but Lady Buckworth let out a laugh.

"A rumor? My dear, Mr. Redmond, it is not a rumor at all! Your parents, as well as Lord Buckworth and I, came to this agreement long ago. It is why we are even within London."

David's spine began to stiffen in anger, but he was aware that these were not the people with whom he should be upset. It was his own parents who knew of his wishes and went against them, regardless.

"That may very well be, Lady Buckworth, but no one's consent is required but my own, and I do not agree to this marriage," he swiveled his gaze back to Lady Georgina, and was startled to find that she was looking up at him with something akin to hope in her eyes. "Please accept my sincerest apologies, Lady Georgina. You seem like a truly lovely woman. It is only that my heart belongs to another."

He heard his words spoken aloud, and, at that moment, consciously realized what he had known deep within him for some time now. He didn't just *care* for Sarah. He loved her. He loved her with all of his being and he couldn't imagine spending another moment, let alone the rest of his life, without her. Suddenly all he wanted to do was finish this conversation, leave this house, and tell her exactly that. If she knew how he felt, would she forget her plans to return to America, and forsake all of it to stay here with him?

He knew of her hatred of London, but perhaps, if he could find some land outside of the city, or talk to his father about living in one of their country homes, she might stay with him there. He had lived in London for most of his adult life now, of course, but primarily it was due to his desire to be on his own. He no longer had that need to be alone — there was a woman with whom he wanted to spend the rest of his life.

But first, Lady Georgina. David returned his attention to the women before him, each wearing an entirely different expression from the other. Unsurprisingly, Lady Buckworth's lips were turned into a grimace, her eyes narrowed, her fingers gripping the arms of the chair so tightly that David imagined she would likely prefer they were currently around his neck. Lady Georgina, however, had her head tilted to the side, her lips curled up in a smile, as though she were happy for him — as if she understood.

"Is your mother aware of this… decision of yours?" Lady Buckworth asked through tight lips, and David nodded.

"I have been completely honest with her from the beginning, Lady Buckworth," he responded, leaning forward in the chair, his elbows upon his knees as he attempted to convey his earnestness. "Both your family and Lady Georgina seem lovely, and whatever man becomes her husband will be most fortunate. I, however, am not that man."

He stood, bowing slightly to the women.

"Please forgive me for any discord I have caused. This was never my intent."

Lady Buckworth said nothing to him — no farewell at all. David would almost prefer angry words that he could respond to than her cold silence, but he took the opportunity to escape as fast as he could.

He was halfway into his carriage, one foot within and the other still on the step, when he heard his name being called and he turned to find Lady Georgina running down the walkway.

"Mr. Redmond," she gasped as she neared, as though she had sprinted the entire way — which he imagined she had, either to get ahead of her mother or because she had needed to make up time after making her excuses to Lady Buckworth. Regardless, he urged her to continue. "I apologize for my mother. You were nothing but honest with us, which I very much appreciate. And I— I understand."

"You do?" he asked, raising his eyebrows, then, sensing the awkwardness of their positions, him so far above her on the steps, he gestured toward the interior of his carriage. "Would you like to sit within for a moment? I will leave the door open."

She hesitated before nodding. "Very well," she said, following him up, taking his proffered hand.

Once they were seated, he urged her to continue.

"I am happy for you and the fact that you have found a woman you truly love," she said, surprising him. He had only had the opportunity to gauge her expressions earlier and he had hardly heard her speak more than three words at once the night they had dinner together, so it was nearly amazing to hear so many at one time now. "I…" she looked down at her hands shyly. "I have found love myself."

"Have you now?" he asked, sitting back into the squabs, crossing his arms over his chest. This was certainly an interesting turn of events. "I am very pleased to hear that, Lady Georgina. Which leads me to ask — why would your parents arrange for you to marry me when there is another who has captured your heart?"

She paused for a moment, as though she didn't know what to say until finally, her words caught his attention once more.

"You truly are not aware of the arrangement," she said, her words not a question but rather a revelation, and he narrowed his eyes at her in puzzlement.

"Whatever do you mean?"

"Oh dear," she whispered, and he leaned in closer.

"Please tell me."

"As you may or may not be aware, my family is in some difficult financial circumstances," she said, somewhat hesitantly. "My father squandered away his fortune on ill-advised investments, leaving my family to sell nearly everything we owned of any worth in an attempt to make it back. I have an older brother to whom all of the estates will be left, but he is already married, so there was no opportunity for him to wed a woman who would provide a substantial dowry."

She stopped talking once more, looking down at her hands. David wanted to shake her, to tell her to continue, but he had enough sense to realize that was likely the last method one should use with a woman such as Lady Georgina — he was liable to scare her away. Instead, he waited, which did not come entirely naturally to him, but he was rewarded for his patience.

"I, of course, have no dowry, which is naturally a problem as I am a couple of years past what would be considered optimal marriageable age," she said. "When my father was last in London, he was sharing his dilemma with your father, who in turn shared his own, as he thought they could come to a mutual understanding."

"Of…"

"Of marriage," she said with a sigh. "Unlike most arrangements, your father agreed to pay mine upon us wedding."

David could only stare at her for a moment before he responded, though the words nearly choked him.

"Are you telling me that my father is so desperate to be rid of me, to see me married off, that he agreed to pay a dowry… for me?"

How embarrassing. How utterly debasing. If anyone ever found out about this…

"I'm not sure I would call it a *dowry*," said Lady Georgina kindly. "Perhaps more of an agreement?"

David ran his hand over his face. Had he really been such an embarrassment to his father? And how did the man think that marriage would change him? Why did it matter?

"But what of your suitor, the man you say you love? Surely if he loved you an equal amount in return, he would pay the dowry for you?"

Lady Georgina looked out the window, her eyes far away.

"He absolutely would — if he could. Unfortunately, he has no access to any money that could even come close to paying a thing for me. He is... not from the nobility."

"Who is he?" David asked, intrigued, and Lady Georgina's cheeks turned bright pink.

"He is a footman within our homes," she said softly. "We fell in love during the summer, when he was at our country estate. It continued throughout the winter. I cannot imagine my life without him, but I also cannot imagine a life with him. My parents, of course, forbid it."

David sympathized with her. He was facing a somewhat similar dilemma, although he was in a better position to do something about it if he so chose. Lady Georgina would likely be held to whatever her parents decided for her.

"I'm sorry," he said, reaching out and placing a hand on her arm. "Truly, I am. If there is ever anything I can do to help you, please come find me."

He gave her the address of his boardinghouse, and then she began to depart the carriage.

"My best wishes to you, Lady Georgina," he said with a wave.

"And to you, Mr. Redmond."

He hoped he wouldn't need them.

CHAPTER 25

*I*t had taken some time, but finally, Sarah found the London townhouse where Lord and Lady Buckworth, as well as their daughter, the beautiful Lady Georgina, were staying. She was surprised when she saw it — if they were marrying their daughter to a son of the Earl of Brentford, she would have thought they would be far wealthier a family. The house lacked any decoration, and had great uniformity with the houses surrounding it.

Not that it mattered — not to her anyway, she thought bitterly.

Sarah took a deep breath. She had been well aware of the hatred Lady Torrington felt for her — one did not need to be particularly emotionally understanding to realize that. She hadn't been prepared for it in a way; however, it was difficult to understand how a woman could hate someone who had nothing to do with the sequence of events that had ended thusly.

With that being said, as much as Lady Torrington's final words had cut deeply into Sarah's very soul, she was also aware that the woman would have said anything to cause her pain and to convince her to leave the house. Sarah's only regret was that she had allowed the woman to see how much her words had affected her.

Before she permitted the pain to filter through to her heart by believing all the Countess had said, Sarah decided she would ascertain the facts. She could have asked David, of course, but Sarah had now allowed enough doubt to creep in that she wasn't sure she would be able to believe what he told her.

So she decided to call upon Lady Georgina. She began to approach the house down the street but stopped when she saw a familiar carriage parked in front of it.

David's carriage. But what was he doing here? She began to take another step forward, but then stopped when she saw a woman running from the house. She was beautiful, her dark hair in an intricate chignon, her dress worn yet still fitting beautifully around her willowy frame. She was chasing after David like a woman in pursuit of her love, and it seemed as though Sarah's heart stopped beating.

Then she saw David stop at the top of the carriage steps, speak a few words with the woman, hold out his hand — and pull her inside.

Sarah could only stare at the scene in front of her. After thinking it through, she had been convinced that she would arrive here and be presented with one of two circumstances — either there would be no one living here by the name of Lord and Lady Buckworth, or she would speak with Lady Georgina, who would tell her that there was nothing between her and David — assuring her that it had all been Lady Torrington attempting to torture her further believing the worst of David.

But now that she had seen the woman — with David — her gut wrenched as she realized that Lady Torrington had been right. And why wouldn't it be true? David was the son of an earl. She had always known that a man like him would never truly be with a woman such as her. Yet with all of his charm, his words of care and concern for her, she had allowed him to convince her otherwise — that she *was* a woman he could be with for more than physical intimacy, that perhaps he could even fall in love with.

She had been wrong. She still had no doubts that he had been truthful — she was sure he *did* care for her, as he had said. Just as one could care for an acquaintance, a friend, or a mistress. The worst of it was that she had been well aware that this was how their time together could result, and she had given him all of her anyway — her body, her soul, her heart.

For she loved him. She knew it now by the way her heart seemed to be torn in two. She loved damn David Redmond, but she would no longer stay and be a dalliance for him while he was everything to her. She couldn't — it hurt far too much.

As Sarah saw the skirts of the beautiful woman begin to emerge from the carriage once more, she finally realized what a fool she must look, standing here immobile as the world carried on around her. She picked up her own skirts — those of one of her best dresses, which she had donned to see her father, a man who clearly had no thought for her at all — and fled.

* * *

DAVID WHISTLED a merry tune as he walked up the Cheapside street to Sarah's rooms. He was conflicted about Lady Georgina's situation — he wished he could help her, yet he could not see how he was in any position to do so, besides marry her yet allow her a relationship with her footman, a man he would have to hire on. That, however, was now inconceivable, for he had plans of his own.

He removed his gloves, noticing his palms were slightly damp in anticipation of seeing Sarah and asking her what would be the most important question of his life. He perhaps should have returned home first and spoken with his father, informing him of all that had transpired with Lady Georgina and Lady Buckworth, but at the moment he cared far more for ensuring Sarah knew just how important she was, how much he wanted — no, *needed* — her in his life.

If his father didn't allow him to utilize one of his country estates — and at this point, David thought it more likely that they would cut him off entirely than actually provide him with anything after the conversation he had just had — then David was sure he could find himself and Sarah a small home in the country. It wouldn't be much, for he would have to determine just how he was going to create income for himself, but he was certain that together, they could make anything work.

After she hopefully agreed to marry him, he would take her to see the Earl of Torrington. He wasn't sure what the man's reception to her would be, but at the very least, David would be there to comfort her if necessary.

David knocked on the door but was disappointed when no ensuing answer came, so he pulled out the key Sarah had left him with and let himself in.

His jaw dropped open in surprise at the scene before him. Sarah was standing in front of her wardrobe, rifling through the fantastic, colorful array of dresses, pulling out only the most utilitarian, drab dresses he had ever seen and throwing them into a heap on the floor behind her, under which, he finally realized, lay her valise.

Her hair was unpinned, flowing down her back, while the rest of the room was in shambles. Her herbs and bottles of concoctions were on the floor beside the valise along with her shotgun and three daggers, while everything else was piled in the corner.

On the small desk lay pieces of paper, each covered in her soft, feminine writing.

She was leaving. The revelation took far longer than it should have to filter through his mind, but once it did, waves of disappointment crashed through him unlike anything he had ever felt before. She couldn't leave — not yet, not until he had said to her all he needed to say.

"Sarah?" he finally called out, and she turned, shocking him when she did, for her face was covered in tears that she angrily and hurriedly brushed away.

David strode across the room in moments, but when he reached his arms out toward her, she stepped away and around him.

"Whatever is the matter?" he asked, shocked at all that lay before him. "Where are you going?"

"I'm going home," she choked out finally, her words as brusque as her current actions. "Where I never should have left."

"What are you talking about?" he asked, wondering whatever could have happened between the time he left her and his return. "Were we not going to visit Lord Torrington?"

"I have been to the Torringtons'," she said, crouching now beside the old, tattered, and patched valise, roughly folding her dresses and skirts and shoving them into the bag as she spoke. "I have my answer. Now it is time to go."

"I thought you were going to wait for me?" he said, perplexed. When had she spoken to Torrington? There was only a short timeframe between when David had left the man and then returned to Cheapside. What could Torrington have said in that space of time that would have so upset her? While David had his doubts whether the man would accept her, he thought Torrington was a decent enough sort who would have done so much more gently than others would have. But by Sarah's reaction, it was as though the man had dumped her out on the street without a word of explanation.

"You have done enough for me," she said, looking up at him for a moment, long enough for him to see the spark in her eyes, shining through her tears. "I release you from your duties."

"You never held me to anything," he said, attempting to maintain his own calm reason. "I chose to be here — to be with you."

"Because you felt beholden to me. Because I saved your life. And then, because I allowed you into my bed."

The room seemed to be spinning around David. Where had this woman come from? For this was not his Sarah, the woman he had come to know, had come to love. No, his Sarah was gentle, kind, loving, and rational.

But then, this was clearly not a typical circumstance.

"Sarah," he said cautiously, taking a slow step toward her. "I am not here because I feel beholden to you in any way. Nor am I here to take you to bed."

"Ah, you are done with me then," she said with a curt nod. "Very well. I understand."

David rubbed his forehead. Never before had he the occasion in which he had to convince a woman of his feelings toward her, for never before had he had any feelings for a woman that were beyond the intimacy she was describing.

He wished he were a man like Clarence, who could find the correct words for every moment. His own always came across so trite.

"Sarah," he attempted again. "I am here for you. Whatever has happened, please tell me, and I will do all I can to help you."

"Very well," she said, rising and crossing her arms over

her chest as she stared at him. "I visited Lord Torrington's home and was told that he was aware of my existence but that he had no desire to want anything to do with me. That my mother was a harlot who he compromised, and then the family forced her to leave due to her situation. Does that tell you all that you need to know?"

David tried to focus on her words, wishing she had waited for him, but her fiery independent streak had obviously felt the need to do this herself.

"I'm sorry," he said, attempting to diffuse her anger, which was likely hiding most of the hurt she felt. "You say you were told this. By who? Torrington himself?"

"His wife. Lord Torrington had no wish to speak with me."

David mulled over her words in his mind. He didn't know Lady Torrington well, but he had a feeling that she wouldn't be enthralled by the thought of a long-lost daughter visiting her husband.

"I would suggest you speak with Torrington himself before you... before you leave," he said, forcing the words out.

"No need," she said, sitting on her bag as she attempted to flatten it enough that she could fasten the buckles on top. "I do not require his approval nor his presence in my life."

"I wish you had waited for me," he murmured, but she shook her head.

"I am capable of doing much on my own."

"I realize that," he acknowledged, beginning to become frustrated himself at the hostility emanating from her toward him. "I thought I could help."

"You have done more than enough."

"But Sarah, how could you just leave? You have all of your friends here in England."

"I have written them letters as none are currently within

London. They have their own lives to live. The ship I would like to take home will be leaving very shortly, within a few days, so I would have no time to visit them."

Tears started to flow from her eyes once more, and David felt like shaking her, to return some sense to her, to make her see that it was not necessary to get on that ship and leave all behind.

"There will be other ships."

"Yes, but I need to leave *now*."

"Why?"

"To get away from this — all of this."

"What about us? What you and I have?"

She snorted slightly, startling him. "What do you suggest, David? That I remain as your mistress?"

"Of course not!" he said, indignant that she would think such a thing. He was willing to give up everything for her, and this is what she truly thought of him? "I've told you how much I care about you—"

"I know you care for me, David, I do not question that," she said. "But how would you continue to *care* for me while you are married?"

"Married? What are you talking about?"

"I have been informed of your upcoming nuptials, for which I simply must congratulate you," she said, and despite her apparent efforts to remain nonchalant, he could hear the pain laced within her words. "I hope you are very happy. She is beautiful."

David stared at her.

"I am not getting married — at least, not to anyone else. Sarah, I lo—"

But Sarah was too upset to listen to what he was saying.

She strode to the door, placed one hand upon the knob, and waved her other toward it.

"Goodbye, David."

"Sarah, I am not leaving," he said, raising his voice now in order for her to hear just what, exactly, he had to say. "You must listen to me—"

A knock resounded at the door, loud enough to interrupt him, and David sighed, exasperated, as Sarah tugged the door open.

A man stood outside, holding the hand of a small child, a girl whose eyes were full of tears.

"Miss Jones?" he said quizzically, and Sarah nodded. "I'm sorry, but my daughter fell today, and her arm doesn't look quite right. She's been complaining of it something fierce, and I was told that you could help. But if I'm interrupting—"

"No, of course not, do come in," Sarah said, ushering them into her room. "It's best to set the bone as soon as possible if required. This man was just leaving."

David shook his head to tell her that no, he most certainly was *not* leaving, but the look she gave him was one that told him if he didn't, there would be consequences.

Very well. If that was what she wanted, he would leave — but he would be back shortly. And this time, he would make her listen.

CHAPTER 26

Sarah made quick work of the little girl's arm. It was a clean break, and easy to set. The girl was a tough one and made little protest considering what Sarah had to do, for which Sarah was grateful. The man told her he had a stall in the market from which he sold vegetables, and if Sarah would like to come by, he would be happy to provide her with anything she'd like in payment for her services. Sarah smiled, thanked him, but then informed him that this would be one of her last days here. Her ship was to sail very soon, and she would have neither the time nor the need to attend the market if she was to make it before departure.

She took a deep breath once she shut the door behind them, finally able to process David's visit, all that he had said and all that she knew to be true. Sarah realized she had been abrupt with him, but if she hadn't, if she had allowed him to become close in both body and mind, then she would be doomed. She couldn't allow his words of charm and comfort, words she clearly unable to resist. This is what had led her to the situation she was currently in, and she would not allow it to happen again — of that, she was determined.

She looked around her now, at the rooms that had been her home for far longer than she could have ever imagined. She had been happy here, in a sense. She had become closer with three women than she could have thought possible, and her heart ached at the thought of leaving them. She sealed the letters she had written to each of them, lovingly running her fingers over the names of her friends. She would write them again, to be sure, and she knew she should tell them of her decision and her plans in person — but if she did, they would likely convince her to stay, at least for a time. In all actuality, had they been in London, she wouldn't have been able to help but to see them, just for one last time. But Phoebe and Elizabeth were each residing at their country estates for the moment, while Julia was at a racetrack else-where in England — likely Newmarket, though Sarah had to admit she had a difficult time keeping up with their schedule.

She would miss them — oh, how she would miss them. But they all had their own lives now and their own families. They might miss her, but it wouldn't be the same. They had much to keep them occupied and she had only been a part of their lives for a few years — they would soon go back to the way things had been before she had ever arrived.

Sarah wiped the tears from her eyes as she gathered her belongings. She would pack the remainder of her things, those she was leaving behind, and give them to another woman who might need them. Perhaps Emily — she was a new mother, and she and Billy had little to their name. Sarah hadn't come to own much, not having the funds to purchase much of anything, but if she could help someone else a bit, that would be best.

Sarah wrote a note to affix to the door for any potential patients who came her way, with directions to where they could find another who could help them. One more night here, she thought with a nod. Then she would be gone. But first, there was one more visit she had to make before she left.

* * *

SARAH HAD VISITED Lady Alexander's London townhome often enough, but she had never been invited any further than the front drawing room, where she would often await Lady Alexander to prepare herself to attend an event. Today, however, the butler led her into a back drawing room, which was styled in rich colors of red and gold, almost oriental in its look. She remembered that Lord Alexander had been interested in all things foreign — in fact, he had died while on a tour of Asia. Sarah was surprised Lady Alexander had kept the room as such, for it might remind her of memories she may not otherwise want to entertain.

"Miss Jones," Lady Alexander appeared in the doorway, elegantly dressed. It was mid-afternoon, so she would have been prepared to receive callers, though Sarah was unsure how much socializing the woman typically partook in. Sarah waited for her to ask why she was visiting when they had no previously scheduled appointment, but Lady Alexander surprised her by leading her into the room, sitting down on the chair across from her and folding her hands in her lap as she gazed upon her studiously.

"I have heard that you are leaving England."

Sarah's eyes flew up to meet Lady Alexander's in astonishment. She had told no one that she was leaving — no one but David. How had she—

"At least, that is what I assume following your conversation with Lady Torrington."

Sara opened her mouth to respond, but no words emerged. She had forgotten that Lady Torrington and Lady Alexander were acquainted.

"She told you of our conversation?" Sarah asked, hearing the hollowness of her words.

"She told me and others within our circle of what she called 'your accusations' and your attempt to discredit her husband's name, coming after their family money. She called you a fraud."

Sarah gripped the arms of the chair in which she sat. "That is not the truth at all!" she said, her words heated, though she knew Lady Alexander should not be the recipient of her anger, but another woman, one not in this room.

Lady Alexander held up a hand. "I know."

Sarah slightly loosened her grip.

"I am aware of why you came to England," Lady Alexander said, her tone devoid of emotion, much more matter-of-fact than Sarah could ever manage.

"Of course, to find my father," said Sarah, as she had told Lady Alexander all of this on their voyage over the Atlantic. "You must know, I only did so in order to find a family connection. I never had any intention of requesting more from him, nor of his family. In fact, I would not have involved his family at all, but Lady Torrington seemed to already know the particulars of the situation and it was she who greeted me."

"I understand," said Lady Alexander, her nose raised high in the air as though she disapproved, though of whom, Sarah had no idea. "However, I know more than you are aware."

Sarah tilted her head at her, confused. "Whatever do you mean?"

"There is someone I would like you to meet," Lady Alexander said, then rose and knocked on the door, as though there was someone awaiting her signal.

The door opened and a woman walked in. She was dressed in far less finery than Lady Alexander, and Sarah wondered for a moment if she was a servant. But she was not dressed as a servant — no, she wore what a woman in the country might wear — a woman who belonged to the lower classes, likely where Sarah herself would fall into were she to remain in England.

The woman's face was pinched, her eyes narrowed as she studied Sarah as though she were some type of specimen. Yet there was something… familiar about her.

Sarah rose in greeting, but the woman said nothing, remaining standing where she was until Lady Alexander took her by the elbow and helped her to the settee.

"Miss Jones," Lady Alexander said, "I would like you to meet Mrs. Baker."

"How do you do?" Sarah asked politely, but the woman said nothing. She only continued to stare at her.

"I should have known," Mrs. Baker finally said, and Sarah reared back as though she had been slapped at the vehemence in the woman's tone.

"Pardon me?" she managed.

"I should have known that after all I prepared for you, you would not be able to follow this through. You're just like your mother — in looks and, apparently, brains or lack thereof."

Sarah looked between Mrs. Baker and Lady Alexander.

"Excuse me? I have no idea of what you are speaking."

"Everything was ready for you. I sent you the letter, I paid for your bloody ticket to come here — do you know how long it took me to save up for that? And all you have managed to do is get yourself removed from his home." She shook her head. "I always have to do everything myself."

"Lucy," Lady Alexander leaned over and placed a hand on the woman's knee, shocking Sarah, for Lady Alexander had never shown her any bit of tenderness. "Perhaps we should first explain to Miss Jones who you are and why you are here."

She turned back to Sarah.

"Mrs. Baker is your mother's sister — your aunt," she said, and Sarah gasped in shock as she returned her gaze to the woman to study her more closely. She did have a similar look to her mother, which was why she had seemed so familiar. Yet her mother had had a much softer countenance, more joy in her gaze than this woman, who seemed angry and bitter.

"Mrs. Baker is also the woman who sent you the letter you received so long ago."

Sarah stared at Lady Alexander. "And you knew?"

Lady Alexander nodded. "I did."

"So you..." as it all became clear, betrayal began to creep into Sarah's soul. "You knew who I was. On the ship. It was not a coincidence that we became acquainted."

"It was not," Lady Alexander said unapologetically. "Lucy and I have been friends since we were children. I knew your mother as well, although we were not... close. I was the daughter of the local magistrate. I actually met my husband while he was in the country with his family visiting the Earl."

"We spent an entire summer together, the four of us," Mrs. Baker said bitterly. "However, years later, one of us became Lady Alexander, the other Mrs. Baker."

"I'm afraid I do not understand," said Sarah, her mind whirling and a swirl of emotions roiling within her belly. "I thought my mother and the Earl were together. Was that not how... I came to be?"

"Yes," Mrs. Baker said. "Because your mother was willing to spread her legs."

Sarah gasped, and Lady Alexander held out her hands between them.

"That's enough, Lucy," she said, then returned her gaze to Sarah. "As Mrs. Baker explained, she and Lord Torrington spent much time together, though it was not romantic."

221

Mrs. Baker began to protest, but Lady Alexander shook her head.

"I am sorry, Lucy, but that is the truth, as you well know." She turned her attention back to Sarah. "Through Lucy, the now-Lord Torrington met your mother and he was captivated by her. They began a love affair, one which, as an observer, I can tell you was felt equally by both sides. Each summer they came together at the estate, until one day, your mother just... left."

"She was pregnant with you," said Mrs. Baker, "And knew the Earl's family would never allow such a relationship."

"You knew of me?" Sarah asked, her voice slightly breaking. Her entire life, she had family and had no idea.

"I did," said Mrs. Baker. "Your mother wrote to me."

"So why... why am I here? Why did you write me such a cryptic letter, and not tell me of all that you knew?" Sarah brought a hand to her forehead as she thought of how much time she had wasted looking for the man when her aunt — and Lady Alexander — had known of his identity all this time.

"Because it quickly became apparent that you were just like your mother — that you would not be out for revenge, as I was."

"Revenge for my mother?" Sarah asked, confused.

"No," Mrs. Baker said sharply. "Revenge for *me*. The Earl had his fun with two country girls — sisters — but it wasn't right. Not at all. It has been years, but he should get what is coming to him — a bastard daughter, to ruin the perfect life he has created. Once you showed yourself to him, I planned to pay him a visit to arrange a deal of sorts. If he provided you with the fortune to which you should likely be entitled to anyway, you would leave his life forever. And, for creating the deal for you, I would receive part of that fortune in turn."

Sarah brought her hand to her breast, rubbing a fist against the place where her chest was beginning to ache. She had come to England to find family. Having none before, she now knew the identity of both her father, as well as her aunt. And neither had proven to care at all about a family connection. One wanted her out of his life, the other wanted to use her for her own gain.

"Mrs. Baker," she said slowly. "I am sorry you feel this way, that you have been slighted by the Earl. I do understand why you must feel so hurt."

Mrs. Baker snorted. "I am not *hurt*. I am angry."

"Very well. I understand your anger. But you must know, I will not ask the Earl for anything. All I wanted was his acknowledgment that he was my father, even if it was only privately to me. I wanted to know what he was like, to have that connection with him. I have been disappointed — by him, and now by you. Do you have no wish for the two of us to better come to know one another? I am your niece."

She heard the break in her voice, but no longer cared. "Do I have cousins? An uncle? And other aunts or uncles?"

"I was not able to have children," Mrs. Baker said bitterly. "My husband is dead, and it was always just me and your mother as our parents died young. I am alone in the world."

Sarah stood, walking over to the woman's chair. She knew what it was like to feel that there was no one else to rely on, and now it began to make more sense why she was so angry.

"I am your family, Mrs. Baker, if you will allow me to come to know you better."

She placed her hand on the woman's, but Mrs. Baker flung it away.

"I have no wish for you in my life, unless it is to bring me my fortune," she said, her eyes so accusatory that Sarah nearly flinched. "You seem to me to be exactly like your mother, and she brought me nothing but pain."

"My mother spoke little of her past," Sarah said softly. "But I do recall her mentioning a sister once. She said that you disapproved of her choices."

"That is an understatement."

Sarah hardly knew what to say. She was shocked at all she had heard since she had walked into Lady Alexander's drawing room. She looked to the woman now, who maintained her stoic countenance, although if Sarah wasn't mistaken, she was looking at her with some pity.

"What will you do now, Miss Jones?" Lady Alexander asked, and Sarah could feel the hot prick of tears at the back of her eyes, but she refused to let them fall until she was well away from this house.

"I will go home, I suppose," she said. "Back to America. There is nothing holding me here any longer."

Lady Alexander nodded and stood.

"I will walk you to the door."

Sarah nodded, allowing herself one final look at her aunt before she followed Lady Alexander. Her aunt sat there, staring straight ahead, and Sarah could only shake her head as she continued on. Once they reached the front door, Lady Alexander turned and surprised Sarah by taking her hands in hers.

"Lucy has become quite bitter over the years," Lady Alexander said quietly. "I am sorry for that. I agreed to help her because I thought this might bring her some closure, but it appears it has only worsened the situation and has caused you some pain, for which I apologize. I wish you all of the best, Miss Jones, in whatever decision you make."

Sarah nodded. It was on her lips to thank Lady Alexander, but then she recalled that the woman had lied to her, deceived her, for what was now years.

"I hope you find whatever brings you happiness, Lady Alexander," she said in all honesty, and then with one last quick nod, she hurried out the door and down the stairs, away from this house and all the secrets it held.

CHAPTER 27

*D*avid was much smarter this time. Instead of darkening Lord Torrington's door only to be turned away by his wife once more, he determined, with some help of a groom who was willing to do anything David required for a few shillings, that he could find the man at White's — perfect.

When David finally tracked him down in the card room after searching through various rooms of the Club, Torrington eyed him somewhat warily as he approached.

"Redmond," he said when David neared his table. "What brings you to seek me out once more? Here with more tales of long-lost loves?"

"Ah…" David replied, scratching his head, "Perhaps we best call it a continuation of our previous conversation."

Torrington sighed, looked over to his two companions and excused himself before standing and motioning for David to follow him to a nearby table.

"The last time we spoke I became caught up in memories and nearly forgot myself," the Earl said as they took a seat. "Please be quick about it today."

"Very well," David said, not taking the man's curtness as a good sign, but forging on nonetheless. "Previously, I asked you about a woman — Mary Jones."

"Yes, I remember well," Torrington responded, although this time he did not seem to be inclined to share any further.

"I told you that I knew Mary Jones through an acquaintance. Well, the truth is, I have never met Mary Jones. But I have met her daughter."

That caught the Earl's attention, as his eyes snapped up to meet David's.

"She had a daughter?"

"She did. I have never met a lovelier young woman."

"She must be like her mother," Torrington murmured, and David nodded. Of course, he had never met Mary Jones, but from the sound of it, Sarah was the woman she was today because of her.

"She is," David said. Then took a deep breath. "Miss Jones — the younger Miss Jones, Sarah — came to visit you yesterday."

"To visit... me?" Torrington repeated, his brow furrowing. He clearly didn't realize the meaning of that statement quite yet.

"Yes," David said, clasping his hands together and leaning over the table toward Torrington.

"Mary Jones left England over twenty years ago to settle in America. There, she had her daughter, Sarah. It was only recently that Sarah learned she had a father in England, and she came here to find him, for no reason other than a familial connection."

The Earl didn't move as he stared at David, the realization of all he was saying finally settling in.

"And then she came... to see me."

"She did."

David reached into his pocket, finding the ring he still held, that he had forgotten to return to Sarah.

"Is this yours, Lord Torrington?"

He set it down in the middle of the table between them, and Torrington reached over, picking it up and turning it over in his fingers. His face still wore an expression of incredulity, as though he could hardly believe what he was seeing.

"This is my mother's family crest," Torrington said, staring at it as he ran his thumb over the crest. "Her father gave it to me when I was a young man. I gave it... I gave it to..." he swallowed deeply. "The woman I thought I would love forever."

"Mary Jones."

"Yes," the Earl said, his word coming out just above a whisper. "I wished to marry her, but it had always been planned that I would marry Lavinia, who is now my wife."

He was silent for a moment.

"I hadn't decided what to do — whether to leave all for Mary, or to see if she would have only what I could offer her while I did what my family asked of me, marrying Lavinia and then one day becoming the earl."

He let out a short, bitter laugh.

"I didn't realize the decision I should have made until it was too late and Mary was gone. I never knew if my father had convinced her to leave or if she had left me of her own accord, but it haunts me to this day."

"From what Sarah tells me, she left so that you would not have to make the decision put before you."

"She would," he nodded and then paused for a moment before looking back at David. "A daughter... I never had any children, did you know that, Redmond?"

David shook his head.

"Where is she?" Torrington asked.

"At this moment? I believe she is preparing to return home to America."

"What?" he said, making as if to rise, his face astonished. "Why, when she has come all of this way?"

David shifted uncomfortably in his chair. He wasn't sure of the current relationship between Torrington and his wife and had no wish to come between the two of them, but he also felt Torrington should know the truth.

"When Sarah came to see you, your wife greeted her. Apparently, she surmised much of the situation and told Sarah that you had no wish to see her nor have anything to do with her."

"She *what*?" The last word came out as a bit of a roar, and many of the other patrons turned to stare at the two of them.

"Sarah tried to make it clear that she is not here for any financial gain, but I believe your wife is quite concerned about what Sarah could do to your reputation as well as your finances."

"Well, I never..." He said, glowering, and David flinched. "I want to speak with her — the girl."

"I hate to be impertinent, my lord..."

"But you will be, all the same."

David took a breath. "What will your response to her be? Would you accept her, or would you turn her away, as your wife did?"

The Earl's gaze slightly darkened as he stared at David.

"I know you ask out of concern for her, which is why I am answering your insolent question," he said. "I have not yet decided how I will greet her nor include her in my life, but I will not turn her away without any acknowledgment of who she is, that I can tell you," he said, and David nodded, satisfied with his answer.

"I'll see if I can find her," David said. "Then I will send word as to where we should meet you."

"Please see that you do," the Earl said, direct yet still obviously flummoxed. As David rose, Torrington held out a hand to stop him.

"Tell me, Redmond, what is your involvement in all of this?"

"Sarah and I have become… rather close."

"I see," said Torrington, as he raised an eyebrow. "How does your family feel of such a thing? I had heard a rumor you were to marry the daughter of Lord Buckworth."

"So my parents would like to believe," David responded, "Though I have told both of them, as well as Lady Georgina, that my heart belongs with another."

"Good for you, lad," the Earl said quietly. "I wish I had done the same."

"Yes, well, the problem is, I don't think Sarah has any wish to have me due to what she believes to be the truth," David said. "I'm not sure if it is best to let her go, or convince her to stay here."

"My choice — even if that choice at the time was to remain hesitant, caught between two worlds — was the wrong one," said Torrington, looking down at the table for a moment before returning his eyes to David. "Whatever you do, son, follow your heart. If you love your Miss Jones and you think she feels the same for you, then do what you can to hold onto her. Convince her of your love. You'll both be the better for it and you'll have a much happier life — one you will enjoy to the fullest. Do not make the same mistake I did, Redmond. Promise me that."

David stared at him for a moment, at the regret that filled the man's face, and he nodded.

"I will be in touch," David said, and then turned and walked away with new resolve.

His mind swirled with the words of both the father and daughter. Sarah had pushed him away, it was true, but he was beginning to realize just how much of that was hurt, rather than the anger she had projected. And as for the Earl... well, David knew he would likely be in much the same situation. He was fairly sure his father would never accept him marrying a woman like Sarah, who lacked a fine pedigree, but David found that he no longer cared. Sarah was worth giving up all for — any financial gain from his father, acceptance from his parents, or a place in society.

The most important thing now was to make Sarah believe in him and his promises.

She was so determined to return to America, but David was unsure if it was the land itself calling her back, or if it was more a matter of a desire to leave England and all that it had held for her.

If it was the latter, he must convince her otherwise. If it was the former... well, he must be willing to leave all and return with her. Could he do it? He, a man who had questioned the thought of giving up even other women for just one alone. He shook his head as he chuckled to himself. Could one woman change him that much?

Yes, he realized. Yes, she absolutely could.

David hurried out of White's, nearly running to his carriage in his rush to leave James Street and make his way to Cheapside as quickly as possible. He knew Sarah planned to leave soon, but surely not immediately — she had said her ship was leaving in a few days, and she would need time to prepare, would she not? She was a woman alone so it wouldn't take long, not like the weeks it seemed to take his family to prepare to leave for the country, but still, it would take some time.

He tapped his fingers on his knees during his entire journey to Sarah's rooms, impatient. Perhaps he should get out and run — maybe he would get there faster. David felt a fool. All that he had known deep within him had surfaced upon hearing Torrington's revelations. Torrington had lost the woman he loved because he hadn't been able to make a choice. David was well aware that he might lose all as well — but now he was willing to risk it, for even if he did, the exchange would be well worth it.

He had the door of the carriage open before it even came to a full stop, and the wheels had just finished turning when he was running up the walkway to Sarah's rooms. He knocked on the door but didn't wait for her to answer before he turned the handle, bursting into the room — only to find it completely empty. David's heart seemed to fall out of his chest as he looked around the barren room, the room in which so much had happened between them over just a few weeks.

He closed his eyes as he remembered the night he had awoken in Sarah's bed as she administered to his wounds, the many nights spent with a sore back from sleeping on the floor as he stood guard over Sarah's door, and the night they had first made love.

A sensation of warmth began to tickle David's eye, and he was astonished when he reached up to find a tear beginning to leak out of it. He couldn't remember the last time he had cried — he must have been a child. Well, he wasn't going to cry now. He was going to find Sarah, tell her of her father, of his own love for her, and his resolve to do whatever it might take to be with her.

He just had to find her first.

CHAPTER 28

*I*t was interesting, Sarah mused, and rather ironic, that she had come all this way to find a connection, only to discover the truth that family was not so much blood, but the people for whom you come to care. In some cases, that could be true relatives, for she and her mother had shared a bond as close as she ever had with any other person.

But then other times, family was the people you created it with. She thought of the people in her village at home, her neighbors in Cheapside, and the three women with whom she had become closer friends than she had ever thought possible. They were all part of her family — much more so than the Earl and Countess of Torrington, or her aunt, all who had proven to be malicious, who wanted nothing of her within their lives.

She thanked the driver of the hack who had conveyed her to port, where she would board a small steamship that would take her out of London to Plymouth. From there, she would board a larger ship that would return her home to Baltimore. She hadn't been sure she would be able to afford it, but upon arriving back at her rooms after her visit with Lady

Alexander and her aunt, she had found within her pockets enough pound notes to comfortably pay for her passage home. Lady Alexander must have tucked it in the pocket within her skirts, Sarah realized. At first, she had been determined to return it to the woman, but she had to admit the temptation to use it to return was far too great, and she had ended up spending it on the ticket, though she vowed to one day repay it, even if she had to send it all the way across the Atlantic.

Sarah didn't think she had ever felt smaller than the moment she stepped out of the hack with her one worn bag and looked at the rows of ships lining the port. She had done the same in New York for the voyage here, of course, but then she had been filled with hope and the belief that she was coming to find the man who had sired her, who had loved her mother more than one could imagine.

Now, she knew the truth.

Sarah had to ask for directions, but eventually, she was directed to a small ship with two masts. The captain himself greeted her as she climbed aboard, and she looked around to ensure that she was not the sole passenger.

"Yer the first to arrive," he said in answer to her inquiring gaze around her. "You have some time to wait still, but you get first pick of berth."

She nodded, thanked him, and then went down to claim one of the bunks before returning to the deck. The ship was clean, though small and rather run-down, but she hadn't wanted to waste much money on the first leg of her journey. She had found the first ship she could at a reasonable rate that would take her out of London, and the captain seemed affable enough, at the very least.

Sarah had known she would be early, but hadn't cared — she had needed to leave London as soon as she could. She was well aware that her experiences here would always be deeply ingrained in her memory, but at the same time the faster she could leave it all behind, the better.

She refused to think of David — of all that they had shared, all that she felt for him, the love that beat within her heart for him that she didn't think would ever die. How she was to live without him now, she had no idea, but she had a far better chance of doing so halfway around the world than if he were simply a carriage ride away.

She looked out over the port, seeing London stretch in the distance. One thing was for certain — she was looking forward to leaving this city behind, to feel the fresh, open air on her face once more. They simply had to leave this dock. And then she would be free.

* * *

DAVID WAS NOT a man who often fell to a panic. But at this moment, he could hardly do anything but.

He had asked all whom he'd encountered within the vicinity of Sarah's residence if they had noticed her leave. A young lad said he had seen her enter a hack with a bag in hand, although where she intended to go from there, no one was entirely sure. Time seemed to be slipping away from David, as he had no idea when she would actually be leaving London, nor how she had decided to go about it. Would she be traveling over land, north to Liverpool, or south to one of the ports? Or would she have taken a ship that way? He had to make a decision, and it was one that would be paramount, for a wrong choice could mean he would not only miss her entirely but also lose her forever.

He returned to his carriage, asking the driver to convey him back to Mayfair. It may lose him precious time, but with the correct direction, he might make the appropriate choice. He earnestly requested the driver to rush as fast as he could, and the man was true to his word, for soon enough they had pulled up in front of Lady Alexander's home.

In all actuality, she didn't seem surprised to see him. David wasn't shown into her home, but rather Lady Alexander came to greet him at the front door after the butler announced his arrival.

"Mr. Redmond," she said, eyeing him up and down critically. "Allow me to make a guess. You are here in an attempt to determine the whereabouts of Miss Jones, is that it?"

"You would be correct, Lady Alexander," he replied, hoping the woman would be more amenable to him today than she was the last time the two of them had spoken. "She has left her boardinghouse, and it appears she has designs to leave England."

"Which would be understandable, would it not?" Lady Alexander asked. "What has she left for her here?"

"So you know of her current... situation?" David asked, surprised that Sarah would have confided in the woman.

"I know far more than you might expect, Mr. Redmond," she said, raising an eyebrow, to which he nodded.

"Though you do not seem inclined to share," he said, no longer caring whether or not he might be offending her.

Lady Alexander raised herself to her full height, which neared David's own, though not quite.

"Unlike what you may believe, Mr. Redmond, I have no wish to see Miss Jones hurt in any way. I am an old friend of her family's, and I did what I thought was right. Whether or not you might agree is another matter, but I feel justified in the decisions I have made. All may not have ended as I would have supposed, but Miss Jones now has all she needs to return to where she is happy."

"Back to America."

"Yes," she said with a nod. "Away from London, at any rate."

"All I need to know is *how* she is leaving London," he said a bit desperately. "To which port would she travel? And how?"

"I can tell you that she has enough funds to sail from London," Lady Alexander said. "Seeing how easily she took to sailing on our voyage *to* England, I would have to guess she is at London's port."

David eyed her critically, wondering if she would steer him incorrectly, but her gaze was more open and honest than it had been before. At this point, he did not have much choice but to trust her.

"Thank you, Lady Alexander," he said, with the slightest of nods as he nearly tripped in his haste to run down the stairs back to his carriage while still acknowledging the woman, who watched him with something akin to mirth in her gaze. "Thank you very much."

The carriage conveyed him as far as London Bridge, where he called the driver to halt and then ran out to look over the port. The sight in front of him made him cringe. The docks were full of hundreds of ships of all sizes, people bustling everywhere like ants below him. How in the world he was ever supposed to find Sarah amongst all of the crowds, he had no idea. But he had to try.

David continued on foot as far as he could, craning his neck this way and that, as though he might become lucky and spot her amongst all of the people, ships, and wares around him.

But of course, it could never be so simple as that.

He found a man, a sailor-looking type, and tugged on his sleeve to capture his attention. "Where would the passenger ships be?"

"There aren't many around here, mate," the man said, but then pointed down a ways. "Try down that way, over where you can see the docks converging. There are a few smaller ships there. But it's getting late in the day. If you haven't booked passage yet, you may be out of luck. Look for a benevolent captain."

"I'll do that," David said as he continued on his way to where the man pointed, running now as he attempted to push his way through the crowds as politely as possible.

David wasn't sure how many times he collided with someone, was cursed at, or became lost through the bustling port, but finally, he came to where there were, as the man had promised, small ships lined up haphazardly. He wished Clarence or Berkley were here with him. Somehow they would know exactly what to do, who to ask, or how to find Sarah within this mess.

David, however, had no idea. So instead he just approached one ship after another, asking of its destination and whether there was a young woman by the name of Miss Jones aboard. He had asked seven different captains with no luck until the eighth finally had a question for him — "To where do you think she's headed?"

"South, likely, if she's sailing. Brighton? Plymouth?"

The man nodded. "There's one leaving to Plymouth in a couple of hours — *The Marjorie*, she's called, after the captain's lost love. It's about a half-mile down, but you better hurry."

David profusely thanked him before taking off at a sprint, spotting the vessel, as it was slightly bigger than the others around it.

Two members of the crew were just beginning to untie the ropes at the docks when David raced up to it.

"Do you have a Miss Jones aboard?" he asked, his breath coming in huffs between words. The men looked at him as though he had gone mad, but he persisted, asking once more. At the very least, his question had halted them in their actions.

"Pretty little thing?" the one asked with a smile that, while certainly not malicious, caused David to want to lean over and wipe it off of his face.

"You could say that," he said.

"Aye, I believe she's aboard," the sailor answered, "But you're out of luck, chap. The ship is sailing and the captain ain't going to want to wait any longer."

"Thank you," David said with a cordial nod as though he was going to adhere to the words and he began walking away, although noting that the gangplank was still down, when he came close enough he ran aboard.

"Hey!" the man yelled, but David didn't wait in his urgency.

"Who are you and what are you doing on my ship?"

The man who came out of the shadows had long dark hair, and was, David could admit, a good-looking man. The top of his shirt was open to reveal a dark chest, and David instantly bristled at the thought of Sarah spending any length of time on a ship with this man — never mind that it wasn't entirely his decision as to what she did or didn't do.

"I'm looking for a woman who I believe is a passenger — Miss Sarah Jones."

The captain crossed his arms over his chest.

"Why should I give you any information about one of my passengers?"

"Please," David said, trying to appeal to the man's understanding side. "I have to find her before she leaves London, or I may never see her again."

"Perhaps that's what the lady wants."

"I just need to speak with her."

"We are setting sail," the captain said with a shrug. "If you'd like to stay on board, then you best buy your passage."

David looked around him, at the two sailors who were

ready to throw the last remaining rope on board, the small plank leading down to the dock, and the river before them.

If Sarah wasn't on board, he would regret this decision for the rest of his life, but at the moment, he had no other option.

"Very well," he said. "How much?"

The captain grinned, clearly seeing the opportunity for an easy extra passage. When he named his amount, David rocked forward.

"For a short sail? Even if I wanted to pay you that much, I do not have it on me, man," he said, and the captain shrugged, as though he was glad he at least had tried.

"What do you have then?"

David rifled through his pockets, finally bringing out a fair amount of notes, which the captain looked over.

"Good enough," he said. "I've one berth left. Doesn't look like you have much to pack away."

The man laughed heartily, and David attempted to swallow his impatience.

"Where is she?"

"I'm not sure I know of who you're talking, mate."

David brought a hand to his forehead. He'd been had. He should have known. Damn, but he had been a fool. He looked behind him, seeing the port was now retreating into the distance.

It was too late. He'd not only likely lost Sarah forever, but now he was bound for bloody Plymouth.

He turned back around to tell the captain exactly what he thought of his deception but was halted in his tracks when he saw a woman's silhouette before him, her face obscured by the setting sun behind her. But he would know that shape anywhere.

"David? Whatever are you doing here?"

CHAPTER 29

Sarah could hardly believe her eyes. David was here, on *The Marjorie*? How he had even known where to find her, she had no idea. And now he was on the ship, which had set sail but moments ago. She could hardly process everything as he crossed the deck to her, taking her hands in his.

"Sarah, thank goodness I found you," he said with a sigh.

"David, the ship is leaving!" she exclaimed, looking back at the shore, which was beginning to recede into the distance.

He shrugged. "I do not altogether care — not as long as you are aboard. Now, had I been tricked, as I initially thought I was—"

The captain snorted behind him, and David turned a glare upon him before returning to Sarah.

"I do not suppose there is somewhere we could go where we could be... alone?"

"Not really," the captain said behind them, clearly enjoying their exchange. David sighed in acceptance of his presence.

"Sarah, you cannot leave England — not yet."

"Whyever not?" she asked, raising an eyebrow. She wanted to be angry with him for following her, but the truth was she couldn't help the relief that flooded through her at the realization that he was here, that she had another chance to see him, despite how angry and upset she was.

"Because Torrington—" he began but then shook his head. "No. No matter what Torrington said, I would be here regardless, pleading with you to remain."

He paused, looking down and then up at her again, desperation within his wide eyes.

"Because I love you. Truly I do, they are not just words, Sarah. This is my soul speaking to you."

"You... you love me?" she repeated, her words just above a whisper, and he nodded, leaning into her, his forehead coming to touch hers so that only she could hear what he had to say.

"I love you with more strength than anything I've ever felt before," he said, searching his mind for the right words. He was far from any poet, and he was well aware that his charm typically stemmed from his physical appeal — he could smile and wink like the best of them, knew all of the lines to attract a woman. But that was not what would convince Miss Sarah Jones of his true feelings.

"Sarah..." he began, struggling but persisting. "Before I met you, I was certainly not a man any would recommend any reputable young woman to tie her name to. I've been irresponsible — foolish, really, in my acceptance of my role as a rake. Sure, I had my fun, but I'm also aware now I likely hurt more women than I made happy. The truth is, I really didn't care about anything — I didn't think there was anyone or anything to care about. In turn, I had no real relationships, no one who truly cared for me. Hell, I was gone for three days and no one even noticed!"

As though she sensed his need to say all he had planned, she simply held onto his hands as he spoke, her steady, even gaze upon him.

He took a deep breath.

"And then there was you. You who took care of me, who gave me more of yourself than I ever deserved. You had faith in me when I had no faith in myself. You shared your secrets with me, gave me your heart and your thoughts. I appreciated that more than you could ever know. I just… didn't use the right words to tell you how much you meant to me."

He closed his eyes tightly before opening them and fixing them upon hers. His green stare warmed her to her very soul, and Sarah mused that she could spend the rest of her life lost in the depths of those eyes.

"Sarah, I know you hate London. I understand that. It's where my life is at the moment, but it doesn't have to be. I have nothing holding me there. I can go anywhere in the world you wish to go. We can live in the English countryside. I can't promise it will be much as I have no idea what my father will allow me after the breaking off of my apparent engagement to Lady Georgina, but I will find a way to work, whatever that may be. We can live in another country. We can sail all the way to America, if that is where your heart is. For my heart is with you, and, as long as you accept it, that's where it will follow."

Her eyes began to water now until tears slid down her cheeks, which he reached out and caught with his index finger.

"Don't cry, Sarah," he pleaded. "Please don't cry."

"These are happy tears," she whispered, and that seemed to somewhat relieve him. "I am so sorry, David, for everything I was upset with you about, for what I accused you of. Instead of being angry with you, not trusting you, I should have simply asked as to whether or not you were truly going to marry Lady Georgina. I should have known you well enough to be aware that you would not willingly enter into marriage, especially to a woman chosen by your parents."

She laughed through her tears at that, and David managed a slightly chastised smile.

"Fair point," he said.

"I was so upset, I let all that I felt cloud my judgment — as well as the feelings I held for you," she said. "Just now I was looking out over the river beginning to retreat behind us, and all I could think of was the fact that you were out there, somewhere, with no idea as to where I was or where I was going, and we would never see one another again. And I knew then, that my heart was out there, walking around with you. I was so disappointed in what I felt were the ultimate betrayals on all sides that I acted rashly and nearly lost everything."

"So... does that mean you love me too?"

"Oh, David, I love you more than anything in this entire world, and yes... I will stay with you. You are home now," she said with a choked sob, and he picked her up and kissed her soundly, twirling her around the deck as he did so, much to the enjoyment of the crew and the few others on board who applauded them and emitted some hoots and hollers.

When he finally released her, she kept her arms about his neck as she looked up at him.

"However did you find me?"

He laughed then. "Dumb luck, for the most part," he said, "As well as an encounter with Lady Alexander." She bit her lip at his words, but then he explained the situation and the fact that Lady Alexander had, actually, pointed him in the right direction, and she softened somewhat.

"Oh, David, I have so much to tell you," she said, but David held up a finger.

"And I you," he said. "But first, and most importantly — I spoke with Torrington."

"Oh no," she said, not wanting to hear another word, but David forged ahead.

"He had no idea that he had a daughter, Sarah. He loved your mother and was devastated when she left. What the Countess told you — that was her own maliciousness. Torrington has no ill will toward you, and, in fact, wants to meet his daughter, the daughter of the woman he loved."

"You cannot be serious," she said, stunned.

"I absolutely am."

"I suppose," she said slowly, "I have already agreed to return with you, so you have no other reason to convince me of such."

"And I wouldn't lie to you, I promise you that," he said, looking around him now, noting that the crowd had finally drifted away, leaving them alone, and he took her hand to lead her over to the railing.

"Are you cold?" he asked, and she shook her head.

"Not in the least."

"Very good, as I have nothing to offer you to keep you warm," he said, laughing, then sobered for a moment. "I wonder whatever my poor carriage driver shall do. Return home, I suppose?"

She looked at him incredulously. "You had no idea you were boarding a ship, then, did you?"

"No," he shook his head. "I boarded the ship just in time, and your captain over here," he pointed his thumb behind them. "Refused to allow me on without passage — a grossly inflated passage, I'll add."

"Oh, David," she said, covering the laughter about to emerge. "I am sorry to hear it."

He shrugged. "It was worth it. So, before we get any further, we should probably decide — where are we off to?"

Sarah looked west into the distance, where her former home had awaited.

"I thought I wanted to return home, back to America," she said, then turned her face back toward him. "But the truth is, I wasn't running toward home, I was running *from* here. I thought that you had betrayed me with Lady Georgina. I thought Lord Torrington had betrayed me by turning me away, just as he had my mother. And I thought that Lady Alexander had betrayed me, pretending to be close to me just so that my aunt could use me."

"What?"

"I told you, there is lots to explain," she said with a hand on his arm. "But I was wrong. About all of it. Yes, of course, there are the Countesses of Torringtons in the world, and women like my aunt, but there are also good people here, truly good people — I have you, and I have three women who will be there for me no matter what is to come. I think, David… I think I would like to stay. But not in London. Outside the city, if we can?"

"Wherever you'd like, my lady," he said with a mock bow, and she swatted him.

"I am far from a lady."

"Yet you are the best woman I have ever known."

She stood on her tiptoes then, reaching up to him, and he bent to meet her.

"So… what are the berths like?" he asked, and she bit her lip, wanting to laugh at him.

"They are fairly small — and not at all private," she said. "Luckily for you, Plymouth is not far."

Suddenly he looked rather concerned. "Where we will have to book a return ticket… and yet I'm afraid I am somewhat short on funds now."

"I hadn't yet paid for my ticket back to America," she reassured him. "It will be enough to cover our passage home."

"I cannot allow you to pay for us."

"I don't think you have much choice," she said with a bit of a laugh, to which he sighed and placed his hands on his hips.

"Very well," he acquiesced. "It will be a loan."

"Very well, but in reality, it's to Lady Alexander, not to me," she said, then smiled at him wickedly. "And perhaps I could be talked into staying for a night or so."

"If you insist," he said with a mock sigh this time, and she laughed at him, then sobered as she studied him.

She thought of all she knew of him, then of all of the warnings with which she had been provided. Never did she think that David Redmond would be a man to give up all that he had loved, for not only a woman, but for her specifically. She knew many would tell her she was a fool, that she should never trust him, but she knew, deep within her heart, that he would never betray her. He had done so much for her, and even when she hadn't believed in him, he had held onto his love for her and had literally searched London until he had found her. She would never have imagined there was a man in the world who would do such a thing for her, but there was — and she had found him.

He held her tight against him, as though if he let her go he might lose her again, but then a voice came from the berths below.

"Can anyone help? My daughter needs someone to see to her — she is coughing something violent!"

David sighed and looked at her with a shrug, and Sarah, unable to ever let anyone by without her help, gave him one quick kiss before rushing below to see what she could do to offer her assistance.

CHAPTER 30

"My wife and I would like a room for the night, please, sir," David said to the man behind the counter, who provided the two of them with the room key as he sent them up to the second floor.

"It has a nice ring to it, doesn't it?" he asked Sarah with a wink once the man was out of sight, and she smiled at him.

"So it does."

He stopped suddenly, turning toward her. It was difficult for David to focus when all he wanted to do was lean down and kiss those plush pink lips that were calling to him. He shifted his gaze to the freckles scattered over her nose and cheeks, but that didn't help, as then his desire changed to wanting to trail his lips over each of them, as though he could connect them with his touch, but then he shook himself out of his reverie. There was something important he first had to say to her.

"I never asked you."

"Asked me what?"

"To marry me," he said incredulously, immediately frustrated with himself, for he was doing this all wrong.

"To marry you?" she asked, her eyebrows raised. "I had thought that was implied."

"Well, yes, but my—" He lifted a hand to his forehead, feeling like a daft idiot. "I cannot believe you nearly let me get away with it."

"I assumed you would remember eventually," she said with a laugh, but then he took her hand and led her up the stairs determinately. The moment the door was shut behind them, he turned back toward her, his face now very serious as he took her hands in his.

"Sarah," he said intently. "My Sarah. Would you do me the honor of being my wife? They say it is for better or for worse, and I must admit that chances are it's going to get very much the worse over the next little bit, once we meet with my father. I may have no money, no way of supporting you, but I shall find a way, I promise you of that. You only have to trust me. With all of that being said, will you still marry me?"

"Of course," she said, raising her cool hands to cup his cheeks. "You know I will."

"I suppose you'd like to wait until your friends are there," he grumbled, and she laughed.

"Yes, I would," she replied. "Just as you should wait for your family."

"I'm not sure about that."

"Whatever happens with them, David, we should start this the right way, by inviting them to be with us as we celebrate our happiness. Maybe then they will see that that's what truly matters."

"Perhaps," he said, though she could tell he didn't believe her in the least.

"Your family… I realize they may not always be what you would wish them to be," she said softly. "But they are still your family. Though I have come to realize lately that family is what you make of it — sometimes they are by blood, sometimes they are of your own choosing."

She looked up at him now, her eyes wide. "My goodness, I just remembered the letters I sent. By the time I am home, my friends will think that I am halfway across the ocean."

"Then what a pleasant surprise it will be for them to find that you are still on English soil," he said with a wink. "Or you could write them again before we leave. If you would ever like to return to America to visit, Sarah, I would be glad to go with you. It would be interesting, I think, to see how people live over there."

She raised her eyebrows at him, and he could tell she wanted to laugh at the thought of him in America.

"What?" he asked, pretending to be offended.

"It is hard to imagine a man such as yourself in the rustic cabin where I grew up."

"Yet you saw me often enough sleeping on the bare floor of lodgings far from where I was raised, and now in an inn near the Plymouth docks. I am a man of many disguises, my soon-to-be Mrs. Redmond."

He said the words in jest, for it was how they had entered this inn, but now that he said them, he had to admit just how much he enjoyed hearing the words roll off of his tongue.

"I like that — Mrs. Redmond," she said, echoing his thoughts, and he drew her closer to him once more.

"As do I."

This time when his arms came around her, they did not remain on her back, but rather drifted down, cupping her buttocks and pressing her against him. He would never forget the feeling of being with her, inside of her, and he desperately longed to do so again.

But she was still so sweet, so innocent, that he didn't want to rush this. No, he should take it slowly, showing her all of the love that she deserved to feel.

He brushed a hand over her hair, slowly removing the pins one at a time, relishing the process as the smooth silky strands cascaded over his fingers. She sighed into the crook of his neck, her breath causing tremors to shimmer down his spine. He found the end of the ribbon that tied her dress together at the bottom of her back, and it took but a few moments for him to release it. He was, at the moment, quite grateful for the fact that she had to ensure her dresses were easy enough to fasten and unfasten that she could do so herself.

As the sleeves of her dress began to slip off of her shoulders, Sarah lifted her hands to David's jacket, releasing his arms from it, before it slid to the floor. As her dress began to pool around her waist, David boosted Sarah up so that she was sitting on the edge of the bed, and she widened her legs so that he was standing between them. He grinned at her forwardness as she tugged him toward her and began to unfasten the fall of his breeches. He tried to step back out of her grasp, for he was sure that if she touched him he would come apart, and he had far more work to do.

"Please?" she asked, looking up at him, and David knew that whenever she looked at him with those warm brown eyes, there was nothing he would ever be able to deny her. He nodded, swallowed hard, and willed himself to maintain control. The moment he was free, his breeches falling down, he made quick work of the remainder of her dress, her stays, and her chemise, before she was sitting in front of him exactly how he wanted her — but she wasn't about to let him have only what he so desired.

No, Sarah now rose so that she was kneeling on the bed, and divested him of his waistcoat and linen shirt. David could have helped her — it certainly would have gone much faster if he did — but he far preferred watching her do the work.

As much as he had enjoyed what was before his eyes, however, when they were finally both free and he pulled her to him, he knew there would never be anything in his life that felt as good as her skin upon his. She was warm, pliant, and her fingertips were light as they ran up the planes of his back, coming over his shoulders and onto his chest.

David allowed his eyes to dip to take in all of her that was illuminated by the glow of the candlelight. Her skin was so soft, dotted in the same beautiful freckles that covered her nose. She was curved in all of the right places, her breasts, her hips, her waist all fitting so perfectly into his hands.

"I think you were made just for me," he said, hearing the desperation in his voice, which emerged as just more than a whisper.

Her lips turned up ever so slightly in response as she tilted her head and gave a little shrug in agreement before raising her face to his, and he took her offered lips, tasting, teasing, loving as he wrapped his arms around her and pulled her in close.

Unlike any other encounter he had ever had, David thought he could simply kiss Sarah forever and be perfectly happy. Of course, he longed for her, but in the same breath if faced with a choice, he would spend the rest of his days holding her in his arms with his lips upon hers as opposed to doing anything else with any other woman.

She, however, was interested in continuing what they had started — and David wasn't one to argue. Sarah broke their kiss, inching back on the bed until she neared the headboard. David crawled toward her on his hands and knees until he was covering her body. At first, she was giggling, but then her expression turned serious once he approached her. She reached up to cup his face in her hands, bringing him back to her once more before he began to make his way south, along her collarbone to her breasts, where he paid attention to first one and then the other. She arched up off the bed toward him, but as much as David yearned to find where he belonged, he first wanted to show her just how good this could be.

He traveled her body with his lips, kissing her, caressing her in places he knew she hadn't been aware could be the slightest bit erotic.

"What are you doing to me?" she groaned, and he grinned, having accomplished his goal. Catching his expression, she glared at him, but then he inched his fingers toward her center, stroked her, and she moaned.

"Are you ready now?" he murmured.

"I was ready the moment we walked into this room."

David chuckled as he found her entrance, slowly sliding inside of her, surprised all over again at how perfectly the two of them fit together. Even their movements seemed to be more in sync than he ever could have imagined.

"Sarah," he groaned as they moved as one, and, in but a few moments, came together in such resounding perfection he wasn't sure that they would ever again be able to match it.

But they would certainly try.

"I love you," he whispered, the words both foreign as well as so completely right.

"And I love you," she returned, a smile on her face, which he returned.

Had anyone told David a month ago that he would be found in such a position, content with the thought of spending the rest of his life with one woman, and only one woman, he would have laughed at their joke. But now that he knew what it was like to have found the one who could make such a thing possible, he realized how idiotic he must have sounded to Berkley and Clarence when he was suggesting to them that perhaps committing to one woman was not the wisest choice.

As he and Sarah lay there blissfully together, however, David's mind began to turn from this moment between the two of them to what was to come. For the truth was, he had only ever been responsible for himself before. Now, he would have a wife to support, and the likelihood was that he would no longer have access to any funds from his father. So what was he to do? David had a fine education, of course, but not really in anything particularly useful. The only occupation that even slightly appealed to him was perhaps that of a barrister, but first, he would require more education — education that he could no longer afford.

"Of what are you thinking?" Sarah asked softly, and he kissed her on the head.

"Nothing, love," he said. "Go to sleep."

"You're worried," she said, as perceptive as ever, and he held her close to him. "What is it?"

"Nothing."

"Tell me — please?"

He sighed. He'd never be able to hide anything from her, he realized, but he supposed he was all right with that.

"I'm only thinking of our future. I know, in my heart, that anything is possible for the two of us together and yet... I've never had to actually support myself before, and the thought of not being able to provide for you nearly rips me in two. I need to find a way to make a living — I'm just not quite sure how to do so as of yet."

"I've always provided for myself, as a healer. I can do the same for the two of us. You can help me, I'm sure — it would be useful to have a man who could move people around, set broken bones," she said, and he knew she was trying to be helpful, but the thought of assisting his wife in her practice didn't quite sit right with him. He had no issue with her continuing to treat others, but he couldn't allow her to provide for him — it simply wasn't done.

"We'll figure something out," he said to reassure her, kissing her on the head. "I'm sure of it."

She nodded and drifted into sleep, but David's mind continued to race. His words had been a bit of a lie — for he really had no idea what was in store.

CHAPTER 31

Sarah could have stayed in bed with David in the Plymouth Inn for days. Perhaps no one would be looking for them yet, but were living on limited funds. Thankfully, Lady Alexander had been more than generous with her offering, but they now had to pay for the two of them to travel back to London — and support them along the way.

"Are you ready for the journey home, love?" he asked.

Sarah looked him over, remembering how green he had become on the ship to Plymouth. He was putting on a brave face, but it was him she was most worried about.

"I am ready for anything," she said, taking his hand. "But are you?"

"Well, I would far prefer to be riding my own horse, that is for certain," he said, a pained expression upon his face. "But, of course, I will brave it. I do not suppose you could come up with a remedy for me?"

Sarah nodded.

"I absolutely can do so, but I wasn't sure how you'd feel about my herbal concoction."

"I trust you."

"Very well, then," she said, reopening her small bag, happy that she had used the precious space for most of her herbs rather than dresses she hadn't thought she would wear again — although she was now remaining in England with hardly a wardrobe to call her own.

She mixed him a drink, and despite the face he made at his first sip, he managed to gulp it down quickly before passing it back to her.

"The stagecoach it is, then," he said, looking sick already, though she wasn't sure if it was from the thought of the journey or just how fast he had finished his drink.

"At least you can ride up top," she said, biting her lip. "I do hate being stuck inside for hours on end."

"It will be quick," he said and then they looked at one another with some conviction that yes, they could get through this — together. "We will likely have much more to face once we return to London and our respective fathers."

"Yes, that is of what I was thinking," she said. "But even if we receive nothing from them, and are turned away..." she shrugged. "We will be fine."

"We will," he said, though even in the light of day, she could tell his worries hadn't dissipated. Sarah could admit that she too felt, of course, a slight bit of unease at all that awaited them. The anxiety of meeting her own father remained, but the outcome of that meeting no longer had as great of a bearing on her future as it once did. For now she had David, and a life ahead of her that she knew would be full of love, no matter what her father had to say about it.

Of course, much more would actually be affected by the reaction of David's parents. For their lives would be greatly changed if his father decided to no longer provide him any support. Sarah had a bit more faith than David, however. While she questioned whether or not they could ever accept a woman like her, a woman born out of wedlock to a nobleman and a healer from a village, she had faith that they wouldn't completely abandon their own son, despite the decision he made.

And if they did, well, they would determine a way forward together. Of that, she was sure.

David clutched Sarah's hand, and she hoped she could impart the same strength to him as he did to her.

* * *

SARAH SAT NERVOUSLY on the sofa, tapping her slipper upon the floor as she waited for her father to arrive. Her father. She could hardly believe the words. David had sent the promised note to the Earl of Torrington the moment they had arrived in London, and she had been shocked when the man had responded immediately with the words that he was looking forward to meeting her.

She could hardly believe it. In fact, she had wondered if it was too good to be true, if she should be worried that something was amiss. David assured her, however, that Torrington, while a man who had certainly made mistakes, as many had, was still a "decent fellow." And that would have to be enough for her.

Sarah had been staying at Phoebe's London home while Phoebe and her family were at their estate for the summer. She had decided to write to her friends before leaving Plymouth, so they would be aware of her current situation. She explained all that had happened in as few words as she could, though it had still taken quite a bit of her coin to purchase the pages that had been required to tell her story.

Phoebe had immediately offered her home once more, for which Sarah was grateful, as her rooms had not been held for her after she had told the landlord she was leaving, and it didn't make sense to find anywhere else to stay for she and David hoped to marry as soon as possible. She had felt rather awkward arriving at Phoebe's home with none of the family about, but the servants had been gracious and Sarah had appreciated their welcome.

David told her he would love nothing more than for her to stay with him, but women were not allowed at the Albany. Besides that, despite the fact that they had basically breached every aspect of propriety there could be, that seemed a line that she shouldn't cross. When he had been at her own lodging, no one had made the association between her as Miss Jones, the woman who attended societal events, and Miss Jones, the healer who lived within. Besides, most of the noble classes didn't spend much time frequenting Cheapside anyway, apart from visits to various establishments, such as the one David had patronized the very night he had been deposited upon Sarah's doorstep.

But people were aware that David was the son of Lord Brentford, and it would be quite obvious if there was a woman staying within.

The Earl had not wanted to meet within his own home, where his wife would be aware and present, and so they decided to meet at the home of Phoebe and Lord Berkley. Phoebe had urged Sarah to avail herself of her wardrobe — as well as her staff — and though Sarah had been hesitant, she had taken up Phoebe's offer today, wanting to appear at her very best. She knew it was slightly silly, for her appearance wasn't likely to change anything, but when she had opened Phoebe's wardrobe and saw the beautiful blue gown at the front of it flowing down from where it hung, she couldn't help herself. It was a slight bit too long, but Sarah didn't think anyone would notice.

There was a knock at the door, and Sarah looked over to David, who gave her a reassuring nod. Everything would be all right, she told herself, as she had for the past hour or so, though the knot within her stomach grew tighter and she could hear her heart beating within her ears. They had told the servants not to worry about callers or tea for the next hour or so, in order for them to be entirely alone for this first time they met.

Sarah stood as David opened the door, her hands clasped in front of her as David greeted the man. She couldn't see him, not past David's frame, but then David stepped away and held out an arm, pointing within. Sarah and Lord Torrington each just stood there, staring at one another for a moment, taking in all that was before them, before he took a hesitant step forward into the room.

Sarah had no idea what to say, nor what she should do. It was not as though she could run up into his arms, but a curtsy also seemed far too formal.

Fortunately, David, who, despite often blundering his way through various situations, seemed to know how to properly introduce new people to one another, stepped in.

"Lord Torrington, I would like you to meet Miss Sarah Jones. Sarah, Lord Torrington. As we have all discussed, we believe, Lord Torrington, that Sarah is your daughter."

"It is a pleasure to meet you," Sarah finally said, and Lord Torrington took a few more steps into the room, finally reaching out to take one of her hands, which he clasped within both of his.

"A daughter," he said, his voice just above a whisper, slightly incredulous.

"I— I believe so," said Sarah, as she pulled out the ring that David had returned to her. "I know David showed you the ring my mother always carried, and from what he tells me you have to say about her and the timing... I can only think it could be true."

The Earl blinked rapidly a few times, clearly attempting

to hold back emotion, which nearly brought tears to Sarah's own eyes.

"Perhaps we might sit down," she said, his vulnerability bringing out the caregiver in her.

He followed her to the sofa. David nodded at her as though telling her all was well and he began toward the door, but Sarah called to him.

"David? Please stay. You are now as much a part of this as anyone."

"If you'd like," he said, and Sarah appreciated the fact that he was willing to do whatever most pleased her in this situation. She would tell him all of this following their encounter anyway, so what did it matter if he were here? She would never have found the Earl without him.

"You look just like your mother," Lord Torrington said, and Sarah returned her attention to him.

"Yet she has your eyes," David noted, and Sarah turned to look at the Earl, whose eyes were, indeed, the very same brown she saw in her reflection.

"My mother had blue eyes," Sarah said softly, and Lord Torrington nodded.

"They were the color of the sky, and they danced when she laughed," he said whimsically. "She laughed often. And loud. That was part of what I loved about her."

"You loved her?"

To hear him say such a thing warmed Sarah to her very soul. Her mother had always told her it had been such a way between the two of them, but Sarah had never been entirely sure whether it was infatuation or true love on the Earl's part.

"Indeed. I loved her very much — I just didn't realize *how* much until it was too late," he said. "But I was hesitant — too caught up with what I knew was right and what I had been told was right. She knew that if I married her, I would give

261

up all that I had known, including my family, my homes, and the earldom. I told her that I had to make the choice, and I didn't commit to her when I should have. I didn't tell her that I loved her, that I needed her in my life. Instead, I asked her to wait. It was a mistake."

His head fell to stare at his shoes, and it pained Sarah to see him so miserable. She reached out and covered his clenched hands with hers.

"I believe she was worried that if you gave up all for her, you would resent her for the rest of your lives together."

"Never," he said vehemently. "I would have been all the happier for it. Like your man here."

They both looked up at David, who returned the Earl's gaze with a shrewd, knowing smile.

"I actually need to thank you, Lord Torrington," David said. "It was because of you, because of our conversation, that I realized the true depth of my feelings in time, and how important it was to follow through on them instead of worrying too greatly about what was to come in the future. While that doesn't mean I am not still concerned about what is to come, I now know that all is possible — as long as I have Sarah."

"That is what is most important," the Earl agreed, a sad smile crossing his face, but then he turned his attention toward Sarah. "I must apologize for my wife. She can be cruel. I can only be grateful that Redmond here found you and told you the truth of the matter so that we now have the opportunity to rectify things."

"She was scared," Sarah said. "Scared that I would take from her a place in your family, or steal from your fortune. That I would ruin your family's reputation. I must assure you, Lord Torrington, that I have no desire to do so. I ask for none of your money, and nor do I intend to share any secret with others regarding who I am to you. I simply wanted to come to know you, if that were at all possible."

"Possible?" he asked. "I would like nothing more. I'm not sure if you are aware, Miss Jones, but I have no children, though I have always wanted them. And even if I did have others, well, that wouldn't change the fact that I would still want to come to know you. You are my flesh and blood, 'tis true, but not only that, you are the daughter of the love of my life, the woman that I always longed for. I shouldn't say that, I know I shouldn't. I am a married man, but my wife and I… well. We were intended for one another since we were children, but not in the way that truly mattered."

"That is fair," Sarah murmured.

"Anyway," he said, waving a hand in the air as if that was not something he wished to discuss any longer, "tell me of your life. Where did you grow up? How did you grow up? Did your mother continue healing? How different was it in America?"

He seemed so eager to hear of her past — almost with childlike excitement — that Sarah nearly laughed. Her heart, however, was breaking over the thought that he obviously was holding onto anything regarding her mother that he possibly could. She would give him the stories he longed for, and hopefully, that would be enough to heal some of the pain he clearly felt.

She began to tell him stories, most of which had him laughing or asking for more. An hour went by fairly quickly for both of them, apparently, for when the Earl pulled out his pocket watch to check the time, he seemed startled.

"I must be going. This has been most lovely, Sarah. I—" He broke off and scratched his head, as though he wasn't entirely sure what to say. "I am glad you came here and found me."

"I am as well," she said, as they both stood in awkward silence, unsure as to what to do next.

"Before I go," the Earl finally said, "Might I have a word alone with you, Mr. Redmond?"

"I would appreciate that very much, my lord," David said, as Sarah looked back and forth between the two of them quizzically.

"We'll be just a moment, Sarah," David said with a wink of reassurance as he led the Earl down the hall and into Berkley's study, leaving Sarah quite perplexed and a little unsure.

CHAPTER 32

*D*avid, of course, was well aware of the protocol of just how to ask a man for his daughter's hand in marriage. What he wasn't sure was how to ask a man when he had just met his daughter for the first time but an hour ago.

"Lord Torrington—"

"I expect you are here to do right by my daughter?" The man asked, worrying David for a moment until he looked up to see Torrington's brow was quirked in some jest.

"Yes," David said with a rush of breath, glad the Earl had raised the subject for him, preventing him from having to do so himself. "We would like to marry, my lord, as soon as possible."

"I'm glad to hear it," Torrington said, and then paused slightly awkwardly. "And you will, ah… be a good husband to her, will you?"

"I will be true and faithful to her, my lord, that I can promise," David said, unable to promise anything, however, of how well he could provide for her as he hadn't yet determined that himself. He could, however, assuage the Earl's fears regarding his previously rakish ways of which the man was clearly aware.

"I'm glad, Redmond," the Earl said. "I had my doubts, but you obviously care for her, and I do appreciate what you have done to bring her back to me."

"Of course, my lord."

"I will arrange for her dowry as well."

"That is not necessary, Lord Torrington, not at all. Neither of us expects it—"

The Earl held up a hand to stop him. "It is something I would like to do, Redmond. I had no idea of her existence through her entire life. Please allow me to do this for her."

"Sarah might not take it. I believe she's worried that you — and others — will feel that it was why she sought you out."

"So let them think it. She is my daughter, and I will do right by her, as I would any other daughter born to me in wedlock."

David nodded despite his surprise. "I think it would mean a lot to her — and to me — if you were able to attend our wedding."

"Of course," Torrington said, as though surprised that David would even have to ask. "In fact, I would be honored to give her away."

"Truly?" David wasn't sure what Torrington's wife or the rest of the ton would have to say about that, but it seemed that Torrington was beyond caring for what they said as much as David was. His heart warmed for Sarah, knowing how much it would mean to her. "She will be both surprised and moved, I'm sure."

"If you need assistance in arranging anything, please advise me," Torrington said. "Now, I must be off, but I would like to arrange another time to see the two of you," he said, opening the door and stepping into the hall, including Sarah in his remark.

When David watched Sarah's happy smile at the man leaving, he knew, deep within, that it had all been worth it. He couldn't wait to see her on their wedding day.

But first, he had one more conversation to take care of.

* * *

DAVID WAS MORE than apprehensive for the next meeting that awaited him. It was not so much that he was worried about speaking with his parents for his own sake. No, it was that Sarah had insisted on accompanying him for this conversation, and he worried that they might say something to insult her. He had not only refrained from speaking to them since he had refused Lady Georgina, but now he was also planning on marrying a woman of whom they had likely never even heard before.

He had informed them that he was bringing a guest, but he had been rather murky on the details of who that guest might be.

Unlike when she had met her own father, Sarah seemed perfectly calm.

"How can you not be worried?" he asked as they strode up the walkway.

"Because your family loves you," she said simply, and David sighed. She was far too optimistic, for he wasn't even sure of the truth of her statement at the moment.

"If they are angry, it is because of me and not you," he attempted to reassure her, but she simply put a hand on his arm.

"It will be fine, David. I'm sure of it."

If only he could have the same confidence.

David was pleased that when they entered the drawing room, his brother, Franklin, and his wife, Andrea, were also in attendance, and they greeted him warmly, though looked slightly confused by Sarah's presence. His parents made even less of an attempt to hide their curiosity.

"And who is your lovely guest, David?" his mother asked with her polite, practiced smile. "I have been quite interested as to who might be accompanying you tonight."

"Mother, Father," he said, his hand on the small of Sarah's back. "Please meet Miss Sarah Jones. She is to be my wife."

The looks that covered their faces was worth the visit, that was for certain. His father nearly choked on the brandy he had just sipped, while his mother's eyes had never been so wide as her mouth formed a round O.

Of all of them, Andrea was the first to break the shocked silence.

"David, how wonderful!" she said, standing from the couch to embrace the two of them in turn.

"Thank you, Andrea," David said, pleased, as he had always been, with his brother's choice in a wife. Franklin followed her lead and came over to shake his brother's hand.

It wasn't long until his parents finally recovered. David braced himself for their disapproval. He was more shocked than he had ever been, however, when he looked up to find that his mother had tears in her eyes as she leaned forward to embrace him.

"Oh, David," she said. "I am so very happy."

"You... you are?"

His father stepped toward him and shook his hand.

"I cannot say, David, I was pleased to hear of your visit with Lady Buckworth and Lady Georgina," he said, holding onto David's hand in a firm grip. Well, *that* was not a surprise. "The repercussions of your conversation have not been particularly flattering for our family's name."

"I realize that, Father, but—"

"But, if you are telling me that you are going to be settling down with a wife, and a lovely one at that," David followed his father's gaze to Sarah, who smiled and blushed prettily, "Then I completely understand."

"You do?" he asked, incredulous. "I thought... I had been under the impression..."

He didn't know what to say until he felt Sarah's elbow dig into his side.

"I am glad to hear it," he finally settled on, and his father nodded, giving him a long look.

"You are a relative of Lady Alexander's, are you not?" David's mother asked Sarah, and now Sarah did look slightly uneasy.

"She is a friend of my mother's family," Sarah explained. "She was kind enough to act as my chaperone throughout the previous two Seasons."

That seemed to appease David's mother for now, though David hoped that with the Earl's acceptance of his daughter, acceptance of Sarah amongst the rest of the *ton* — including his parents — would soon follow.

"David, would you come speak with me and Franklin in the study for a few moments before dinner?" his father asked, to which David hesitated. He had no desire to leave Sarah to his mother just yet, although Andrea, at least, was here...

"Go ahead," Sarah assured him softly, and he reached out to squeeze her hand before he followed his father, sitting in front of the mahogany desk next to Franklin with some trepidation.

"When I had determined you would marry Lady Georgina," his father began, "I had also begun to make other plans for you."

David's spine stiffened. His father had more than enough plans for him lately, and none were to his liking.

"As you know, we have a few different estates around England. One of such estates is Gracebourne near

Cambridge."

David nodded. He knew it well. It was one of the smaller of his father's estates, but he had always enjoyed it. The nearby village of Hauxton was warm and welcoming, while the estate itself was just large enough.

"It's yours," his father said, and David stared at him in shock.

"Pardon me?" he asked, before looking over at Franklin, who grinned at him.

"It's yours," his father repeated. "I had always planned to give it to you once you settled down some, proved you were keen on taking responsibility. It was why we were trying to push you to marry Lady Georgina. She seemed a respectable sort of girl, pretty enough, and we were hoping you would be taken with her."

"I realize that you must be quite disappointed in my rejection of her—" David began, but his father stopped him holding up a hand.

"When I first heard the news, yes, I was," he said, leaning back in his chair as he fixed his stare on David. "However, I was actually also proud of you."

David furrowed his brow as he stared at him. "Proud of me?"

"Yes," his father said with a nod. "You did the right thing by going there to tell them the truth. Instead of shirking away from the responsibility, allowing the family to believe that you were going to go through with the marriage. You looked them in the eyes and told them the truth."

"Which I wouldn't have had to do if you had listened when I told you that I was not interested. I was also not pleased to hear you felt you had to pay someone to wed me."

His father shrugged, unperturbed. "Perhaps. I thought, however, you were denying her because you were resisting our efforts, not because you had your own plan in mind. As for the payment, what does money matter when it comes to your children's happiness?"

David sat in silence for a moment, processing all that his father had just shared with him. Franklin leaned over to give him a reassuring pat on the shoulder.

"All will be well, brother," he said. "Forgive Mother and Father their machinations."

"Did you know?" David asked him, and Franklin looked slightly chagrined.

"Part of it," he responded. "But I had faith all would work out."

"I know you likely aren't pleased with the thought of living outside of London," their father said now, and David shook his head in response before he could continue the thought.

"Actually, Father, it's perfect," he said. "Sarah has never lived in a city before she came to London, and she is not keen on remaining here, a place where she has never felt comfortable. I had promised her we would live somewhere in the country, I just wasn't sure how I was going to do it. I had yet to come up with a profession I was suited for. I had actually thought perhaps I could become a barrister, but that would require an education, which I could never afford on my own. I think, however, I should like looking after my own estate."

"You would?" Franklin asked, surprised, looking over at his brother. "That was the one aspect of Father's plan I was unsure of — you, living in the country looking after an estate. It seemed to be the last thing you would enjoy."

"Sometimes, things change," David said simply.

"I think I like this Sarah of yours," Lord Brentford said as he stroked the gray beard that covered his face. "She has brought out a side of you I haven't seen in many years."

David cleared his throat and looked down at his hands for a moment before meeting his father's eye.

"I realize that I have not been the son you have likely wished for. I must admit I had my own frustrations with you and Mother, but I do understand your lack of faith in me."

"We only wanted you to find happiness and stability in your life, which you certainly weren't finding at The Red Lion," his father said, and David slightly cringed. He hadn't been aware that his father knew exactly where he had been spending much of his time.

"I do not believe I will be frequenting The Red Lion much more anytime soon," David said, and his father laughed.

"That sounds like a wise idea, son, particularly if you are interested in a happy marriage."

"That," David said resolutely, "I most certainly am."

CHAPTER 33

*S*arah blinked back tears as she placed her hand on the arm of her father. Her father. It was amazing how much could change in a few short months. She had spent so long here in England searching for him that she could hardly believe that all she had been searching for had actually come true.

Despite the Countess' more than obvious disapproval of her, Lord Torrington had welcomed Sarah into his life, inviting her into his home for dinners and even claiming her as his daughter to any who asked. It was rather astounding, really, David told her, and far from usual for an earl such as Torrington to claim a daughter who had been born outside of marriage.

But the Earl had clearly always been keen to have a daughter, and so he welcomed Sarah into his life as he would any other child born to him. It was far more than Sarah could have ever asked for, and she had been equally as surprised by David's parents. They seemed to feel that if she was accepted as the daughter of the Earl of Torrington, then they would accept her just as well as their daughter-in-law.

Lady Brentford had, perhaps, been a little too exuberant in the wedding plans for Sarah and David, but if that was the largest of Sarah's worries, then she could accept that. She had finally convinced Lady Brentford to hold the wedding in the small country church of St. Edmond in the village of Hauxton, where her new home was located.

She had asked that it be a simple affair, with only family and close friends, but it seemed that Lady Brentford had quite a few close friends.

That, however, didn't matter. What did matter was that Sarah's father and her friends were in attendance and that it was David Redmond who stood waiting for her at the end of the church's aisle.

"Are you ready?" her father asked, his voice low in her ear, and Sarah nodded as she smiled up at him. She was more than ready. She was dressed in a long, flowing cream gown, a garland of flowers about her head which matched the assortment of violets and sunflowers in the bouquet within her hands.

Sarah looked up, caught David's eye, and, with her father beside her, began to take slow yet purposeful steps toward him, her smile growing ever wider as she approached.

The vicar began the proceedings, and when he came to the line where he asked David, "Wilt though love her, comfort her, honor, and keep her in sickness and in health; and, forsaking all other, keep thee only unto her, so long as ye both shall live?" David smiled at Sarah through the first part, but his expression became hard when someone in the pews let out a laugh at the thought of David forsaking all others.

David shook his head, mouthing "Lord Hartley," with an eye roll, but then all of his levity fled. He gripped Sarah's hands within his own, stared deeply into her eyes, and fiercely claimed, "I will," which was enough to silence those who watched them.

Sarah believed him with all of her heart, and that was all that mattered.

* * *

THE WEDDING BREAKFAST following the ceremony was held in their home — their *new* home. The estate had not been often frequented in the past few years, and the staff seemed thrilled to welcome their new master and mistress.

David was still becoming used to the idea that this was his. Never in his life had his father mentioned the possibility of any of his properties becoming David's, and David had always assumed that they would all go to Franklin, who was certainly the man best suited to become the master of it all. But Franklin, apparently, was more than happy with the others he would someday inherit from his father, in addition to the property where he currently lived as well as his town-house in London.

The manor had been built some fifty years prior and held more than enough space for David and Sarah's purposes. She had been most pleased to discover a beautiful wood extending behind the house, and the village was but a short walk away.

"All who may need me can easily find me," she said enthusiastically, and David had to laugh, for what other woman would be so eager to have villagers calling upon her at any hour of day or night? But that was Sarah — and it was why he loved her, which he told her so now, and she simply laughed and shook her head.

"Well, Redmond?" The Duke of Clarence said now, as he stood with David, Lord Berkley, and Eddie Francis in a corner of the drawing room. "Do you now understand why we chose to forsake all for one woman?"

"I more than understand," he said with a laugh. "A few months ago, had you told me I would be here, in my own estate with a wife of my own, I would have laughed at you — or cried, perhaps. I'm not entirely sure. But now... now everything has changed."

"That's what happens when you find a good woman," Berkley said with a bit of a sigh.

"Or the woman finds you," added Francis, and they shared a laugh as they looked at the enjoyment in front of them — especially the four women who sat across from them, the women who held their hearts.

SARAH SANK BACK into the soft cushions of the settee. As much as she adored having her friends here with her and welcomed David's family into their home, she had to admit that she was also looking forward to the time when it would just be the two of them, alone together at last. But for now, she appreciated the opportunity to have some time with her three friends, whom she knew she might not see again for some time.

"Well, your David Redmond has certainly surprised me," Elizabeth said from where she sat across from her, and Sarah gave her a somewhat reproachful look. "I'm sorry, Sarah, but from what I knew of him, he was certainly not the type of man to commit to just one woman. Who am I to speak of such things after all that happened with Gabriel in the past, I realize, but still, Mr. Redmond had quite the reputation."

"Reputation isn't everything," Sarah argued.

"No, but it can say much about a person, or an institution," Elizabeth said. "Wouldn't you agree, Phoebe?"

"I think fact matters most," Phoebe said practically. "That is why we report on various issues — so that we can share such information with others, which then allows them to decide for themselves what they may think or feel about an issue."

"Fair enough," Elizabeth said with a bit of a shrug, and Sarah smiled to herself.

"How do you find life on the road with a little one?" Sarah asked, changing the subject as she looked to Julia, who smiled prettily.

"Oh, just fine," she said. "We love being around the horses and the other families for part of the year. Besides that, we often find ourselves in London for most of the time, or if Eddie has not far to go, we stay home. We do like to be together, though, and I must admit that I find it hard to miss a race."

"Particularly after you have trained the horse," Phoebe said pointedly.

"Exactly," Julia said. "Will you continue your practice?" she then asked Sarah, who nodded enthusiastically.

"Absolutely, if the villagers will have me," she said, tilting her head to the side. "The housekeeper doesn't see why they wouldn't — she said they have been lacking someone who can aid them, and she's hopeful I would be welcomed, though she thinks they may be unsure about coming to the wife of the Earl's son for treatment."

"I'm sure as soon as the first meets you, all of their worries will be swept away," Phoebe said confidently, and Sarah smiled at her in thanks.

"I do hope so," she said. "How do you fare, with motherhood and the newspaper?"

"As well as always," Phoebe said, smiling wide now. "Rhoda, my editor, remains remarkable, which provides me plenty of time to do what I must at home, though I cannot imagine giving up the paper entirely. Which had me thinking — we could freshen up some of our columns. Perhaps, in addition to our column on horse racing, we could use a couple newer items. Elizabeth, we could have one on finances, for there are many women — widows and the like — who are left with financial burdens they must learn to handle, and have no prior knowledge on how to do so. And Sarah, while I realize that we cannot prescribe entire medical knowledge as much is on a case-by-case basis, perhaps you could include some basic remedies or ideas on the treatment of common ailments. What do you think?"

Even if they did not think her ideas to be grand — which they certainly were — Sarah thought they had no choice but to agree, so enthusiastic was Phoebe about her scheme.

"I would love to," Sarah said, "assuming you would do most of the writing portion. I can't say it is my strongest skill."

"Of course," Phoebe said. "Send on what you come up with and I will work with it."

"I would enjoy it as well, I think," agreed Elizabeth, and Phoebe clapped her hands together, just once, in appreciation.

"Wonderful!" she said. "Start as soon as you like, and simply post your submission to me as Julia does."

As she sat back in the chair, Sarah looked around at her friends with a smile on her face.

"We are fortunate," she said, and they turned to look at her to see to what she was referring. "It is not often that a woman has the opportunity to marry a man she truly loves. Even rarer is the chance to follow her passions, to do what she enjoys and be supported by her husband. Look at us — we have all found the man we love while doing what we love. It is rather extraordinary, is it not?"

They nodded in agreement, and then Julia's grin somewhat widened.

"And then there are the children," she said.

"Wait until it's your turn," Phoebe said with a wink, and Sarah blushed, for she had a feeling that may be coming very, very soon.

EPILOGUE

S arah had seen many ill people within her lifetime. But never had she seen anyone truly as green as David when the ship pulled into Baltimore's harbor.

The poor man had a case of seasickness that even Sarah's remedies could only offset, not completely prevent. The fact that he had suggested — even insisted — on this trip to America proved how much he truly did love her, for a week in such a state was not one she envied.

"This really wasn't necessary," Sarah said as the two of them stood at the rail, the port becoming ever larger as they approached.

"But it was," David said, covering her hand on the rail with his own. "I needed to see where you come from, love. You know all of me — my life, my family, the homes where I grew up. I have seen none of your background. Besides that, I know there are people here you must see again, are there not?"

She turned to him, her eyes watery.

"There are. And I thank you."

"We also know that our home is in good hands, so there is nothing to worry about."

There had been quite the dramatic turn of events shortly before their departure to America. Lady Georgina and her footman had run away and eloped, much to the delight of both David and Sarah. David had hired her husband as a steward within his estate, and the arrangement was working out wonderfully. It was an interesting position for Lady Georgina to have changed such positions in life, but she was happy, and she and Sarah had gotten on well together.

Her own stomach lurched, and she gripped the rail ever harder.

"Are you all right?" David asked, and she nodded. "Seasickness?"

"No," she said with a shake of her head, but she wasn't quite ready to tell him just exactly what it was that was causing her stomach to roil in pain. Not with all of the passengers around, nor with the ship just beginning to dock.

When it finally bumped to a stop, Sarah heard David let out his breath, as though he had been holding it since they had left England. She smothered a smile as they reached land, and she thought he might nearly collapse upon it.

"The village you call home..." David said, clearly trying to hide his wariness regarding more travel. "How far would you say it is?"

Sarah nearly laughed but held it in for his expense. It wasn't that she found his illness to be humorous — it was more the desolate expression that covered his face.

"It is a few hours away," she said, "But if you would prefer, we could hire horses instead?"

"Yes, please," he said, sighing in apparent relief, and this time she did laugh. He managed a rueful chuckle. "Is it that obvious?"

"Your displeasure in travel of nearly any sort? Yes, absolutely. But it is entirely understandable."

Riding, however, seemed to revive his spirits, and by the time they arrived in the village where Sarah had grown up, he was back to his usual self.

"Sarah..." he said as they rode through the greenery that lined the road, which became more of a path the closer they came. "This is beautiful."

The familiar path brought a sense of peacefulness that settled deep in Sarah's soul. As she glanced over at David, however, she realized that while this would always be the most special of places to her, where she had grown and spent so many days of happiness with her mother, it was no longer home. For home was now wherever David was.

"This is the village," she explained. "We took a short cut around the town. Each has been growing, though it seems even the village has expanded since I have been gone."

She could hardly believe her eyes. The village that had been but a few homes when she left had grown from one road to a square of houses.

"Sarah?" She turned to see a woman running toward her from one of the houses on the edges of the village. "Sarah, do not tell me that is you?"

Sarah dismounted and ran toward the woman, the two of them embracing for a long while.

"Mabel!" she said. "It is ever so good to see you."

It truly was wonderful to see her — as well as the other villagers, those she knew greeting her warmly. Sarah had missed these people, her home, but she had to admit she was somewhat relieved. She had been worried that when she returned, she would feel that this was her true home, one she had left behind to be with David, but now that she was here... she knew that this would always hold a most special place in her heart, but life was not complete by living here. It was completed by the man whom she was with, and she had never felt so lucky as she did now to have David by her side.

She had been shocked to find her little cabin nearly as she had left it, though many of her supplies had been disturbed at some point in time.

"This was home," she said to David. "But it doesn't feel that way any longer."

"No?" he asked, raising his eyebrows as she turned to him.

"No," she shook her head as she walked over to him, lifting her hands to lay them on his chest. "Home is with you. With our family. Our *growing* family."

She met his eyes then, waiting for the moment when her words registered with him.

"Our growing… do you mean, Sarah? You are… we are…"

She laughed at his inability to put into words what he thought and felt, yet she knew all the same the sense of both shock and amazement that was coursing through him, for it was likely quite near to what she had felt herself when she first suspected.

"We are having a baby," she said, her words just above a whisper, and David's arms came around her and held her close. He finally drew back away from her to look into her eyes once more, and she smiled when she saw that his shone with tears. Sarah wasn't sure how long they would have stayed like that, holding one another and revelling in what was to come, but they turned when they heard a knock at the door.

"Sarah?"

"Abigail? Is that you?"

Sarah could hardly believe her eyes. Abigail, who had been but a girl when she left three years ago, had grown into a young woman. She had often followed Sarah around, interested in her treatments, picking herbs, and creating remedies for all that ailed the villagers.

"It's me," she said, a shy smile crossing her face. "I came to apologize."

"Whatever for?"

"I took some of your supplies. After you left, whenever the villagers needed help and the town was too far away, I did what I could. I have not nearly the knowledge that you do, but… well, I have done what I can."

Sarah's heart was full of both admiration for the girl, as well as a slight bit of regret that she hadn't sooner recognized Abigail's interest and trained her better. But she had seemed so young, and Sarah hadn't wanted to place such a burden upon her. But, apparently, she had anyway, purposefully or not.

"Tell you what," Sarah said. "We are here for a week or so. I promise to devote my time to providing you with any knowledge I can — and maybe you can teach me a few things. I know it's not a lot of time but—"

"Oh, that would be so wonderful," Abigail said, grasping Sarah's hands. "I will take all of the expertise you can offer me."

Sarah smiled at her, then noted the bundle Abigail had left at the door.

Following her gaze, Abigail smiled shyly.

"Fresh blankets, as I figured yours could use some airing," she said. "If you and your…"

"Husband. This is my husband, David," Sarah supplied, introducing the two of them, and Abigail blushed at his greeting.

"If you and your husband require other lodgings, please let me know and we can find somewhere for you."

"Fresh bedding is perfect," Sarah said, with one more hug for the girl. "Thank you, Abigail, for everything."

David wrapped his arm around Sarah's waist as they watched Abigail walk away from the cabin.

"You feel a sense of relief now, do you not?"

Sarah nodded into his shoulder.

"I think this is what was keeping me from truly feeling settled — the thought that I had left something behind here, left these people without any care. To know that Abigail is here, watching out for them... it leaves me with a sense of peace, to know that I haven't left them alone."

"You're a good woman," David said, kissing the top of her head. "The best I have ever met. I do not think there is a heart larger than yours on this side of the Atlantic or the other."

"And it's full of you," she said, turning her head to accept his kiss upon her lips. "I love you, David Redmond. My home is with you, wherever that may be."

"And mine with you. I love you too, Sarah. Now, and forever."

THE END

* * *

DEAR READER,

There we have it! The fourth and final book of The Unconventional Ladies series. If you read all the way through, I hope you enjoyed each story. Sarah's book is all about finding love and family in the most unexpected places and I hope it struck something within you.

If you enjoyed this series and are looking for something else to read, then might I suggest The Bluestocking Scandals? It is a series featuring women who have set aside their search for love in favor of professions nearly unheard of for women in the Regency era. But what happens when stubborn men — and love — finds them anyway and takes them unawares? I have an excerpt from <u>Designs on a Duke</u> in the page after this one.

If you haven't yet signed up for my newsletter, I would love to have you join us! You will receive Unmasking a Duke for free, as well as links to giveaways, sales, new releases, and stories about my coffee addiction, my struggle to keep my plants alive, and how much trouble one loveable wolf-looka-like dog can get into.

www.elliestclair.com/ellies-newsletter

Or you can join my Facebook group, Ellie St. Clair's Ever Afters, and stay in touch daily.

Until next time, happy reading!

With love,
Ellie

* * *

Designs on a Duke
The Bluestocking Scandals
Book 1

HER SECRET WILL SAVE A LEGACY. **But it could also break her heart when faced with a duke caught between two identities.**

The daughter of a famed architect, Rebecca Lambert has been raised among the nobility yet understands the circumstances of her birth. Becoming an architect is a dream, not an option, until she must assume an identity to protect her father's name.

No one was pleased when Valentine St. Vincent was

shockingly named the Duke of Wyndham -- least of all Valentine himself. He has always led with his fists, but now he must become the man his brother was supposed to be.

When Valentine hires Rebecca's father, she takes on the work herself. But as she spends more and more time at the duke's homes, she finds herself hopelessly falling for a man she can never have. For the Duke of Wyndham must marry a woman for her dowry and respectability -- two things Rebecca can never provide.

Will Rebecca and Val resign themselves to the lives chosen for them, or those they were born to live?

AN EXCERPT FROM DESIGNS ON
A DUKE

LONDON ~ 1820

*T*he door knocker appeared to be frowning.

Rebecca tilted her head to better study the gigantic lion that stared her in the eye. This one was quite stoic and serious, its eyebrows narrowed in anger and, perhaps, a bit of worry. If the duke was attempting to discourage visitors, then he was certainly achieving his purpose.

"A door knocker should be welcoming, should it not?" she asked her father, who was making his own study of the front exterior of the house.

"It's a shame, really," he murmured, looking around. "A house of this size, in the middle of London, kept secret from all eyes for years now. Look at the gardens on the southern side! But Becca, this house… why it's not finished!"

"You're right," she said, her eyes widening. From afar it looked rather extravagant, but upon closer examination, all of the finishing details had not yet been completed. "We shall see what the interior holds. But Father, let's not tell him any of our thoughts on his home until we further determine just why he has asked us here."

"He quite obviously wants to hire us!" her father exclaimed indignantly. "I am in high demand, Becca. High demand! I have heard much of Wyndham House, you know. There were plans for it to be rather grand, but there is no need to determine just why it wasn't completed, for it is quite obvious. Clearly the initial design was flawed. The duke must know that I will *not* simply follow another's designs."

"Father, we need this commission," Rebecca said, tapping her foot nervously, hoping that her father would move on from his passionate criticism of what could be one of the grandest mansions in London.

All knew of Wyndham House, as it covered one of the largest footprints of any home in the city. But its fame was partially hinged on the fact that it had become something of a mystery.

It was nearly a decade now since the first brick had been laid, but for the past eight years, no one besides servants had set foot in it. The recently passed duke had been quite ill during his final years, and his visitors consisted solely of caretakers as he had no immediate relatives.

Which was partially why the dukedom had passed into the hands of this man, a far-removed cousin, who apparently had been unaware that he would someday become one of the most powerful men in England.

It was all quite intriguing. But Rebecca was intent on dismissing all of the gossip and fascination that surrounded the new duke and focusing on the task at hand. It would take all of her concentration to do so.

She took a deep breath as the door swung open.

"Good morning," said the man Rebecca assumed to be the

butler, though he was much younger than any butler she had ever met.

He was tall, handsome in a boyish way, and had a spark in his eye as he looked Rebecca up and down before turning his gaze onto her father.

"You must be Mr. Lambert," he said. "I am Dexter. Do come in."

Rebecca and her father stepped into the foyer, both of them immediately more interested in their surroundings than any of the human inhabitants.

The foyer was designed to impress but was lacking the details of a completed room. A dome in the ceiling had yet to be ornamented, and Rebecca thought that a gold inlay would make it sparkle like the sun. Perhaps with diamonds. There were cutouts in the wall for statues, the arched doorway beyond providing a glimpse of a grand staircase. How much better would it look, Rebecca mused, to be rid of the wall and have the staircase greet the arrivals? Something worth a discussion.

When they had finally finished their initial review as Dexter waited patiently, the three of them stood staring at one another.

"Is, ah, the duke in residence?" Rebecca finally asked. The butler, who stood before them, was unexpectedly hesitant.

"That's just the thing, Miss…"

"Lambert. Mr. Lambert is my father."

"Ah, yes, Miss Lambert. The duke was supposed to be here to meet you, but has not yet returned home."

"I see," Rebecca said, though, in truth, she was rather annoyed. So the new duke, despite his supposedly common upbringing, had already become like the rest of the nobility. "Shall we wait?"

"Of course," he said, though he made no move to show them into the house.

"Is the drawing room available?" she suggested with a raised eyebrow.

The butler looked rather flustered.

"Perhaps the parlor would be better."

"Very well," Rebecca said, willing patience.

So they were to be relegated to the parlor. Apparently they were not fine enough quality to be shown to the drawing room.

It was likely under the duke's own instructions. Rebecca had been around more than her fair share of the nobility as she had spent her life following her father from one commission to another. In some homes they were seen as upper servants, though her father had gained much respect over the years, the better his name became known. *She* was most often looked right through, seen almost like furniture.

"You see, Becca?" she heard her father murmur in her ear. "Unfinished. Ragged. Shameful."

He was right on the first two accounts. Despite the fact the house had been standing for a decade, many of the walls were bare, unadorned, some of the ceilings half-painted. Draperies covered some windows but not others, and furniture that had been accumulated had the look of that which was to have bided time until new furniture was procured.

That day had obviously not yet come.

They passed through the foyer and then into a long chamber that Rebecca guessed was to be a ballroom. It was currently empty except for two long tables, upon which sat a curious collection of objects.

She was so busy looking at their contents that she walked right into her father, who had stopped to stare at everything in front of him.

"What in the…"

"Father," Rebecca warned, cutting him off. Just then a jar

of green liquid on the table began to bubble, and Rebecca took a step backward, pulling her father with her.

Just as it exploded with white foam shooting out the top of the jar, a tall, slim woman dressed in green raced into the room.

"I'm so sorry," she said, clearly flustered as she attempted to push back some of the strands of blonde hair that floated around her face, though she refrained from touching her skin with her gloved hands. "I didn't know we were having company and I should have had this in another room. That being said, I think I am close to—"

"Jemima!"

"Oh, Mother!" the woman whirled around as an elegantly dressed white-haired woman *sailed* into the room — Rebecca didn't think walked was an adequate description. A strong floral scent wafted around her like a cloud.

"Hello there," she said, waving a hand in front of her demurely, giving Rebecca the idea that the woman hailed herself near to royal status — which, Rebecca supposed, she now was, as the immediate family of a duke. "You must be the architect. Please, do wait in the parlor. We look forward to our discussion. Dexter, please show them in. And next time, perhaps walk them the other way, through the drawing room?"

"Very well, Mrs. St. Vincent," he said with the slightest of bows and he waved a hand in the air, bidding them to continue to follow him.

Rebecca and her father exchanged a look, but Rebecca shrugged and urged her father to continue, though they both jumped at the bang that exploded from the table behind them.

"Sorry," the younger woman — Miss St. Vincent— said with a cringe and a bit of a wave before she returned to her work.

"How very curious," Rebecca's father murmured as they finally entered the parlor.

While this room, too, was not yet complete, Rebecca was drawn to the large Venetian window on the far wall, which overlooked the back court. A huge green expanse flourished beyond, though there was much potential to expand the gardens. This should be the focal point of the room, Rebecca thought. The furniture should look out beyond the window, the remainder of the room simple and unornamented.

The door opened behind them, and Rebecca turned, hoping to see the duke so they could be on with it, but instead it was the woman she assumed to be his mother.

"Wonderful to meet you, Mr. Lambert," she said with a wide, practiced smile on her face, as though they had not just encountered one another in the ballroom. She took a seat in one of the mismatched chairs, this one a royal-blue uphol-stered mahogany one that had been home to many bottoms, artfully arranging her expansive, clearly expensive, skirts over the chair so they fanned out evenly. "I am Mrs. St. Vincent and my son is the Duke of Wyndham."

"A pleasure to meet you," Rebecca's father said, his prac-ticed charm emerging as he bent to kiss the woman's hand, though she pulled it away before he was able to do so.

"Yes, well. My son was supposed to be here to meet you, but unfortunately, he was called away on very *urgent* matters. As you may know, we have only recently arrived at this home in London, and as you can see, there is much to complete. I know my son has more particulars in mind and will review them once he arrives, but obviously the house has the potential to be *quite* opulent."

"Actually, Mrs. St. Vincent, we haven't seen much of it," Rebecca said, growing rather impatient. They hadn't much time to waste waiting. "Perhaps while we wait, we could tour the house?"

"And you are...?" she asked, fixing her pointed stare on Rebecca.

"Miss Lambert. I assist my father as his secretary."

"Oh. How unusual. Well. I suppose Dexter can show you around, if you must see it now."

They rose and Rebecca followed her father out. He began chattering away in Dexter's ear, and Rebecca followed behind, pulling out her sketchbook and making notes as well as drawing sketches and designs as she went.

The style was Palladian with a hint of neoclassical, she realized as they wandered through, and she wished she was able to better question the duke as to what had happened over the past decade. At least the current duke was willing to pay for additional work. While her father may have blamed shoddy design, the truth was evident. The previous duke had run out of money.

She poked her head into one room and then the other. It was a travesty, really, and Rebecca wondered what the country estate looked like. Stripped of all its finery, perhaps, in order to attempt to pay to keep up appearances? No wonder this place remained a mystery.

She stopped for a moment, attempting a quick drawing, when suddenly she realized how quiet the hall had become. Rebecca looked up to find that her father and Dexter were nowhere in sight. Drat. She had become too caught up.

She quickly ascended the staircase in an attempt to catch them, but the upstairs corridor was empty as well. Rebecca put her ear against one door and then the next, but there was no sign of them. There was, however, a door slightly ajar at the end of the hall. She continued toward it, pushing it fully open to reveal a long, wide bedchamber. The windows were covered in heavy navy draperies, the bed itself taking up a large portion of the room. Goodness, how large was the duke that he needed such space?

Curious, Rebecca walked further into the room, though she was aware that this was likely not one of the rooms Dexter would have included in his tour. But she couldn't help herself. She loved studying how people lived. And, unlike many rooms in the house, this chamber was obviously occupied.

There was a small dressing room and another door that Rebecca assumed connected to another bedroom. She pushed it open, finding the bedroom entirely bare. So there was clearly no *her* grace. Rebecca was about to retreat when she heard a heavy tread in the hallway, the steps coming closer and finally entering the room.

Not the wandering, unhurried steps of her father. Not the quick steps of Dexter.

It must be the duke.

Her heart began to race at the thought of being caught in the bedchamber of one of the highest peers in all of England. How would she ever explain herself? Rebecca did the first thing that came into her mind.

She hid.

KEEP READING Designs on a Duke on Amazon or in Kindle Unlimited!

ALSO BY ELLIE ST. CLAIR

The Unconventional Ladies
Lady of Mystery
Lady of Fortune
Lady of Providence
Lady of Charade

The Unconventional Ladies Box Set

Reckless Rogues
The Earls's Secret
The Viscount's Code
Prequel, The Duke's Treasure, available in:
I Like Big Dukes and I Cannot Lie

The Remingtons of the Regency
The Mystery of the Debonair Duke
The Secret of the Dashing Detective
The Clue of the Brilliant Bastard
The Quest of the Reclusive Rogue

To the Time of the Highlanders
A Time to Wed
A Time to Love
A Time to Dream

Thieves of Desire

The Art of Stealing a Duke's Heart

A Jewel for the Taking

A Prize Worth Fighting For

Gambling for the Lost Lord's Love

Romance of a Robbery

Thieves of Desire Box Set

The Bluestocking Scandals

Designs on a Duke

Inventing the Viscount

Discovering the Baron

The Valet Experiment

Writing the Rake

Risking the Detective

A Noble Excavation

A Gentleman of Mystery

The Bluestocking Scandals Box Set: Books 1-4

The Bluestocking Scandals Box Set: Books 5-8

Blooming Brides

A Duke for Daisy

A Marquess for Marigold

An Earl for Iris

A Viscount for Violet

The Blooming Brides Box Set: Books 1-4

Happily Ever After

The Duke She Wished For

Someday Her Duke Will Come

Once Upon a Duke's Dream

He's a Duke, But I Love Him

Loved by the Viscount

Because the Earl Loved Me

Happily Ever After Box Set Books 1-3

Happily Ever After Box Set Books 4-6

The Victorian Highlanders

Duncan's Christmas - (prequel)

Callum's Vow

Finlay's Duty

Adam's Call

Roderick's Purpose

Peggy's Love

The Victorian Highlanders Box Set Books 1-5

Searching Hearts

Duke of Christmas (prequel)

Quest of Honor

Clue of Affection

Hearts of Trust

Hope of Romance

Promise of Redemption

Searching Hearts Box Set (Books 1-5)

Christmas

Christmastide with His Countess

Her Christmas Wish

Merry Misrule

A Match Made at Christmas

A Match Made in Winter

Standalones

Always Your Love

The Stormswept Stowaway

A Touch of Temptation

For a full list of all of Ellie's books, please see
www.elliestclair.com/books.

ABOUT THE AUTHOR

Ellie has always loved reading, writing, and history. For many years she has written short stories, non-fiction, and has worked on her true love and passion -- romance novels.

In every era there is the chance for romance, and Ellie enjoys exploring many different time periods, cultures, and geographic locations. No matter when or where, love can always prevail. She has a particular soft spot for the bad boys of history, and loves a strong heroine in her stories.

Ellie and her husband love nothing more than spending time at home with their children and Husky cross. Ellie can typically be found at the lake in the summer, pushing the stroller all year round, and, of course, with her computer in her lap or a book in hand.

She also loves corresponding with readers, so be sure to contact her!

www.elliestclair.com
ellie@elliestclair.com

Ellie St. Clair's Ever Afters Facebook Group

Printed in Great Britain
by Amazon